LOVE OUT LOUD

ALLIE SAMBERTS

Editing by Mandi Andrejka at Inky Pen Editorial Services

Cover Design by Lorissa Padilla

Chapter Header Art by Lorissa Padilla

alliesambertswrites@gmail.com

www.alliesamberts.com

For Deven—
The way you've supported my art for *more* than twenty-five years
means more than you'll ever know.

For Joe—
No one is part of Drama Club until they come to a meeting.
Thanks for asking me.

For Chris—
Thanks for reminding me that you're never too old to do cool stuff.
I wish I had listened earlier.

For Tim—
Thank you for encouraging me to choose myself.

And for anyone who is feeling the winds of change—
May you spread your wings and fly.

Author's Note

WHEN I SET OUT to write this book, I intended it to be a love letter to theater. I wasn't a theater kid, but I was in band and for a long time I was a dancer, so I've been around the performing arts for as long as I can remember. And all of my friends were theater kids. Many of my adult friends are still performing. I even took on directing the school plays at my first teaching job, and I've been coaching my school's Speech Team for over a decade. I still geek out over audiobooks. And as a parent now, my children are starting to take the stage. Some of the best moments I've ever had have been onstage, backstage, or in the audience.

In short, watching characters come to life is a magical experience, and I wanted this book to capture some of that magic.

Over the years, theater and speech have given me a soft place to land. When I've felt at my lowest, the people in these groups have opened their arms to me, unquestioningly and without fail. It has been a privilege to be even a small part of young actors' journeys, too. I've seen kids who are floundering without a clear sense of direction join Drama and flourish.

Now, in my forties, I'm also seeing a lot of women around my age reject the confines of their jobs and upbringings and chase dreams they've long thought dormant in hopes of creating a better second half of their lives. I am one such woman—I'm publishing these books, after all.

Lark and Lennon's story is special to me for this reason. It's about belonging and passion, both in life and in love. I'd even go so far as to call it cozy. But—and please stop here if you don't want potential spoilers—if you know me at all, you can expect that my characters deal with some heavy things. They drink, smoke marijuana, use profanity, and have adult relationships. There are explicit scenes meant for mature audiences in chapters twenty and twenty three. I believe these are crucial to the development of my characters, but you can do whatever you see fit with that information.

Lark was a young mother; she is now divorced and sending her child off to college. There is discussion of divorce and loneliness in these pages. Lennon is a product of a complicated childhood. His parents were not bad people, but they often left him alone when he was younger, and he struggles with anxiety and abandonment issues. All of these things are discussed on page. There is also the death of a beloved childhood dog in the past.

My hope for this book is that it helps you love out loud. We are products of our pasts, but not beholden to them, as Lark and Lennon discover. I hope your laughter and love are big, booming sounds—larger than life. And I hope these pages feel like sunshine and joy during a time when we all need it the most.

PROLOGUE

LENNON

Twenty-Two Years Ago

"Okay. It's almost showtime, people. One more time!" An excited, tinny voice comes through my headset. "Five till places."

A chorus of "Thank you, five" follows. I add my own, then mentally run through my cues. Even though I've done this a million times, I want it to be perfect.

"Here we go," the voice says a few minutes later. "Lennon, bring the house lights down."

In the booth at the back of the high school auditorium, I use my index finger to slowly slide the dimmer switch on the light board all the way down until the space is in complete darkness. The chatter of the audience quiets. A baby wails somewhere near stage right, and someone shushes it gently.

"Spotlight," the same voice demands, and another slider glides under my fingertips, illuminating Davey McMan, a short, goofy sophomore wearing a bowler hat and a vest over a thin, white shirt. He tips his hat back and greets the audience with his normal charisma. The audience laughs like they always do, and I bring the spotlight down.

"Curtain." This is where the magic starts. My heart beats faster in anticipation. In the dim light of the stage, the green velvet curtain slides open in fits and starts as Tim pulls the rope from backstage.

"Music," the voice in the headset barks. The orchestra conductor, Mrs. Smith, raises her arms to cue the quartet sitting on the stage as well as the rest of the musicians sitting in the pit. They're a mix of student musicians—some of them friends of mine—and hired professionals to fill in the gaps. The trumpet player onstage brings the instrument to his lips, using the head of a plunger to make a *wah-wah-wah* sound. And with that, the final performance of my high school career has begun.

Our assistant director continues to read cues through the headset, but we've practiced this so many times, it's practically second nature. Sliders glide under my fingers as I turn mics on and off, going mostly off muscle memory. Student actors in the chorus all dressed in various black leotards, shirts, pants, and skirts walk to and fro, singing their parts behind Anne Jensen, who is hamming up her opening solo at center stage.

There's a quick transition into a softer song, and I lean forward in my chair. I can just make out the vague outline of a young woman standing perfectly still at center stage. The voice demanding a spotlight vaguely registers as I slide the center spot up to illuminate her in all her glory. Short blonde hair in pin curls. A black leotard with lace sleeves that cover her arms in a nod to the adjustments our school administrators demanded we make to this show. Black tights and high-heeled shoes.

The musicians vamp a bit as they wait for her to pop her head up and step forward, her signal that she's ready. "Mic two, up," the voice comes again. This time, I'm glad for the cue. I had been lost in her. I'm always a bit lost in her.

Her chest heaves for two bars. That's it. Just two bars. But I hold my breath for what feels like a lifetime waiting for her to steal the show like she always does.

Her head comes up, and she smiles the most brilliant smile I've ever seen. She's not faking it, either. She's at home on that stage, always has been. She once described it to me as a high unlike any other. This is our last performance before we graduate, and she's now let the pit vamp for longer than usual, so I know she's soaking up every minute.

Her blue eyes are sparkling; I can see them even from here. Her joy is contagious. I'm suddenly aware that my cheeks hurt because I'm grinning, too. She's completely in her element there, at center stage, ready to own the audience. Give it one song, and she'll have them in the palm of her hand.

Her eyes glide over the auditorium, taking everything in. Then, she finds me. She always finds me, because she's my best friend.

She steps forward, and Mrs. Smith cues the pit. Her smile widens a fraction. Just for me.

And that's when it hits me.

I'm in love with Lark Caspian.

CHAPTER 1

LARK

PRESENT DAY

I've barely filled my mug with coffee when my phone rings from where it sits face down on the counter. I rub some of the bleariness from my eyes as I flip it over to see a picture of my best friend, Lennon Hollis, lighting up the screen. His eyebrows are raised, and he has shoved a marshmallow into his mouth. The white edge of it sticks out between his lips, and his cheeks are puffed out like a chipmunk. It's an old picture from the last time I saw him—on my thirtieth birthday, about ten years ago. He hates it, which is why I made it his contact photo.

I glance at the clock on the sage-green wall of my living room as I swipe to answer the call. It's six o'clock in the morning Michigan time, which means it's three Los Angeles time. He's probably just getting home. Sure enough, as his real-life face pops on the screen, I can see his bare shoulders and a pillow behind his head.

"Good morning," I say brightly.

"Maybe for you," he grumbles. "I haven't been to bed yet."

"Aww," I intone with mock sympathy. "No pretty woman to keep you company today?"

He levels a glare at the screen. "You act like I'm bringing home a different woman every night."

I return the look he's giving me in silence. It may not be every single night, but it's frequent enough. Not that it bothers me per se, but it has led to more than one awkward phone conversation when some hot California blonde walks out of his bathroom wearing his shirt and not much more.

"Anyway." He sighs and settles further into his pillows. "I just wanted to see how my favorite person is doing on this fine Monday."

I lean the phone against the fruit bowl on the kitchen table so I can grab a banana from it. It takes me a few tries to get it to stay facing outward so he can still see me as I make breakfast. I spread peanut butter on toast and cut the banana so it lies in slices on top of it. "Things are good. Three more weeks until the term is over, and then dragging Devin across the finish line to her graduation." I pause what I'm doing to give him a meaningful look.

Lennon chuckles, and his image shakes on the screen. "She's a good kid."

"Even good kids get senioritis."

He glances behind me, his gaze bouncing over the white-washed space of my townhouse kitchen and snagging on a few of my plants that rest on top of the cabinets. "Is she still sleeping?"

I shake my head. "She just left for an early run with her friend. There are still a couple of track meets left, and they're both determined to hit a personal best before the end of the year."

Lennon narrows his eyes in disbelief. "She's voluntarily out for a run at six in the morning—*before school*—and you're going to accuse her of having senioritis?"

"Your memory is slipping in your old age. You of all people should know that senioritis is an affliction that only affects one's academic studies, not one's extracurricular activities," I counter. I remember dragging a certain someone over that same high school finish line when we were seniors, even as he threw all of his effort into our final show together. From the look on his face, he remembers it, too, and he wisely decides not to push the issue.

"Speaking of the end of high school," I continue as I slice another banana over peanut-butter toast on a second plate. "Are you planning on coming in for her graduation, or no? I have to make dinner reservations pretty soon."

Lennon wrinkles his nose, and I know before he says anything that he's going to decline. This is how it goes with him—he says he's going to think about it, evades conversation about the topic until he can't put it off any longer, and then he says he can't. It's definitely part of the reason why we haven't seen each other since that marshmallow picture was taken ten years ago, though I suppose I'm just as much to blame as he is, not having the time or money to get on a plane and fly out to LA after using most of my extra funds to fly Devin out to New York when she was younger, sometimes staying for a few weeks if she asked me to.

It's also why I've already made graduation dinner reservations without him.

"I can't," he says, then follows that up quickly with his explanation. "I'm working on a few projects that are supposed to wrap right around then, and I have to be available."

I take a bite of toast and chew it slowly, letting him wince apologetically at me for a little while longer. After I swallow, I can finally speak. "Are you sure it's not because Richard will be there?"

He raises a hand, palm out, but he has to move the phone a little farther away from himself so I can see it. The angle allows me to catch a glimpse of the tops of the trees on his tattoo—an outdoor scene that I know goes from his elbow to his shoulder—and his very defined pecs. His hours at the gym are paying off. The man works hard and plays hard—that's for sure.

"I swear, it's not. I actually wouldn't mind seeing Dick again."

I raise an eyebrow at Lennon's use of Richard's least favorite nickname but don't bother correcting him. Richard and I dated in high school before getting married shortly after college, so Lennon has known him for almost as long as I have, and they've never really gotten along. My mom used to tease me that Lennon was jealous of him, but I'm sure that wasn't it. I've always suspected Richard needled Lennon out of envy at our closeness, but not the other way around. Lennon and I have never been anything more than friends since we met during our freshman year. It's not that I never found Lennon attractive, even when he was scrawnier and less muscular than he is now. It just never came to that, and when Richard and I started dating during our junior year, I figured it was fine. If Lennon had wanted to make a move, he surely would have by then.

But Lennon's distaste of my ex grew even more when Richard and I went to the same college. Lennon always thought I should have struck out on my own. And based on the fact that I found myself pregnant just before graduation from undergrad, maybe he was right. The fact that Richard and I got married when we found out I was pregnant didn't do much to change Lennon's mind, and when Richard and I ultimately decided to split when Devin was seven, I think Lennon was mostly happy. And then, when Richard took a new job and moved out to New York, Lennon seemed relieved. Now that Richard is out there with his new wife and their five-year-old son, I really only see him when we exchange Devin at the start and end of the summer.

Whatever I was going to say as a retort is lost when the door to the townhouse opens and Devin comes in. She's wearing a bright yellow sports bra and skin-tight black running shorts, and she's dripping sweat. I grimace as a few drops of it hit the tile floor, but she grabs the towel she left at the door and dries herself off before slinging it around her neck.

"How was your run?" I ask her.

She grumbles something incoherent as she wipes her face off with her towel.

"That good, huh?"

She just trudges over to the refrigerator and grabs a bottle of water. Her throat works against huge swallows as she chugs half of it in just a few seconds. When she pulls the bottle away from her lips, she wipes them with the back of her wrist, though I don't know what good that does her. It's been an unseasonably warm and humid spring southern Michigan, which I know is part of what has Devin so frustrated. She was counting on a temperate spring to help bring her times down, but all physical activity is harder in this heat.

"Hey, kiddo," Lennon says.

Devin perks right up at the sound of his voice. They don't see each other in person very often, but he's always been part of the family, in a way, and he's one of her favorite people. Like an uncle who lives miles away and pops in for a holiday or special occasion once in a while, but who also calls all the time.

"Hey, Lennon." She smiles brightly at him as I hand her the plate with her toast on it. "Let me guess. You just got home from the club?"

He winks at her, flashing her his neon Los Angeles smile. "You got it."

I frown at her. "What do you know about 'the club'?"

Devin's smile drops as suddenly as it appeared. She shoots me an exasperated look. "Mom, please. I'm eighteen."

I raise my hands, palms out. "My bad. I didn't realize the entirety of adult knowledge was dropped into your brain upon your eighteenth birthday."

Devin rolls her eyes so hard I'm surprised they don't fall out of her head. Luckily, Lennon can see the attitude brewing from miles away—literally—and jumps in. "I hear you've been working on your pace. What are you at now?"

"Well, I beat Molly at the 400 this morning, which has never happened before," she says, her mood lifting a little.

"That's great!" Lennon beams with pride.

Her shoulders droop again as she leans on her elbows so she can see the phone screen better. "But I finished in sixty-two seconds, so not even close to my best."

"Sounds pretty fast to me," I mumble. Devin and Lennon both give me annoyed looks this time, so I back away to pour another cup of coffee.

"Hang in there, kiddo. You know that race day adrenaline will kick in and give you a little rocket boost," Lennon reassures her.

It seems to work, because I see her smile out of the corner of my eye. "Thanks." She shoves half the toast into her mouth, then says around her mouthful, "Gotta shower!" Then she waves at him and locks herself in the bathroom.

Lennon yawns. "See? Good kid."

"She is." A familiar pang hits my chest when I remember that her graduation means she'll be leaving soon. She and Molly and a few of the other kids in her grade are headed to Europe for a senior trip, and then she'll fly directly to New York to spend the rest of the summer with Richard per our custody agreement before moving into her dorm at NYU to study journalism. I'm about to be an empty nester at forty. Well, *almost* forty. One more month for that, too.

"You okay over there, Songbird?" Lennon's gentle voice snaps me out of my musing.

I blink a few times before offering him a half smile. "Yeah." His phone is slipping down slightly, and his eyes are drooping, so I don't offer any more. "You should get some rest. I have to get going anyway. Early class and all that."

He yawns again, and I avert my eyes from the flash I get of the inside of his mouth. Gross.

"Okay. Talk soon."

"Love you," I say as I move toward the phone to hang it up.

He responds the same way he always does, the same way he has for at least twenty years: "You're my favorite."

The last thing I see before I hang up the phone is Lennon grinning sleepily from his side of the country.

Chapter 2

Lennon

The nice thing about freelancing as an audio engineer is that I can mostly make my own hours and take whatever projects interest me. Usually, if it pays, it interests me enough to take it on. And I know what I'm doing, so most of my leads are from word of mouth. I've built an enormous client list in the twenty-or-so years I've been working, and I've had the opportunity to work with some amazing people on really cool projects. Podcasts, independent films, audiobooks, recordings of live and studio performances—you name it.

The not-so-nice thing about freelancing as an audio engineer is that I live in LA, which is amazing but fucking *expensive*. And while I could probably afford to live on my own—and should, at forty years old—it's a lot nicer to have the cushion that a roommate provides. The only problem is that most guys my age have settled down. And my roommates keep settling down themselves.

So when my current roommate, Bobby, comes home from a weekend in Napa as I'm grilling a couple of burgers on our balcony and tells me he proposed to his girlfriend and will be moving out at the end of next month, I have to swallow a groan about what the hell I'm going to do to cover his half of the rent in order to give him a proper congratulations.

"I know it's not the best timing," Bobby says as he cracks open a beer and sits in one of the wicker seats. "I'll help you find another roommate if you want."

"No, man. It's totally fine. I'm sure there's someone out there who's looking for somewhere to live." I flip a burger and press down on it with the spatula. It sizzles satisfyingly. I smirk. "I found you, didn't I?"

I don't mention that he's my fifth roommate since I moved in here ten years ago. I had my misgivings about him since he was only twenty-five when he moved in and the last twenty-something regularly had loud parties well into the morning. I'm not one to turn down a party, but even I have my limits.

Bobby takes a swig of his beer and nods as if that settles it. I suppose it does, for him. What can I do? Demand he stays here until the end of his lease? I suppose I could, but I'm not interested in listening to him fuck his girlfriend—sorry, fiancée—through the walls after their wedding night.

I shrug it off. I'll figure it out somehow. I always do.

***

"What do you mean she needs to get her tonsils out?" I shut my bedroom door behind me and pinch the bridge of my nose. This day has gone from bad to worse. "Isn't that something you do when you're a kid?"

"Apparently not," my friend, Noah Baker, says from the other end of the phone call that interrupted beers on the balcony with my soon-to-be-former roommate. Noah is an audiobook producer at Luminaudio Productions, where he works with narrators and independently published authors to bring their books to life. It's how we met when I was fresh out of college and he was starting up the company. I worked on a few projects with him when I first graduated, and we just kind of hit it off. He used to regularly hit up the bars with me, back in his single days. Now he's married with a couple of kids, and he's taken his nights out down to a few of drinks once a month. Still, I consider him my closest friend in LA.

I actually pitched him this current project, and I think he took it on as a favor to me. It has been nothing but a headache since we started. I honestly wouldn't be surprised if he never wanted to work with me again. The author, Jessica Jordans, is an acquaintance of mine, so I vouched for her with Noah. Luminaudio accepted the book before it was even published, and when it debuted, it skyrocketed to the top of the charts. Now the company wants the project done as soon as possible, but Jessica has been dragging her feet for a month. She's been very particular about the narrators, but since the book is such a hit, the directive from everyone has been to keep her happy at all costs. We finally had narrators picked last week and were scheduled to start recording in a week or two, but apparently not anymore because one of them needs some useless appendage removed.

"How long is the recovery time on that?" I ask, knowing full well if it were only a week, Noah wouldn't have even bothered calling me.

"Could be two weeks, could be six. But she wants to remove herself from this project all together, just in case. She doesn't want to ruin her voice." I can hear his exasperation over the phone. "I think this thing is cursed."

"No kidding." I sigh. "Okay, so what are our options?" This project can be delayed, but it cannot die, especially now that I need the money to cover my potentially solo rent for a few months.

Noah makes a noise low in his throat, and I know what's coming next isn't going to be good. "I don't know if we have any," he says tightly. "We already ran through our entire roster of available narrators in the first round of auditions. There's no one left, and anyone who would be available has probably heard about this project by now. They won't touch it with a ten-foot pole."

"Can we hire off your roster?"

He grumbles again, and I can hear a scraping sound as he runs a hand through his beard. It's his signature move. I'm actually surprised he has any chin hair left with how much he tugs on it.

"The investors aren't going to like it," he starts slowly. "But they won't want to lose this thing. It's projected to do really well, especially with Silas already signed on for the male narrator. I can make a few calls."

"I appreciate it. I don't want to lose this one either, if we can help it."

He's silent for a moment. "You don't happen to know anyone who could do this in a pinch, do you?"

I laugh humorlessly. "Casting's not my specialty."

"Oh, come on." He forces a lighter tone. "In all your hookups, you haven't met some wannabe starlet who's dying to get her foot in the door?"

"Narrating an audiobook is hardly a foot in the door," I counter.

"A gig is a gig," Noah replies.

He's not wrong. LA is filled with people who moved here to try their hand at acting, only to find out it's much harder to rocket yourself to stardom than it seems on TV. There are probably thousands of people who would kill for this opportunity, but the thought of going back to the drawing board and auditioning again—unknowns this time—has my stomach clenching.

Noah must be reading my mind, because he says, "And I think it'd help appease Jessica if it were someone you recommended. You were the one who ultimately got her to pick people to begin with." He pauses before practically singing the next bit, as if he could keep the words from coming out. "You have a way with her."

"Oh my god," I groan. "Stop."

"She likes you."

"Who doesn't?" I deflect.

Noah huffs. "Does it get heavy carrying that giant ego around with you everywhere?"

"It's why I have to work out, man. Gotta stay in shape to lug it with me."

The truth is that Jessica probably does want to sleep with me, but I would never. She's far too young, and frankly, she's almost definitely more interested in what I can do *for* her than what I can do *to* her, which is not a dynamic I like in the bedroom.

"Okay, well, we have a meeting tomorrow. I'll see what everyone says and let you know. This might delay us a month or more, and I probably can't keep Silas from taking another job in the meantime."

Silas Matthews is the male narrator Jessica finally settled on. She actually cast him first, which is no surprise. He's incredibly sought after. It probably also helps that he's good looking and charming. Losing him would mean the whole project would likely fall apart. I don't particularly like the guy, but I have to admit, he does good work.

"He can't record his part now?"

"I can't ask him to commit the time to a project we don't know is happening. You know that," Noah chastises.

He's right. I do know that. A guy can dream, though.

"Fine. I'll go through my little black book and see if anyone comes to mind," I say as I pace to the other side of my bedroom.

Noah snorts. "You're getting old. No one has a little black book anymore."

"It was a metaphor, asshole."

"Whatever you say. Talk tomorrow." He hangs up, leaving me staring at my phone screen.

I flop onto my bed in defeat. Seven-thirty on a Sunday evening, and the week ahead is already shaping up to be a disaster. I could find someone to go out with me and drown my worries in drinks and loud music, but the only person I want to talk to is two thousand miles away and likely already asleep.

Ever since we were kids, Lark has had a way of making shitty situations feel less awful. When I was sixteen, we had to put my dog down. Daisy was a golden retriever my nomadic parents had bought for me as a puppy in a rare fit of guilt about moving me around the country whenever the wind blew a certain way or a job opportunity came up. That dog had been with me through three moves, my early adolescence, my first breakup, and a hell of a lot more.

Lark loved Daisy, and Daisy loved her. There was no question about it. Even when Daisy's arthritis got so bad she could barely make it out of her doggy bed, she'd come padding over to Lark whenever she came over. I have a picture of the two of them sitting in the grass at a park, just looking out at nothing. But when we put Daisy down, Lark was there. She held my hand in silence while I tried—unsuccessfully—not to cry. And then when it was all over, she went home for a few hours. I remember thinking I just wanted her to stay, but I understood that she needed some space. Turns out she crafted a whole shadow box with pictures and Daisy's favorite toy Lark had swiped from my room.

I would have stolen her collar, too, but you wouldn't let it out of your sight, she had said. I laughed then—a huge, wet sound that caught me completely off guard. I still don't know why I thought that was so funny. Something about Lark has just always made it easier to laugh.

I could use a laugh right about now. This certainly isn't at the level of losing Daisy. I'm not even all that worried about losing my apartment or this gig. I'll find something else if I have to. But it complicates things enough to be really inconvenient.

Ten-thirty Michigan time isn't too late to call her, probably, and I really want to see her face, so I push the Call button without thinking too hard about it. I sit on the edge of my bed while the phone rings a few times.

When she answers, the room is dark. I can barely see the outline of her face in the ambient light from her screen, and she's clearly in bed.

"Shit, I'm sorry. I didn't mean to wake you," I say quickly.

"You didn't." She's not facing the screen, and her voice is heavy. Not with sleep, I realize, but with sadness. A quiet sniffle confirms it.

I sit straight up in my bed, my knuckles going white as I grip my phone. "Lark, are you crying?"

"No," she says obstinately. She wipes her cheek with the back of her hand. "Maybe."

"What's wrong?" I ask. "Who do I have to kill?"

She huffs a laugh. "Father Time?"

I'm not getting it, but I can play along until I do. Just like that improv class she made me take in high school. *Yes, and...*

"He's a dirty thief," I grumble as my hand loosens on my phone.

She wipes her face again, then finally turns to look at the screen. Her nose and eyes are puffy and red, indicating she's been at this for a while. One minor inconvenience and she's the first person I want to talk to. She's been crying for what looks like a long time. Why didn't she call me?

"I'm fairly certain it was only a few weeks ago that you were coming out here for my thirtieth-birthday-slash-divorce party. Devin was eight. *Eight*, Lennon. Second grade." Her voice wobbles on that last part, as if she's on the edge of breaking down again.

"She was a spitfire. She sassed me the whole time I was there."

Lark sniffles again. "She'd still sass you. You know, if you ever came out here again."

I don't miss that not-so-subtle dig, but that's not the issue here, so I ignore it. Instead, I jab her right back. "Just like her mama."

That was not at all the right thing to say based on Lark burying her face in her pillow and shuddering.

"Oh no. I'm so sorry," I groan, rubbing a hand over my face. I'm not winning at much today. "I meant that as a compliment."

Her shoulders shake for another minute as I internally kick myself for picking the wrong time to throw out my sarcasm. I watch as her short blonde hair falls over her cheek, fully obscuring her face from me.

Finally, she turns to the camera. I fully expect to see more tears glistening down her face, but she's smiling and her blue eyes glitter with mirth. "You're the worst." She chuckles.

"I don't know why you put up with me."

"Habit, mostly." She sighs heavily and shifts so she's lying on her back and holding the phone above her face. Even swollen from crying, she's beautiful. She always has been, like a bright light in the darkness.

The mood has shifted, and the worst of it seems over, so I risk asking, "What's going on, Songbird?"

She turns her big blue eyes away from the camera, staring at her ceiling. "When did I get old, Lennon?"

I reel back a bit, then fall against my own pillows. "Nope. Nuh-uh. If you're old, then I'm old, and I'm not old, so..."

Lark rolls her eyes, then glares at me as best she can through the screen. "We're forty."

"I'm forty. You're still thirty-nine."

"Close enough." She pauses, and her gaze falls as if she's lost to thought again. "This isn't exactly where I saw my life going."

She doesn't let herself admit it very often, but getting pregnant with Devin changed the entire course of her life. Not in a bad way, but she had her sights set on professional acting after college, and once Devin was here, that was off the table for a while. Her parents would have helped, but Lark is so fiercely independent that she refused to ask. Plus, between school and work, she wanted to be home with her baby as much as she could. Throw in a divorce and a pandemic that shut down theaters right around the time Devin was old enough for Lark to get back into it, and she never really got the chance.

But one thing I know for sure about Lark is she always feels worse when she lets herself admit that Devin interrupted her plans. The guilt of wishing, even for a second, that things had worked out differently pulls her deeper into her sadness for days at a time. I won't let that happen if I can help it.

"Well, you're not dead yet." As soon as it's out of my mouth, I give myself a mental facepalm, and I backtrack. "What I mean is you have a lot of life ahead of you. Devin is graduating, and you'll have time to do whatever you want."

Her lip wobbles again at that. "I'm going to miss her," she whispers, as if even giving it full volume could keep her from what's coming.

"I know," I say, because I do.

A few more tears slink down her cheeks, and she squeezes her eyes shut against them. She rolls to her side and takes the phone with her. I imagine us both lying next to each other in the same bed, not two thousand miles away. I put my hand against the other pillow on my queen-sized bed, wishing her hand were there so I could hold it until this passes.

Lark clears her throat, and I can practically see her zipping up that part of her sadness and packing it away for later. "It's not like I can just jump back into acting anyway," she says, changing the subject. "Who is going to hire a forty-year-old woman who hasn't been onstage since undergrad?"

It doesn't matter that Lark is still an absolute knockout, with her blonde ringlets and big ocean-blue eyes. This industry sucks for women over a certain age, and there's no use trying to pretend otherwise, no matter how gorgeous she is.

She was the most beautiful girl in our high school, and that's an objective fact. Everyone loved her. Why she settled for that asshole, Richard, is completely beyond me. She could have had any guy she wanted. And no small part of me blames him for Lark's current state. He couldn't even step up to be enough of a partner in raising his own daughter for Lark to have time to pursue her passions. He never thought acting was a good enough profession for her. I remember him telling me that she'd grow out of it eventually once when we were all home for the summer. Which was after he more or less told me to get lost for her sake at the end of our senior year.

"Well, one thing I know, Lark Caspian, is that you are the most determined woman I've ever met. Not everyone can get a master's degree while caring for a newborn and land a job as a professor at a university—"

"Community college," she corrects me.

"Tenure track, though," I counter right back.

She screws her lips to the side, conceding. Point goes to me, because I'm right. It's a coveted position no matter how you slice it, and she got it while balancing Devin on her hip.

"Regardless," I continue, "if there's anyone who can figure out what to do next, it's you. The curtain's not closing on the show; it's just the start of the next act."

Lark groans. "If I had known you were going to bust out theater metaphors, I wouldn't have answered the phone."

"I'm glad you answered," I say softly. "I like being here for you. Why didn't you call me if you were feeling like this?"

The screen bounces as she shrugs. "I didn't know if you were out, and I didn't want to interrupt your fun."

I search her eyes as best I can through the screen. Ten years without looking at her in person is too long, but neither of us has been able to get away. I make a mental note to see if I can shift a few things around now that this audiobook is probably dead on arrival to make it to Devin's graduation.

"It's never an interruption when it's you." I try to infuse as much honesty as I can into those words, because I mean it. I'd do a lot more than leave a bar if she asked me to.

She shrugs again. "I was just having a moment, you know? It'll pass."

It's not worth pushing, so I just nod. "You're my favorite person in the world. You know that."

She covers her mouth against a huge yawn. Her eyelids start drooping. "It's late here, and I have an early morning." Then, her eyes pop open wide again. "Wait. *You* called *me*."

I laugh lightly. "I did, but it's not important. Go get some sleep. We can talk tomorrow."

"Okay," she says slowly. I can tell she wants to protest, but sleep is going to win. "Good night, Lennon."

"Good night, Lark."

I hang up and flip onto my back and clasp my hands over my chest to feel the gentle rise and fall of it with my breathing. I stare at my ceiling for a long time, wishing I could fix this for her. Or even just give her a big hug. Maybe steal some of Devin's stuff and make her a shadowbox. Or get her an audition somewhere.

The realization that I might be able to solve both of our problems dawns on me slowly as my bedroom darkens completely with the setting sun. It's so obvious. I can't believe I didn't think of it while we were on the phone. I must have been too consumed with her emotional state to see the solution that is so clearly staring at me.

Lark could narrate this audiobook. She's done some voiceover work before, so she knows the basics. It would give her something to do, let her scratch an itch, and allow me to keep this project.

I remember Jessica's picky nature with a groan. It's probably a slim chance that she'd allow an unknown actress like Lark on this project. Then again, Lark can charm anyone if given the chance. Maybe I just need to warm Jessica up to the idea.

I pick up my phone to call Lark back but remember how exhausted she looked when we hung up earlier. She's probably already asleep, and it isn't worth waking her up for an opportunity that isn't a sure thing. I'll run this by Noah and Jessica tomorrow and then call her if they seem on board.

But I have a good feeling about this. For once, I have the opportunity to make Lark feel better, not the other way around, and the possibility makes me fall asleep with a smile on my face.

CHAPTER 3

LARK

I TAP MY PENCIL on the mousepad that sits next to my laptop as I wait for the clock to tick from two fifty-nine to three o'clock. The longest minute of the day, and the reason we switched the analog clock out of our office to a digital one that doesn't count seconds. I had commented one too many times that I thought it was broken, and in a fit of annoyance, my office mate, Hannah Laurent, plucked it off the wall and tossed it into the garbage can. The next day when I came in, there was a new digital clock sitting on the window ledge between where our desks face each other.

It's an odd setup for an office, but it works for us. When we decided to share the space, we were thrilled, but we kept fighting over who got to put their desk near the only window. We compromised by facing our desks to each other, so we can each turn to stare aimlessly outside when we need to.

Finally. Three o'clock and the day is over. I reach across my desk to where hers meets mine and triumphantly flip the end-of-year count-down from six to five. Five more school days before we get a break. And then the fall term begins, and the countdown starts over again.

Hannah eyes me over her dark-rimmed glasses. "Don't you have your evaluation meeting with Carl this afternoon?"

I groan and violently lean back in my chair. It squeaks in protest and rolls back an inch. "Yes. God, who schedules a meeting on Friday afternoon?"

"You." Hannah's brown eyes don't leave me as she reaches out to flip the number back to six. She shoots me a sardonic smile and tosses her long auburn hair over her shoulder before returning to the stack of papers on her desk. "Day's not over," she singsongs.

"Oh, come on," I whine. "I have to go to Devin's track meet right after my meeting, and flipping that number is a bright spot in an otherwise endless string of monotonous days."

"You're so dramatic." Her voice is cartoonishly flat, and she doesn't look up from the papers in front of her. She makes a large circle with her green pen, then notes something in the margin.

"As the Intro to Drama professor, it's kind of a job requirement," I counter.

"I hope you have it listed on your resume," Hannah says drily. She teaches the introductory rhetoric classes every student has to take at Arbor Hills Community College, and we've been close friends since she started here about ten years ago. When the school cut funding five years after that and had to repurpose some buildings, they lumped all the humanities together in one place, which is when we decided to make the best of a bad situation and become office roomies.

"I do, in fact. Right between my master's and my lack of stage-acting experience." I hadn't meant for that to come out sounding so bitter, but

I'm still feeling a little raw from the pity party Lennon interrupted last weekend. I'd probably feel better if I were able to talk to him again, but between the end of my term, Devin's year wrapping up, and a three-hour time difference, we've been playing phone tag all week.

Hannah looks up to give me a small sympathetic smile, and I'd probably feel better if I just talked to her about it, too, but there's no sense in dwelling on any of this anymore. I can't build a time machine, so I may as well just look to what's next. And right now, that's a meeting with Carl.

I push myself up from my desk with a whimper. I might not be forty for another few weeks, but I sure *feel* forty today. My back cracks as I straighten it.

"You sound like a glow stick," Hannah muses, her attention turned back to her papers again.

"You look like a relic." I flick a corner of the paper she's working on. "I can't believe your students haven't revolted against your handwritten essay tests yet. You're five years younger than me. What are you doing grading on paper?"

She smacks my hand away. "Don't you have somewhere to be?"

"Yes." I sling my giant tote bag over my shoulder. "Don't miss me too much."

"I won't," she promises, but she looks up and smiles, genuine this time. "Good luck."

"You *mean* 'break a leg,'" I correct as I'm almost out the door.

She does actually roll her eyes at that. "It's not a performance."

"'All the world's a stage,'" I quote with a flourish. She wads up a piece of scrap paper and throws it at me, but I easily sidestep it.

"'The fool doth think he is wise,'" she returns. At my impressed look, she frowns. "Why are you shocked? I have degrees in English literature. Several. You drama people don't corner the market on Shakespeare."

I consider her with narrowed eyes for a moment. "You win," I concede. "I don't have a comeback."

Hannah cackles and pumps her fist in victory as I close the door behind me on my way out.

The department chairs' offices are in their own special building across the quad. It makes no sense to me for them to be so far removed from the people they oversee, but office space is slim pickings, and if the college wants their department chairs lumped together, that's a decision above my pay grade. I take my time crossing the grassy space, enjoying the warm sun on my face and the activity of students milling about either on their way to Friday activities, home, or studying before night classes. The scent of lilac greets me, and I stop along the sidewalk to breathe it in deeply. It smells like springtime—like life is blooming all around me. I can't help but hope my life might be blooming along with it.

Slightly rejuvenated after that little jaunt outside, I pull open the heavy door to the building and bound up the two flights of stairs to Carl's office. His door is open, but he appears thoroughly engrossed in whatever is on his desk, so I knock on the doorframe.

He looks up at me, his eyes magnified by his strong reading glasses. This coupled with his slight, wiry stature kind of makes him look like a bug, and it's jarring no matter how many times I see it. Before coming here, he made a living playing either comical or villainous sidekicks. The work never dried up for him because he was able to fit the part so well just by being himself, but he decided he wanted to pass on the knowledge he had gained from his time onstage in a more stable job.

Thankfully, he removes his glasses before waving me over to a chair in front of his desk. "Lark, come on in. Close the door behind you, if you want."

I leave the door open and cross the room to the armchair facing his desk. He riffles through a huge stack of papers on his desk, looking for something. For the second time today, I'm left wondering when the people in this place will join the times and go digital.

"I had your evaluation paperwork here just a second ago..." he mumbles. Papers drop to the floor in his haste to find what he's looking for.

I lean over to pick them up and place them back on the edge of his desk. My phone vibrates in my bag as I do so, which reminds me to silence it. I take it out and glance at the screen, unsurprised to see Lennon's marshmallow-stuffed face lighting it up. Tag, I'm it.

"Here it is." Carl holds up a piece of paper in triumph. I click my phone to Silent and slide it back into my bag. He skims the paper, nods to himself, then sets it on top of another pile on his desk. "No surprises here. Another excellent evaluation." He eyes me carefully, as if he's not sure if he wants to say the next thing but he has to. "We'd love to see you branch out, though."

I straighten in my seat, leaning forward. This is exactly the segue I was looking for. "I'd also love to branch out. I know the Acting II classes are opening up with Monique retiring, and I have thought about a few shows I could maybe direct—" I cut myself off as Carl's lips tighten to a fine line.

"The Acting II classes are going to Paul," he says.

"Paul? He's been here half as long as I have."

"And has twice the field experience. Lark, we've been over this. You need to get back out there. Do some actual acting so you can bring that experience into the classroom. That's what I mean by branching out." He reaches to push his glasses up the bridge of his nose before he must realize they're no longer on his face.

I keep my voice even as I say, "You and I both know no one is interested in hiring someone as old as me for any of the fun roles."

"Even doing some community theater would help."

I raise an eyebrow. "Would it put me on the same playing field as Paul?" I try to keep the disdain out of my voice when I say his name but fail miserably.

Carl doesn't miss it and levels me with a warning look. "He's been in an off-Broadway show."

Yes, and he won't let anyone forget it. But I don't say that, because that would surely only make me look as bitter as I feel. I actually don't say anything. There's nothing I *can* say. Paul didn't spend his twenties changing diapers and finding pacifiers, and I did. That's all there is to it.

Carl stacks a few papers and taps the edges of them against his desk. "He can't out-teach you, Lark. You're excellent in the classroom, and the students love you. But the college wants the instructors to have more experience at the upper levels of coursework." He shrugs as if this is out of his hands, even though I know he could fight for me if he wanted. "Think about it. Are you teaching this summer?"

I shake my head slowly, not wanting my voice to betray me. I had opted out of teaching summer courses to be around to help Devin move before I knew she'd be taking a few weeks to backpack across Europe with her friends and then moving herself in with Richard until classes start. I'm still sore about that, too. Not at Devin, just at the universe for its cruel humor.

Carl nods once as if everything is settled. "Consider using that time to do something to take your career here to the next level." He starts riffling through his papers on his desk again, and I think I've been dismissed.

There's a lump rising in my throat, and I try not to look too dejected as I swallow it and stand to make my way back outside. The sun doesn't feel as rejuvenating anymore, but I do my best to shake it off. I can't have Devin thinking I'm bringing bad mojo to her track meet, or she'll blame me if it doesn't go as well as she hopes.

Thinking about Devin has me checking my phone as I pick up my pace to my car. Lennon's marshmallow face is silently lighting up my screen again. I'm not normally irritated with his calls, but this is getting a bit excessive. I grit my teeth and answer just as I'm sliding behind the steering wheel of my Honda. It connects to the speaker system as soon as I start the car. "Hey, listen, I'm on my way to Devin's meet—"

"I've been trying to get ahold of you for a week," he interrupts, a bit breathless.

"Sorry," I say, though I'm not feeling entirely apologetic. "The end of the school year is a little nutty—"

"Yeah. I get it. Do you have a minute right now, though, or..." He trails off.

I grind my teeth at his second interruption. He could just get to the point, but he's not going to without my permission, so I say, as brightly as I possibly can, given the circumstances, "I'm on my way to the meet, so I have"—I check the clock on the dashboard—"three minutes. What's up?" I back out of my parking space.

He takes a deep breath. "Okay. Before you say no—"

"No," I jump in.

He's silent for a moment, and I can feel the smile tugging at my lips as I inch through the intersection and onto the main road outside the campus. Banter with Lennon, I can do. It's as natural as breathing, and it goes a long way to make me less unbalanced.

"Lark, come on." He's trying to sound manly and reasonable, but there's an unmistakable whiny edge to his voice. He sounds so much like teenage Lennon that my heart skips.

"Sorry," I say again, and I mean it this time. "Go ahead."

"I have an idea. A proposal? No. Maybe a proposition." He's muttering now, trying to find the right word, but before I can pipe in to tell him to spit it out, he does. "I have this project. An audiobook. Two narrators. The female narrator had to drop out because she needs her tonsils removed, so I talked to the author and some people, and they'd like you to do it. Well, to audition. But we're in a bind, and you said the other day that you wanted to get back into acting. No, you didn't say that. You were sad about Devin leaving, but you kind of implied that you wanted to do something else and—"

"Lennon! Good lord, take a breath. You're making me nervous just listening to you." I swing my car around into the only parking space left at the high school. I can hear the crowd cheering through my closed windows. A glance at my clock tells me the meet just started, which means I have a little time before Devin's race.

"Let me get this straight," I say slowly. "You need a female audiobook narrator because someone is getting their tonsils out?"

"Yes."

"And you know the author well enough to suggest your high school friend should take on the role?"

"Jessica. Yes. Sort of."

There's a puzzle piece sliding into place. The name isn't familiar, but it sounds like someone Lennon may have spent some horizontal time with.

"Right. So you told *Jessica*"—I don't even try to hide the disdain in my voice—"who I am sure is very young and pretty, that your old hag bestie might be a good fit for this project in some kind of misguided white-knight moment to save me from my own impending empty-nest midlife crisis. Is that about right?"

He's silent for so long I check to see if he's hung up. He hasn't.

"I don't even know which part of that to respond to first," he finally admits.

"This is not one of your better ideas," I say flatly.

"It's a great idea." He sounds offended. "You're not teaching courses this summer. Devin is going to be traipsing around Europe with her friends and then headed to New York. You've done some voiceover work before. All you need is a microphone and a closet."

"You want me to spend my summer in a closet narrating a book. For Jessica." I am losing my grasp on reality with every minute this conversation carries on, so I turn off my car and press my phone to my ear so I can at least make my way closer to the track.

"I haven't slept with her, if that's what you keep implying."

"I think 'the lady doth protest too much.'" I really need to teach something more advanced, if only so I can stop analyzing Shakespeare in Intro to Theater. Just for a semester.

"There was no protesting. I said it one time."

"I don't care if you've slept with her or not. It's just a little weird that you're asking me to do this. You're in LA. Home of starlets and fame-seekers. Surely there's someone out there who can do this in a pinch." I arrive at the entrance to the track and smile at the security guard on duty. He waves me through.

"Look, you rattled me the other night, Lark. I felt really bad for you. And if we're being honest, I could use the money from this one. It's a big project. Bobby got engaged, and it would be a nice cushion in case it takes a while to find another roommate."

There's another puzzle piece sliding satisfyingly into place. Two, actually: pity and money.

I sigh heavily, pausing while the announcer's voice booms over the speakers, ushering in the next event. "I'm at Devin's meet, so I have to go. But I don't think this is in the cards for me, Len. Even if I got a mic and locked myself in the closet, I live next to a bunch of rentals in a college town. It's loud. It's why I quit voiceover work years ago."

The first runner crosses the finish line, and the crowd erupts just as Lennon says, "So come to LA. Do it here."

I plug my other ear with my finger. "I'm sorry. It sounded like you just said I should come to LA. I can't hear you over the crowd."

"I did," he shouts. "Come out here. I've got a room now that Bobby is leaving, and the studio has recording space. You've got time off and an empty place." He pauses as the announcer states the next event. "And I miss you," he adds once it's quiet again.

I miss him, too. Desperately, sometimes. Like the other night when I was lying on my side, pretending he was in bed next to me, giving me a hug I so fiercely needed. He gives the best hugs. They're the kind that completely envelop you and make you feel like absolutely nothing can touch you or harm you ever again.

"This is...a lot," I finally admit. It's a ridiculous idea. There's no need for me to go all the way to LA to record an audiobook. But I'd be lying if I said I was completely uninterested. If a little bit of Michigan sunshine in the quad earlier gave me some pep in my step, imagine what sunny Los Angeles could do for me. Not to mention that recording an audiobook could open more doors in the industry, which might satisfy Carl.

Though based on the slight crack I'm sure I heard in Lennon's voice when he said he misses me, I don't think this visit would really be about any of that. It'd be about spending time with my best and oldest friend. The rest of it would be a bonus.

Lennon's voice scatters my thoughts. "Yeah, of course. Take some time to think about it and call me later, okay?" He sounds nervous, and maybe a little dejected. Knowing him, he had this wild idea and thought it was so amazing there's no way I could turn it down.

But he knows me as well as I know him, so he should have been prepared for me to have to think it through.

"Okay," I say.

"Tell Devin she did great," he adds quickly.

"She hasn't run yet."

"I know. Doesn't matter. Whatever she does will be awesome. Okay, talk later."

Devin's event is up next, so I say a hasty goodbye, but for the first time in a long time, I feel like I'm standing at the edge of something really exciting. And it's not just the personal best Devin runs while I scream and jump up and down. Her teammates all rush onto the track at the end of her event, hugging her. She greets each of them in turn but makes sure to shine her smile up at me in the stands.

I'm so proud of this kid—and proud of myself for doing a good job raising her. She'll always need me, and I'll always be her mom, but right now, I have a chance to be just Lark again. Not Professor Caspian. Not Mom. Not even Lennon's Songbird. And the idea of it is so attractive, I'm having a hard time finding a reason not to go.

For the rest of the meet and long after we get home, eat dinner, celebrate with ice cream, and she retires to her room to call her friends, I try to talk myself out of it. I even look for flights thinking they'll be prohibitively expensive, but they're surprisingly reasonable. I decide to sleep on it because hasty decisions aren't my MO. But as I close my eyes, a giddy sensation washes over me.

I'm going to LA.

And I get to spend a summer with Lennon.

CHAPTER 4

LENNON

> Lark: What is the book called? I'll buy it so I can read through it.

> Lark: Or does Jessica have a scene she can send me for an audition?

I COULD BARELY SLEEP last night. I didn't bother going to the club, even though Noah invited me out for Friday night drinks. I hadn't meant to ask Lark to come out to LA for the summer. It just kind of slipped out. But now that I've said it, I'm having a hard time thinking about anything else.

Even though I know sensible and sturdy Lark would never.

And yet I can't help but hope.

So when I roll over and see Lark's texts, my heart starts galloping. Is it possible that she might actually agree to this?

Which is also about when my heart bottoms out. I hadn't thought to mention that Jessica's novel is a spicy romance. Or rather, I had thought to mention it. I just didn't feel like shouting it over the ambient noise from Devin's track meet.

Better she goes into this with her eyes wide open, I suppose.

> Lennon: It's called Sizzling Secrets by Jessica Jordans.

I chew on my lip while I watch the three dots appear and disappear at the bottom of the screen. Finally, a message comes through.

> Lark: No way.

> Lennon: Yes way. I can send you a PDF so you don't need to buy it.

> Lark: No need. I own it.

The next message is a picture of Lark holding up a copy of the book next to her face. She's flashing an amused grin.

> Lennon: I didn't know you were a fan.

> Lark: I saw it everywhere. I was curious. I haven't gotten around to reading it yet, but I will.

> Lennon: I'm suddenly nervous about this.

> Lark: Why? Does she give away your bedroom secrets in it?

> Lennon: I didn't sleep with her.

> Lark: My bad. I forgot. I'll record an audition of a few pages at the office later today and send it over. Cool?

I stare at that message for a lot longer than I should. Ultimately, I hit the Call button at the top of the screen. The phone rings once before Lark's face lights up in front of me.

I don't even bother with a hello. "So, you're coming?" I feel like a kid on Christmas morning—excited that I might get exactly what I wished for, but also not quite sure what's coming.

Lark chews her bottom lip. "Were you serious about it?"

"Hell yeah, I was serious about it. I'd love to have you here, Songbird. I'm already making a list of all the things I want to show you."

"What if Jessica doesn't like the audition?" There's a little trepidation in her voice, but I don't miss the slight emphasis she adds to Jessica's name. I decide to ignore it.

"She will. She'll be grateful we found someone last-minute." That's probably not exactly true, but I've been in meetings with Jessica all week and she did agree to listen to Lark's audition, which is something. "You'll knock it out of the park. I'm sure of it." I'm trying not to sound too overeager, but the idea of having Lark here for the entire summer is making me smile like an idiot.

"I guess if she doesn't like it, I'm back where I started, which isn't so bad." She looks off to the side as she says it, muttering more to herself than to me.

My heart cracks open. This isn't the confident, self-assured Lark I went to high school with. When did that happen?

"She will love it, and either way, you're coming out here for the summer." Now that I've gotten my hopes up about spending time with her, I'm going to ensure that it happens. Audiobook or no. "You don't need a reason to hang out in LA for a few months."

Her eyes snap to the screen. "You're the reason." Then she says, quieter, "You're the reason whether I record an audiobook or not."

We stare at each other through the phone for a while, soft smiles creeping up both our faces.

I'm the first to break the silence. "I'm going to hug the shit out of you when you get off that plane."

Lark's smile turns mischievous. "Is that a promise or a threat?"

CHAPTER 5

LARK

I SHIFT RESTLESSLY IN my office chair. It squeaks, and I catch Hannah's lips tightening into a thin line, though her eyes stay trained on her computer screen. I refocus my energy on my own monitor to try to input the grades from the final I gave yesterday, but the letters aren't registering. Can I just give everyone an A? Surely this would make all parties involved happy—I could be finished with grades, the students would get a bump in their GPA...

No. I can't. For a million reasons, not least of which is because an adjunct professor in the math department was fired a few years ago for grade inflation. But also because once I eventually come to my senses, I'll kick myself for allowing Cade Peyton—resident class clown and king of doing the least amount of work possible to eke out a C minus—to get a better grade than he deserves.

I skip down to the P's on the roster and enter his grade while I'm thinking about it. His percentage comes out to a 69.7, which will round up. *That little...*

Hannah clears her throat loudly enough that it's obvious she wants my attention. I slowly drag my eyes away from my screen to meet her brown ones, which are narrowed on me.

"What?" I ask after a few seconds of silent staring.

"What is wrong with you today?" she finally asks exasperatedly.

My chair squeaks again as I rear back in it. "Nothing. Why?"

"You haven't stopped fidgeting and grumbling to yourself since you came in here. You are an absolute cacophony of noises over there, and not in a good way."

Running through the past hour in my head, I have to admit she's probably right. I have been fidgety today. I was up late last night trying to persuade myself to click *Buy* on the plane tickets to LA. It's not that I don't want to go; it's just that I'm not sure it's the best idea. What if staying with Lennon for two months is weird? We've never roomed together for longer than a weekend before. What if Jessica doesn't like the audition I send? Not that I've recorded that yet, either. I can only hype myself up to do one thing at a time. What if Lennon wants to spend time at the beach? Of course he'll want to spend time at the beach. It's Los Angeles, for fuck's sake. It's basically the whole reason he went out there in the first place. And here I am without a single swimsuit to my name. What if...

"Am I attractive?" I blurt out without thinking.

Hannah barks out a harsh sound that I think is a laugh, but it's hard to be sure. She slaps a hand over her mouth, then smacks her other hand over that one as if she can physically contain more of those sounds from escaping.

I frown deeply and find a pen to play with on my desk so I don't have to look at her eyes, which are now undoubtedly full of mirth. "Damn. I mean, I know I'm older and have popped out a kid, but I didn't think it was that bad."

Hannah's shoulders fall away from her ears as she removes her hands from her mouth and rests her elbows on her desk. "Shit, no. I'm sorry, Lark. I didn't mean it like that. That was just maybe the world's most unexpected question."

"Not if you're in my brain," I grumble.

"Well, I'm not in your brain, so how about you walk me through how you got there?" she asks, her voice overly sympathetic as if she's trying to make up for her outburst.

I take in a deep breath, hoping the extra oxygen will help organize my thoughts. It doesn't.

"I might be narrating an audiobook this summer."

Hannah blinks a few times, then stares at me blankly. When I don't elaborate, she pinches her brows together. "You do know no one can actually see you narrate an audiobook, right?"

I let out a frustrated puff of air. "Of course I know that."

She closes her eyes and draws in a slow breath through her nose as if she's counting to ten and trying not to lose it. When she opens them again, her expression is carefully neutral. "Are you asking about whether or not your *voice* is attractive? Because when you're saying things that make sense, I happen to think your voice is super hot—"

"No," I interrupt, shaking my head. "No. Okay, let me back up. Lennon asked me to narrate this audiobook. Or rather, audition for it."

One corner of her mouth ticks up as if she's suddenly very interested in where this conversation is going. "High school Lennon?"

"How many Lennons do you know of?" I ask, my voice flat.

"Aside from John?"

Even though Lennon's hippie parents did, in fact, name him after the famous singer, he hates the comparison. Unluckily for him, it's the first thing anyone brings up whenever they meet him. Richard used to call him Johnny when we were in school, until I made it clear that we couldn't date unless he stopped antagonizing him. Now he only uses the nickname when Lennon's not around.

I raise an eyebrow, unimpressed. "I'm not dignifying that with a response." Hannah chuckles to herself while I pin her with a glare. "From what I can gather, he's the sound engineer for this project. The original female narrator has to get her tonsils out, and Lennon doesn't want the project to die, so he asked if I could do it."

"What's the book?"

"Irrelevant to this conversation." I don't want to share that information if I can help it.

"Incorrect. I'm an English professor. Books are always relevant to the conversation."

I sigh. "*Sizzling Secrets* by Jessica Jordans."

Hannah's eyes practically bug out of her head. Her jaw slackens, then her mouth curves up into a sinister smile. This is exactly why I didn't want to tell her.

"No fucking way," she practically whispers.

"Oh, so you've heard of it," I ask drolly.

"Heard of it? I've read it twice. That book is..." She fans herself as she leans back in her chair.

I bury my face in my hands and groan. "Fuck," I mutter.

Hannah pops up in her seat to tip forward again. "She self-published and topped the charts."

"I know." My voice is muffled by my palms.

"She's had publishing houses beating down the doors for rights but won't sell because she's making too much money."

"I know."

"Lark. Honey. This could be huge for you." Her voice has an edge of excitement I don't usually hear from her, and it makes me peek out at her through my fingers. Her eyes are wide, and her eyebrows have shot up her head. It would maybe be encouraging if she weren't so overeager.

"No pressure," I grumble as I hide behind my hands again.

"Okay, okay, okay." She waves at the air in front of her as if wiping the conversational slate clean. "Lennon thinks you'll be good for this project, and you're going to audition, but you're worried about sounding attractive while narrating a sexy audiobook?" she guesses.

Her eyes go impossibly wider like something just occurred to her. She picks up the framed picture I have of Lennon from my desk, the one of him standing in a sleeveless shirt and board shorts next to his Jeep with a gorgeous beach and the ocean behind him. His tattoo stretches in black ink from his elbow to just under his shirt, and another one of a compass is visible on his forearm underneath it. He's squinting into the sunlight and smiling an easy smile, his shirt is tucked to give a hint at washboard abs, and his dirty-blond hair is mussed up and wavy from the salt water.

She studies it and turns it to me. "You're worried about Hot Lennon from high school listening to you narrate a sexy audiobook since he's the one who has to do all the edits and sound mixing and all that? Because if that's the case, don't be. I think this could actually be good for you to maybe break through something in your relationship with him—"

"Good lord, Hannah. No. Stop." I put up my palms to face her as if that could put a dam in this river of her thought process. Truthfully, I hadn't thought about Lennon listening to me narrate the steamier parts of this book, and now that the seed has been planted, it has my heart trying to beat nervously out of my chest. "At least, I *wasn't* worried about that, but now that you mention it, it's super weird, and I don't want to go." I don't even want to touch whatever she meant about breaking through something in our relationship. I can only deal with one problem at a time.

"Wait," she backpedals. "Go where?"

"Los Angeles. When he brought it up, I told him it's hard to record here. The college kids are loud, even over the summer. So, he suggested I go to LA, stay with him for a while, and record out there. If they want me to do it, that is."

She waves this away. "They'll want you. Even if they weren't desperate, your voice is perfect for Gia."

"Who's Gia?"

Hannah blinks at me a few times in disbelief. "The woman from the book," she says, as if that should be obvious. To be fair, it probably should be, but I haven't had a chance to read any part of it yet.

"Oh. Thanks."

"Okay, then you're worried about Lennon seeing you again after, what, a decade or so and not thinking you're hot?"

"Fuck, Hannah. I do not care if Lennon thinks I'm hot! It's Los Angeles, where beautiful people go to play. There will be time at the beach, possibly in a bathing suit. People will see me. *Men*, specifically. Attractive ones." I circle my hand in the air in front of us, willing her to put the pieces together.

She tilts her head and regards me. "Let's say I believe you when you say this is about men in general and not one man in particular." I start to protest, but she talks over me. "And let's also say I can put away my lecture on body positivity and self-love about how every body is a beach body for just a minute."

"Super excited to hear that lecture before I leave for the day," I mutter.

"Oh, I'm sure you are. Regardless of all that, I'm going to say this only one time, because I truly do not think it matters one bit, but I can tell it's wearing on you."

Yeah, that and a bunch of other things now that we've had this conversation, I say to myself.

"You, Lark Caspian, are smoking hot. And not 'hot for almost forty' or 'hot for a mom.' Not even '*I have to say this because you're my friend hot.*' Objectively hot. This"—she waves a hand up and down indicating me—"is princess-level shit. Giant blue eyes. Blonde hair that is only ever in ringlets, and I'm still not sure how you do it after knowing you for the better part of a decade. Adorable freckles."

This is starting to get weird. "You're making me sound like Shirley Temple," I grouse.

"That's because I thought commenting on your bombshell curves and long legs would make it awkward. But that's true, too. You could have any guy you wanted, including Hot Lennon."

"Can you stop calling him that?"

"Why? Jealous?"

I blink at her. "No."

"Okay." She says it like she doesn't believe me, then she laughs.

"I'm so glad my distress is a source of amusement for you," I intone.

Her expression falls to one of sincerity. "It's not. I swear." She takes in a deep breath, then lets it out slowly. "Listen, I have so much respect for you. Raising an amazing kid, getting your master's, landing a full professorship here, not to mention all the shit you had to deal with while you were doing it. But I've never seen you date. Or, for that matter, perform. I kind of thought you'd get back into at least one of those things when Devin got older, but you didn't. And it's none of my business why," she clarifies quickly, "but this is a chance for you to do both. Maybe you won't hook up with Hot Lennon. But you can do something I know you love doing, and maybe bang a Los Angeles himbo in the process. And then come back and tell me all about it." Her words are crass, but her smile is genuine. I return it, even as my stomach flops with new fears I didn't know I had until just now.

"You're right," I admit. "I think half the reason he suggested this in the first place is because he caught me in a midlife-crisis moment and felt bad. He's trying to shake me out of it." I shrug. "And I probably agreed because I do need this. *Not* to 'bang a hot himbo,' necessarily, but to do something...else. Just for a little while."

Hannah nods sagely as if she came to that conclusion a while ago. Who knows. Maybe she did. Maybe everyone knows more about what I need than I do. I just wish they'd loop me in on it every once in a while.

"Okay, so what's first? Getting you a bathing suit that'll turn heads?" she asks.

I laugh, and some of the butterflies in my stomach calm slightly. "I suppose the first thing I need to do is record my audition. He didn't tell me what to record, so I guess I'll send the first chapter?" I honestly have no idea what the right way to go about this is.

Hannah's expression goes blank again, then she suddenly starts to cackle.

I lay my palms on my desktop, trying not to clench my fists in irritation. "What?"

She dabs fake tears away from her eyes. *Over-acter*, I think.

"You haven't read the book yet, have you?" she asks through her residual laughter.

"No," I admit. "I bought it when it came out, but I haven't had a chance to read it. I was going to thumb through it today to make some character notes, but then I got roped into this conversation." I raise an eyebrow at her.

She hasn't stopped laughing, though it seems like she's trying to hold back. "The book opens with the couple hooking up in a storage room closet."

"It does not." Maybe if I say it, I can will it to be true.

Hannah snorts, then covers her mouth again. "It does."

I drop my forehead to the desk in front of me, then bang it a few times for good measure. "I can't do this."

"It's a brilliant example of starting a story *in medias res*, actually," Hannah says in her best professor voice.

"I seriously can't do this," I say louder, though it's still directed at the floor.

"You can, and you will." She's all business now, and I'm wondering where that was a moment ago. It would have been more helpful than her hysteria. "Come on, slugger. I'll help you find a good passage to send in, and you can get it recorded here before you head home for the night."

***

After a lot of back-and-forth and some procrastination with a discussion about who is going to watch my townhouse while I'm gone, Hannah ultimately ends up offering to house-sit and then persuading—ahem, bullying—me to go ahead and record the first chapter. I do it right in the office because I don't have access to a recording booth, and Lennon had said it didn't matter. They just need to hear my voice.

Hannah wasn't lying about it starting right in the middle of the action, so to speak, and even though she wisely excuses herself while I record it, I don't know if my face has ever felt so hot for so long in my life. I blush through the entire thing like some kind of prude.

I send the unedited take to Lennon before I can overthink it. It'd be his job to edit it anyway, so as soon as I get a take that's as clean as possible, I let him have it. I shut down my computer and put my phone on silent before heading home. If Lennon listens to this and calls me, I don't want to know about it. I need some time for the flames licking my cheeks to calm down before I talk to him.

By the time I pull into our garage, Devin is already home. When I open the front door, I'm greeted by the scent of garlic, onions, and tomatoes. I toe off my shoes and drop by bag near the door before making my way to the kitchen. Devin is at the stove, her dark ponytail bouncing as she dances back and forth in front of the stove. She's stirring what looks like marinara sauce, and there's another, larger pot of boiling water next to it.

"You cooked dinner?" I try not to sound incredulous, but this almost never happens. "What's the occasion?"

She glances over her shoulder at me and smiles. Her coloring is Richard's—dark hair and eyes, an olive skin tone, and no freckles to speak of—but her face is all mine. Large eyes, full pink lips, and a heart-shaped face ending in a cute, pointed chin. *Princess-level shit* indeed. Maybe Hannah had a point earlier today. I know I'm biased, but Devin is a beautiful girl. Maybe, if my genes had anything to do with that, I'm not so bad myself. I straighten my posture a bit as I sit in the kitchen chair.

Devin shrugs as she turns back to the stove. "Coach suggested I try carb-loading this week before our last meet, so I stopped at the store and figured I could handle making pasta." She pauses like she's unsure if she should say the next thing, but then she goes for it. "And I'm going to have to cook for myself pretty soon, anyway."

Well, that hurt like hell. I rub my chest as if that could take the pain away.

She whips around as if she knew the knife she just threw hit a bullseye. "Plus, you work so hard. I wanted to, like, show my appreciation or something," she adds quickly.

I can't help but chuckle at that. "Gee. Thanks, kid."

She slinks into the table, leaving the pasta to cook and the sauce to simmer. "I'm sorry, Mom. I know you're going to miss me." She chews on her lip as her gaze falls to the table. "I'm going to miss you, too. I think it kind of just hit me today that in a few weeks I'll be gone and..." She trails off. Her dark eyes start to shine with unshed tears. I reach out a hand to cover hers where they're clasped on top of the table. "What are you going to do?" she asks quietly. "Will you be lonely?"

I blink away my own tears at this unexpected and completely unprecedented display of teenage empathy. *She's a good kid*, Lennon's voice echoes in my mind. I pat her hands a few times.

She's the best kid.

I huff a small laugh. "Funny you should ask, actually. I wanted to talk to you about that tonight." The kitchen timer goes off. "Let's get some food first, huh? It smells amazing."

Devin preens at the compliment. She jumps up, insisting that I stay seated so she can serve me. She doesn't have to tell me twice. I settle in and let her bring a plate of pasta to me.

I'm going to miss her like hell. Which makes me all the more certain that I need to do this thing in LA, if only to get my mind off of how much of a hole she's leaving in my life.

Once we've eaten a bit and I've sufficiently embarrassed her with compliments about how delicious the food is, I lay out the entire opportunity Lennon has presented me with. I try to ham up my excitement so she can stop feeling bad about leaving me, but I find I don't have to try very hard to make it sound like I'm thrilled to be taking this on. I gloss over the spice level of the book, but Devin is too smart for that. She asks what book it is, and I tell her. She doesn't seem fazed, but when I tell her it's a bit explicit, she levels me with one of those exasperated, teenage looks.

"Mom. I know," she says.

I narrow my eyes at her. "What do you mean you know? Have you read it?"

She makes a disgusted face. "No, but I don't live under a rock." She pushes some pasta around on her plate and avoids eye contact with me when she says, "And some of my friends have."

It never occurred to me that narrating this audiobook might have implications for Devin, and I mentally smack myself in the forehead for not considering it sooner. "Would it bother you to have your mom working on this?" I ask carefully. "I can use a stage name if you'd rather."

Devin takes a bite and chews thoughtfully, considering the question. I find myself holding my breath, waiting for her answer.

She swallows and her dark eyes meet mine, determined. "You're doing this. That's not even a question. I don't know how you've lived so long without seeing Lennon in person. If I didn't see Molly for ten years, I'd be so sad." Her eyebrows pinch together. "And I think it's cool you'll be narrating this book. You deserve to have your real name on it." She shrugs again, as if this is no big deal. "Anyone who gets weird about it isn't worth my time anyway."

My smile stretches across my face, wide and open. I'm sure if we were in public, it'd embarrass the hell out of her, but in the privacy of our home, she returns it. I'm not quite sure how I got so lucky with her, but she's the best thing that has ever happened to me.

"I'm so proud of you, kid," I say.

"I'm proud of you, too, Mom." She stands and collects my empty plate, so she isn't looking at me when she says it, but it fills me up all the same.

CHAPTER 6

LENNON

His hands skate down my back, cupping my ass and squeezing tight. I angle my hips so I can feel his hardness pressed up against me, right where I need it most. A thrill passes through me at the effect I'm having on him, though I shouldn't be surprised. He was the one who grabbed my hand and led me into the storage room closet. We certainly weren't coming in here to talk. Still, knowing a man wants me the way Marcus does is its own kind of high.

We don't have much time before someone comes looking for us, so I make quick work of the buttons

on the fly of his jeans. I reach my hand into them,
circling it around the smooth, hard length...

I RIP MY EARBUDS out of my ears and lay my palms flat against my
desk in front of me. My breath is coming in rapid pants, and I have to
consciously work to get it under control. I don't even want to think
about what's going on between my legs. If I acknowledge that, then I'll
have to admit that my best friend's voice gave me a hard-on, and I don't
know if I can do that quite yet.

I don't think I've ever heard Lark sound like this. Her voice was husky
and overflowing with sultry longing. It sounded like she had just woken
up, but not exactly like when my phone call rips her from a deep sleep.
More like a lover had roused her with a line of hot kisses down her
neck. I find myself wondering if she would, in fact, sound like this if
someone woke her in that way, and I have to clench my fists against
another unexpected wave of desire.

My phone rings from where it sits on the desk next to me. Saved by the
bell.

"That was phenomenal," Noah says when I answer it. "Holy shit, Len.
What a find. Where has she been all my life?"

"Michigan," I grind out with more roughness than I intend.

I had excitedly sent Lark's audition over to him before listening to it
myself, not thinking she'd have started with the first chapter. In retrospect, I'm not sure which chapter she would have started with instead.
I'm proud of Lark for nailing this audition, but at the same time, I'm
regretting my hasty forwarding of her email to Noah. The edges of rage
creep up around me at his obvious infatuation with her voice.

I need to get a fucking grip. Noah is *married*, for fuck's sake. With
children. He doesn't want her like that. He just wants her to narrate this
book. And regardless, Lark isn't mine.

She is mine, though. My best and oldest friend. My high school savior and confidante. My Songbird. My favorite person in the world. Just not mine in any kind of way that would excuse me feeling like *this*.

Noah doesn't hear any of this in my tone, though. He just clucks from his end of the line and says, "With a voice like that, she should be out here. Or at least doing this full time. I want to get her on our roster—"

"Whoa," I cut in. "I know you're excited. I am, too. But let's see how this one goes, okay? She might not even like doing this, and I don't want to scare her off."

I can practically hear the wheels in Noah's head turning. "Yeah," he says slowly. "I like that. Play a little hard to get. Make her want it as much as we want her."

That isn't at all what I meant, but I let it go. "Right. Okay, so do you want to talk to Jessica about this or..." I trail off before offering to do it myself. I really don't want to get any more involved than I already am.

"Yeah, we'll take it from here. I'll have our intern do some practice editing on this file for extra experience. You said Lark is coming here in two weeks? Any way we can move that up a bit so we can get started sooner? Provided Jessica approves. Which, honestly, if she hears what I'm hearing, she will."

"Her daughter is graduating high school, and she's coming as soon as she can after that. I don't think we can move it up."

"Oh. No, probably not. High school graduation is a big deal. I get that. Okay then, leave this with me, and I'll keep you posted. But man, I'd really love to meet her when she gets here. Do you think you can arrange a meeting?"

"A meeting?" A little kernel of anxiety starts to form in my stomach. This is turning into something bigger than I suggested it would be when I first broached the topic with Lark, and I'm quickly losing control of both this situation and my libido. Is he going to woo her and try to get her to move out here to pursue acting as a career? I'm sure she would have died for an opportunity like that in another life, but he's kidding himself if he thinks he can drag her away from that professor gig she worked so hard for. No, I need to take this down a notch.

I breathe in to a count of four and out at the same speed to try to tame my suddenly racing heart. "She's my friend. You're my friend. We'll get together for lunch or drinks or something casual."

"Right. Yes. Even better. Okay, Len. Thank you. Talk soon." He hangs up without waiting for a goodbye.

I set my phone down and pinch the bridge of my nose. If Lark is going to do this thing, and it sounds like she is, I'm going to have to get it together, and fast.

It's not the first time I've had to get a handle on my desire for her. I still don't know why she gave me the time of day when we first met. She certainly didn't have to. She's always been the most beautiful girl I've known.

I was the new kid freshman year. My parents had decided to move in the middle of September, well after school had already started. Why they traded the big blue skies and wide-open spaces of Wyoming for the dingy, gray streets of eastern Michigan, I'll never know. But I was pissed about it and had stubbornly decided I wouldn't bother trying to make any friends this time. The only place there was room for me was in the back of each classroom, so I spent the first three weeks sitting quietly there. Forget about friends at lunch; I ate alone. I kept to myself, determined to create as few ties as possible.

About a month into the move, I ended up after school waiting for someone to pick me up. It's unclear if my parents had something to do and didn't tell me or if they had simply forgotten about me. I figured wandering around the school was better than sitting with a bunch of emotions I didn't want to have, so I started walking. No one stopped me. No one asked me what I was doing. No one even cared I was there. It was like I was invisible.

The sound of gibberish coming from down the hall greeted me as I rounded a corner. It was too weird to even be a foreign language. Figuring I was invisible anyway, I followed the sounds to a classroom with the door propped open and looked inside. The desks had been moved out of the way, and there were about fifteen students standing in a circle shouting words at each other. Someone must have messed up or something, because they all started laughing or good-naturedly punching one of the kids in the arm.

"Hi," came a voice from behind me.

I turned around slowly, wondering who could see me if no one else seemed to be able to. A girl with long blonde hair and huge blue eyes was standing there, smiling up at me.

I looked to the left and right to see who else she could be talking to. No one was there. I pointed at my chest. "Me?" I asked.

"Yes, you." She giggled, and it was a magical sound. Warm. Sparkling. *Beautiful*, some little voice said, springing up in the back of my head. She was really pretty, I realized. And for some reason, she was talking to me.

"Uh, hi," I said uselessly.

"I'm Lark." She stuck out her hand with her long, thin fingers pointed toward me.

By the grace of whatever in the universe is holy, I had the good sense not to stand there like an idiot. I took her hand in mine and shook it. "I'm Lennon."

She tilted her head, and I steeled myself for what I knew was coming next. *Like John?* It came without fail, every single time I met someone new.

But instead, she smiled again, like it was easy for her to do so. Like she never had to think about whether or not she was really happy. She just *was*.

"I like *L* names," she announced. "Lark and Lennon. Sounds musical, doesn't it?"

It took me so much by surprise that I gaped at her for what felt like multiple minutes. She didn't seem uncomfortable by it, though. She stood there, her tiny frame unabashedly taking up as much space as it could with her shoulders squared and her back ramrod straight. It was clear to me that she was the type of person who was not only used to people looking at her but who liked it when they did.

Must be nice to be seen like that, I thought. I sort of wished some of her visibility would rub off on me.

"You want to play?" she asked, nodding toward the doorway where the kids inside had started up their nonsense words again.

"Play?"

"This is Drama Club. You know, the theater kids? We're doing improv games today." She adorably scrunched up her nose. "It's a little weird, but it's fun once you get the hang of it."

"Oh," I said, my shoulders falling heavy with regret. "I'm not part of Drama Club." I would have given a lot just then to spend more time in her presence, and I would have settled for joining this group and at least having something to do until someone remembered I existed.

She bounced forward on her toes, leaning closer to me as if she were going to tell me a secret. "No one is part of Drama Club until they come to a meeting. And look at you, here for a meeting." She ticked her head toward the door. "Come on. I'll teach you how to play."

With that, Lark bounded past me over the threshold and into the classroom. The circle parted and made room for her, absorbing her into its circumference. I hesitated at the doorway, sure there was no more room for me in a circle that already looked complete.

A teacher I hadn't noticed spoke up from the corner. "Lark, is your friend going to be joining us?"

She looked at me from her spot in the circle but didn't hesitate. "Yeah, he is. Everyone, this is Lennon."

"Hi, Lennon," came a chorus of voices. They spoke together like a well-oiled machine. Or like a cult. It was a little disconcerting, if I was being honest. But I also desperately wanted to be a part of it.

"Hi." I waved like a total dork and considered turning right around and walking back out in that moment. And yet the circle broke and opened up a spot next to Lark. For me, I belatedly realized. They were allowing me to be a part of this, no questions asked, which was exactly what I wanted not two minutes ago. I'd be an absolute moron not to step in.

So I did.

My phone ringing cuts through my reverie. As if my memories have summoned her, Lark's picture lights up my phone screen. It's a candid shot I snapped of her the last time we were together. Her head is tipped to the sky and laughter is bubbling up out of her. It's one of those pictures you can almost hear. *Warm. Sparkling. Beautiful.* Still so easy for her to be happy, even when things are hard.

It's not a video call, which must mean she doesn't want to see me after sending that sexy-as-hell audition. That's fair. I'm not sure I'm ready to see her, either. My face might still give too much away.

I answer the call on speaker. "Hey," I say a little too brightly. I immediately grimace.

"Oh, great." She knows. "You listened to it. So that's weird now."

"Uh…" I trail off.

"I don't want to know what you thought," she says quickly. "That's not... We're..." She pauses to find her words. "We're not going to talk about that right now."

I laugh softly at her discomfort. Not because I think it's funny, but because I'm relieved it's not just me. She laughs, too, and somehow that's enough to kick us back into our normal rapport.

"What's going on, Songbird?"

Her laughter is cut short by a sigh. "Listen, I know you have a room at your place opening up, which is why you want me to stay with you. But...um...I was thinking, maybe that's not a great idea."

I frown and run my hand through my shaggy hair. I should probably get a haircut before she gets here. "Why not?"

She lets out a low hum. "Because of your..." She trails off again. "I don't want to cramp your style."

"What style?" I ask, genuinely confused and a little nervous. I mean, yes, I need a roommate, but I have been ridiculously excited about the prospect of uninterrupted time with Lark. Movie nights on the couch with popcorn. Watching the sun set from the balcony. No worry about traffic or transportation.

Lark makes a noise that can only mean she's frustrated at having to explain herself. "What if you want to bring someone home?" she asks as if the words have been ripped from her in a whoosh.

I bark out a laugh, mostly because I hadn't even thought about this—not because I thought it'd be fine to bring women home with me while she's staying here, but because I'd never do that. It wouldn't even be a thought.

"I'm not bringing anyone back here this summer, Lark. I can promise you that."

"I don't want to be the reason you're not having any fun," she insists.

I don't miss a beat. "You're the fun." Then, I consider what that must have sounded like and backtrack quickly. "Not that you and I would be... I just mean that..."

She laughs a big, hearty laugh. It's so loud through the phone speaker that I wince. "I knew what you meant."

"What if *you* want to bring someone back?" I tease. "There are a lot of hot guys out here."

"So I've been told," she grumbles, but before I can ask what that's all about, she says, "That's not a thing I do."

"Mmm," I hum. "Never say *never*."

"I'm going to go ahead and say *never*," she replies. If I'm not mistaken, I hear a tinge of bitterness in her tone.

My phone beeps with an incoming call before I can explore that topic with her. I look at the screen, and I'm shocked to see Devin's name scrolling across the top of it. She doesn't call me often, though she knows she always can if she needs something. If she's calling, it must be important, and it must also be something she doesn't want to loop Lark in on.

"Hey, I'm getting another call. Work thing," I lie. "Can I call you back later?"

"Oh, no need. I'm going to book my flights right now. I'll text you the info."

"Awesome," I say before clicking over to Devin's call. This one is a video call, so her face fills the screen as soon as I answer. "Hey, kiddo. Everything okay?"

"Yeah." She puts her chin in her hands. A quick glance behind her tells me she's in her bedroom. It's still lined with some of the same boy-band posters from her childhood, along with a rack of track medals she's acquired over the years.

"What's going on?" I ask, since she doesn't seem like she's going to be forthcoming with the reason for her call.

"I just talked to my mom about her staying with you this summer."

"Oh yeah?" I ask, leaning back in my chair. She seems to be working up toward something, and I don't want to push.

"I think it's great. She needs something like this. Major props to you for suggesting it."

A little bubble of pride rises in my chest. There's something about the approval of a teenager that feels better than any other kind of accolade. But she's still a teenager, so I have to play it cool. "I'm glad."

She scratches her head and looks off to the side in uncertainty before pinning her gaze to the screen, resolved. "Take care of her, okay?"

Not resolved. Worried. She's about to shift into something totally new, but so is her mom. Things are changing fast for both of them. I'm sure she's worried about herself, too, but she clearly wants to make sure her mom is okay before she steps out on her own.

Devin is the sweetest damn kid to ever exist.

"You know your mom is really precious to me, right?" I ask around a sudden swell of emotion.

She nods cautiously. "I think I do."

"I've known her longer than you've been alive," I remind her. "She met me during a really important time of my life and made me feel like I belonged somewhere. I hadn't ever felt that before."

Devin smiles. "Yeah, she does that."

I grin back. "It's taken me over twenty years, but I'm going to return the favor. I think..." I stop myself, not wanting to worry her any more than she already is. "Your mom loves you more than anything in the world."

"I might be tied with you," she smirks.

I tilt my head back and forth. "Maybe. But if it came down to a death match, she'd be rooting for you."

"That's morbid. But I think I get what you're saying. I don't want her to be lost without me here."

I carefully consider my next words. "Your mom is the strongest, most determined woman I've ever met. She won't be lost without you, kiddo. But I think, maybe, she needs a little break to do something for herself. What do you think?"

Devin nods vigorously. "I'm so excited she's doing this. She needs it." She chews on her bottom lip. "I just want to make sure someone is watching out for her while I'm gone, you know?"

"I know," I say gently. "I promise you I'll take care of her."

"Thanks, Lennon." She moves as if she's getting ready to hang up, then pulls back again to pin me with a look. "Oh, and please don't tell my mom I called you. She'll lecture me about staying out of her business or whatever, and I can*not*."

I laugh loudly and easily. This kid reminds me so much of her mother at that age—so audacious and unassumingly funny. It's no wonder she's so amazing.

"Your secret's safe with me."

CHAPTER 7

LARK

DID I SCHEDULE MY flight to Los Angeles at around the same time as Devin's flight to Munich so I could go with her to the airport and hug her goodbye?

Yes, I did, I have no shame.

In retrospect, this may not have been the best of ideas. I should have gotten her ready to go and sent off to Germany for the first leg of her trip, then come back and gotten myself ready. In my defense, I didn't want to spend much time alone in our townhouse after she left. I felt like I might lose my nerve if I had any time to sit with my own thoughts. And that may have been true, but the result is one of the most hectic weekends I can ever remember.

Devin was supposed to have packed everything she needed for the first month of school so we could send it out to Richard and have it waiting for her when she got there. I was going to meet her out there after I got back from LA to help get her settled in her dorm and bring anything she inevitably forgot.

She did not, in fact, pack anything. So, a bunch of things happen in very quick succession: Richard and his new wife, Rachel, come in in time for graduation—and a little bit of a vacation away from their five-year-old son, RJ. We watch Devin walk across the stage, we all go to a very nice dinner together, and then Richard insists on taking her shopping for dorm essentials. Never mind that this is my last weekend with her for two months. Never mind that he was supposed to do this with her when she came back from her trip. Never mind that she has nothing packed to send back with him.

But when she pins me with her puppy-dog eyes and promises she'll do the packing when she gets home, I cave. Which leaves me alone and packing for myself. It would be nice if I weren't in the middle of about three existential crises.

One, my daughter is leaving for college, and I'm going to miss her like hell.

Two, I still don't have a bathing suit.

And three, suddenly none of my summer clothes are cute. Which I don't understand, because they were cute last year.

Three-B would be that I don't have time to shop, which means I'm going to have to either find two months' worth of excuses for not swimming or go with Lennon. I'm not sure which is more embarrassing.

Lennon calls, interrupting at least twenty minutes of me standing uselessly in front of my closet with an open—and empty—suitcase. I answer it gratefully.

"What do people wear in LA?" I ask by way of greeting.

"Um...clothes?" is his response.

I glare at his image on the screen. "Can you be a little more specific?"

"Probably not," he says. When I shoot him another look, he holds his hands up in front of the camera. "Okay, okay. I'll try. It's usually warm and dry. Sunny. It gets cool by the water at night or in the morning. I'd say bring some jeans and sweatshirts, shorts, T-shirts, tank tops. Normal summer stuff. The recording studio is super casual, too, so any of those things would be good. And then, I don't know...pajamas? Leggings? Do women still wear leggings?"

"You can pry my leggings out of my cold, dead hands," I say flatly.

"Well, there you go. Leggings. Whatever you need to feel comfortable is fine. And I have a washer and dryer in my unit, so you'll be able to do laundry without much hassle."

"I just want to look cute," I admit, scrunching up my nose.

Lennon laughs heartily. "You're always cute."

"You know what I mean," I whine. "I want to fit in."

He gets serious when I say that. His smile is replaced with an intense look, his hazel eyes piercing through all two thousand miles and a phone screen to send chills up and down my spine. "You, Lark Caspian, never have to worry about fitting in. You're the one who makes people feel like they fit in, not the other way around." He leans back, adopting an air of nonchalance, though I can still see his muscular shoulders are tense. "And besides, you're with me. No one is going to question what you're wearing."

"Okay," I say quietly, then louder and more confident. "Okay. That helps. Thank you." I start taking some things that seem appropriate for the weather he described out of my closet and place them in the suitcase.

"So, do you mind if we talk business for a second?" Lennon asks as I work.

"Sure." I pull out a blue cotton sundress and examine it for a minute.

"Yes. Bring that," he pipes up.

I frown at it on the hanger. "Am I going to need a dress?" What am I thinking? Dresses are good for a million situations. "Never mind. Okay, I'll bring it."

"Anyway, the team loved your audition. Jessica thinks you may even be more perfect than the last narrator we had, which is saying something because she's picky as fuck. Basically, you nailed it."

I pause what I'm doing to look at him, and I can't help the grin from spreading across my face. Lennon matches it with one of his own, though his looks a bit more self-assured than mine feels, as if he knew all along I'd nail it. I hadn't been as sure.

"So, I got the gig?" I ask.

"Not only did you get the gig, but my buddy, Noah—you remember me talking about him?"

"The producer?"

"Yeah, that's him. Anyway, he wants to meet you." Lennon winces. "He probably has a whole pitch or whatever, but I warned him to tone it down until this project is over."

I stop what I'm doing and put my hands on my hips as I face the camera. "What kind of pitch?"

Lennon runs a hand through his sandy hair. A lock of it falls over his forehead, but he doesn't bother pushing it out of the way. It makes him look boyish, and a little soft spot opens up in my heart.

"He wants to see how this project goes, but my guess is he's going to want to get you on his roster of people to call to narrate other books."

"All from that one audition?" I ask, incredulous.

Lennon shrugs. "He's been at this for a while. He knows talent when he sees it."

He says it as if it's the most normal thing in the world. As if my talent is a given, not something I've let languish in the eighteen years since my last real performance. That unwavering confidence he seems to have in me settles some of my nervous energy.

I realize after what must be an awkward minute on his part that I've been staring at him, smiling a goofy smile. But he's just returning it, waiting patiently, his eyes glimmering with what I think is pride.

It strikes me just then that I cannot wait to see his eyes in person again. Gorgeous hazel with speckles of gold and brown. I used to spend as much time as I could looking at them without letting on that's what I was doing. Or maybe he knew and let me do it anyway. Either way, I can't wait to look at them again.

"Sorry," I say. "I got lost there for a minute. So, everything is falling into place?"

Lennon clears his throat as if he had been lost, too. "Right. Yes. Couldn't have planned it better. Noah and Jessica want to meet with you as soon as possible. This isn't a normal thing they do, but like I said, they love you. I used Devin's graduation as an excuse to hold them off as long as I could. They're chomping at the bit, though. I don't want to overwhelm you the minute you get out here, but it would get them off my back if we could meet them for lunch after you land."

I looked Jessica Jordans up on the internet, and she is gorgeous. Young, with long brown hair that's always perfectly wavy. Slim but athletic. One-thousand-watt smile. I can't say I'm excited to meet her and watch her fawn all over Lennon, because I'm sure she will. Who wouldn't? Everyone would, if the women he's had in and out of his life are any indication.

I take two more dresses out of the back of my closet and lay them next to my suitcase.

While I can't say I'm excited to meet Jessica, I try to sound as enthusiastic as I can. "Oh. Sure. Yeah, that sounds good."

"Perfect. Thank you. I'll make it up to you by taking you somewhere really cool or—"

"You don't have to do anything special," I cut him off. "Just being with you is going to be more than enough."

He tilts his head. "I want to, Songbird. I want to show my favorite person in the world around my favorite place in the world."

I can't help a smile at that. It sounds like exactly what I need.

***

Richard and Rachel leave as soon as they drop Devin off from their shopping trip. He grouses about carrying all the stuff they bought her back to New York, and I have to bite my tongue so I don't mention that he could have saved himself the trouble by following the original plan.

Devin is a tornado of activity from the minute he leaves right up until I'm wheeling my suitcase to the front door and shouting up to her room that we need to get going.

My phone dings with a message just as Devin tosses a duffel bag down the stairs.

"I hope there wasn't anything fragile in that," I mumble to myself as I check my phone.

> Hannah: Delivery for you!

What does that mean? I pull the curtain over the porch window aside and see a package on my doorstep. Hannah's car is in the street, but she pulls away quickly. She stops down the street, and my phone dings again.

> Hannah: I knew if I were still here when I gave it to you, you wouldn't take it. I'll be back a few times this week to check on the place.

What in the world? I open the door to get the box, then slide my finger under the tape keeping it shut. Inside is a bathing suit. A red one. Two pieces, though the bottom looks big enough to be high-waisted. I hold it up against my torso. It'll probably fit.

> Lark: You didn't have to do that.

> Hannah: Do you have a bathing suit?

> Lark: No.

> Hannah: You do now. You're welcome. Have fun.

I laugh and, shaking my head, open my suitcase just enough to slip the bathing suit inside.

***

Somehow, I hold my tears back long enough for Devin to round the corner toward her terminal. Molly had texted her that she was already there and waiting, but Devin spent an extra few minutes with me, even though I could tell she was excited to go.

As soon as she's out of sight, the waterworks start, and they don't stop until I'm in the air. I pull *Sizzling Secrets* out of my carry-on to take some notes, and I try. I really do. But I end up mostly watching the puffy clouds pass underneath the wing of the plane from the window, counting down the minutes until I get to squeeze my best friend.

CHAPTER 8

LENNON

I BARELY SLEEP. I'M pretty sure I see every single hour tick off on the clock, and when I finally roll out of bed thinking I can at least get in a quick session at the gym before heading to the airport, I look about as exhausted and excited as I feel.

I'm nervous to see her. Which sounds so stupid, but I can't help a little anxiety sneaking through. I see her every day, pretty much, on video calls. But two whole months with her in my apartment is going to be different. Wonderful. Amazing.

After I get home from the gym, I take a quick shower and stand in front of my closet, wondering what to wear. Suddenly, I know exactly what Lark was talking about the other night when she said she wanted to look cute. Ten years apart, and it doesn't matter that she's seen some variation of my wardrobe on a screen almost every day. She's going to see it in person. I want to look good for her. I want my shirt to be soft when I hug her. I want her to think I haven't changed much, even though I know I have.

Fuck, this is ridiculous. I run a hand through my still-wet hair. What difference does it make if I look good or not? She's my best friend. She doesn't care what I look like.

I grab a white shirt and blue chino shorts and throw them on. I eat some breakfast, and then it's time to go get her.

But right before I leave, I go back and switch out my shirt for a softer one. Just in case.

***

The entire drive to LAX, I psych myself up. When we were younger, I used to be able to drink in every detail of her face. And I would, when she wasn't watching. She was beautiful beyond all measure.

The last time I saw her in person was ten years ago for a weekend, and most of the time was spent occupying Devin. One night, we sat on her couch after Devin had gone to sleep. We leaned our heads against the back of it. She curled her knees up under her chin and hugged them toward herself. I folded a leg under me and used the toes of my other foot to play with the fibers of her carpet—something tactile to ground me, otherwise I would have floated away on the high I got from listening to her talk and having her close to me.

I still can't shake the residuals of the feeling I had when listening to her audition. It's both like listening to her that night ten years ago, and not. I've always needed Lark. She's always been sunshine for my soul. My anchor.

But after listening to her audition, I didn't just need her. I *wanted* her. Craved her presence. I haven't listened to it again because I'm not a masochist, but every time I think about it, something I can't name grips me. It takes a lot of conscious effort to get whatever it is to loosen up.

Knowing she's disembarking the plane right now—that I'm going to see her in fifteen minutes—has that same feeling creeping up through my stomach and clutching my heart.

It's just anticipation. Residual anxiety that I still feel in stressful situations even after years spent working with a therapist, maybe. Anyone would feel this way after not seeing their best friend for a decade. I'm sure it'll go away as soon as I lay eyes on her.

There is no way I'm letting the first time I see her be as she's slinging suitcases into my trunk and jumping into the passenger seat to avoid the ire of other people in the pickup lane. My mother didn't teach me much, but she taught me enough to know that you don't let a lady carry all her bags across an airport terminal. So, I swing my Jeep into the nearest parking space I can find and walk as quickly as I can to baggage claim.

I see her before she sees me. She's not hard to spot, even with her back to me. Her short blonde hair falls in perfect curls as she reaches up to tuck a piece of it behind her ear. She's wearing pink leggings, a black T-shirt, and gym shoes. She stands tall, her back straight and her shoulders squared. Lark was never one to slouch. I don't even think the word is in her vocabulary.

Disbelief rocks through me. It stops me in my tracks. I suddenly understand what people mean when they say, *Pinch me.*

She's here. Right in front of me. And my feet are glued to the spot.

I wish I had thought of something witty to say when I first saw her. Something she'd remember forever.

As if she knows someone is watching her, she turns around. Slowly. So achingly slow. It's like I'm watching a movie and holding my breath, immobile and waiting for her to see me.

And then, she does. Her big blue eyes lock on mine, and an even bigger smile stretches across her face. She seems stuck, too, for a moment.

Until she suddenly sprints the few feet between us and crashes into me, wrapping her arms around my torso and burying her face into my chest.

"Lennon," she sobs.

I wrap my arms around her, one hand on her upper back and one cradling her head, pressing her into me as if I could fold her all the way into my heart and keep her there.

Her shoulders shake as she cries. Warm wetness seeps through my shirt. All I can do is hold her. Feel her hair weave its way through my fingers. Smell the bright citrus scent of her shampoo. It takes me right back to a different airport and a different time—eighteen years old and holding her just like this. Both of us embarking on our own journeys, going our separate ways, making promises that we'd never lose each other.

And we never did.

"You're here," I laugh, and I'm surprised to find it's wet. The top of her head is shimmering with my own tears. I allow myself to kiss them away and breathe her in more deeply.

"I'm here." Her voice is muffled by my shirt.

"How was your flight?"

"Well, I miss Devin and I'm overjoyed to be here with you, so...neutral?" She tilts her head up to look at me. Her eyes are rimmed with red, and it's clear she didn't just start crying the minute she saw me.

I narrow my eyes at her. "I don't think that's how that works."

Lark shrugs. "It's not *not* how that works."

I thumb a couple of renegade tears off her cheeks, chuckling at her logic. "Do you want to postpone this lunch? I'm sure everyone would understand."

She shakes her head, her lips pressing together so hard, they almost turn white. "No. I want to get it over with." Her eyes go wide, and she removes a hand from my back to clamp it over her mouth. "I'm emotional. That came out wrong."

I tip my head back and laugh. Something loosens in my chest. But my left arm is still slung around her shoulders, she's still holding on to my waist, and that feeling is clawing its way up to my heart again. It must not have been anticipation.

I try to ignore it as I say, "That's pretty much how I feel about these things, too. All of them, not just this one. We have a couple of hours, and I didn't plan anything in case you wanted to just settle in. What do you want to do?"

"Oh, there's my suitcase," she says, pointing to an old, battered, navy blue bag. It looks like it's held together by duct tape and a prayer.

I step around her to gingerly pluck it off the carousel. "I'm surprised this thing stayed together in the air."

"Me, too. Devin took the nice set, and I didn't have time to get anything new." She tucks a piece of hair behind her ear again.

I throw her carry-on over my shoulder and try to kick the suitcase onto its wheels, then realize too late that it doesn't have wheels. So, I pick it up and look at her expectantly. "Where to, madam?"

"Madam?! I have another month until I'm officially old, thank you very much." She reaches for the handle of the suitcase. "And you don't have to carry that."

I twist myself so it's out of her reach. "I know I don't have to. I want to."

Lark eyes me up and down with an eyebrow raised and her lips quirked to the side. "I suppose it wouldn't kill you to put those biceps to good use for once."

"That's the spirit," I say sarcastically. That giddy feeling surfaces again. It feels so good to banter with her in person. It's like a piece of me has come back, and I can be whole again.

She winces. "Would you mind terribly if I showered and changed? I don't want to meet these people looking like I just got off an airplane."

You look more beautiful than any woman I've ever seen, I want to scream, but I don't. She'd probably turn right around and get back on the plane if I did, and besides, I'm not sure what has gotten into me today. I need to cool it, and fast.

I scrunch up my nose and start walking toward the exit. "Probably a good idea. You kind of smell."

"Like roses, you mean." She matches my stride as we walk outside into the warm summer air.

No, like citrus and sunshine, my mind screams again.

I'm just happy she's here. I'm sure this excitement will wear off in a few days. I toss her bags into the back of my Jeep and turn around to find her standing close to me. She flings her arms around my middle again. I belatedly realize I should hug her back before my arms circle her.

"Sorry," she says. "This shirt is just really soft."

I huff a laugh. "Well, lucky for you, I have plenty more soft shirts where this one came from."

CHAPTER 9

LARK

My hair whips—probably unattractively—around my face as Lennon drives us in his open Jeep back to his apartment. I settle in and enjoy it. It's Lennon; I don't have to be on all the time with him. It's nice to be around someone who has known me at my most awkward and still wants me around.

It doesn't take too long to get to his apartment. We take the stairs up to the second floor, where he walks down a short hallway and opens a door. Inside, directly to the left, there's a small galley kitchen with a bar-height counter and a couple of stools on the other side of it. Past that is the living room. Unsurprisingly, he has a giant television mounted on the wall. We walk a little farther to a sliding glass door that opens up to a balcony. There's only a sliver of a view between buildings, but it's a nice outside space with a grill and some wicker couches around a small table.

He takes me back inside and toward the front door. There's a narrow hallway there with a bathroom on the left and a quaint little bedroom on the right. Lennon rubs a hand over the back of his neck. "This is the smaller of the two bedrooms, and the bathroom isn't attached. We can switch if you'd rather—"

"No, this is great," I say as I belly flop onto the bed. It's ridiculously comfortable and smells like clean laundry. "Yep, this is amazing."

He chuckles. "My room is just down the hall, and I have a bathroom in there, too, so at least we don't have to share." He's looking around as if trying to see the space through my eyes.

I sit up on the edge of the bed. "It's perfect, Lennon. Seriously."

Lennon drops his hand and smiles sheepishly. That expression makes him look so young. If it weren't for the muscles and tattoos peeking out from under the sleeves of his shirt, I'd think we were back in high school.

"Okay. I'll just be..." He waves in the direction of his room. "Let me know when you're ready."

The shower feels really good. I'm not only washing away the airplane smell but also a morning's worth of tears, and I emerge completely rejuvenated. I riffle through my toiletry bag to find my hair products and hair dryer, makeup, and several different vials of anti-aging creams and serums. I'm sure half of those are as good as snake oil, but I'm not taking any chances.

I take my time getting ready, then stare at the bathroom door as I clutch a towel around my torso. The sudden realization that my clothes are in my bedroom descends on me like a cloud. In retrospect, that was pretty stupid. Lennon could be anywhere. He could see me wrapped in nothing but a towel as I walk between the bathroom and the bedroom. We've always been close, but not hang-out-in-nothing-but-a-towel close.

There's nothing to do but make a break for it, I guess. And buy a robe as soon as I can. I roll my eyes and grumble to myself that we're *friends*, dammit, and he's not thinking about me like *that* anyway, so what does it matter?

Even if my mouth went dry and my heart tried to beat its way out of my chest when I first saw him at the airport. Even if standing there, watching him sling my bags into the back of his car, I had a sudden urgent desire to trace the tattoos rippling over his biceps with my fingers.

It's just because I missed him. That's all.

I open the bathroom door and stick my head out to look left, then right. The coast is clear, so I quickly walk the three steps to my bedroom and shut the door behind me.

When I emerge again, I'm fully clothed in the blue sundress Lennon told me to bring. I feel like a new woman.

I make my way to the kitchen to pour myself a glass of water. Lennon is sitting on the couch, scrolling on his phone. He doesn't look up when he chuckles and says, "Turns out there's not much to do when I don't have you to call."

Laughing, I walk over and sit next to him. When he puts his phone down and looks up at me, he goes completely still. He stares at me for a long moment, his face completely unreadable. What is he doing, looking at me like that? I know I probably look a lot different than the last time he saw me—softer around the middle, saggier around the eyes—but I had been clinging to Hannah's assessment of my looks for weeks. Was she lying to spare my feelings? Am I so different that I've caught him off guard?

I tuck a piece of hair behind my ear, suddenly really self-conscious. "Do I look okay? I can change or—"

"Absolutely not," he says, his voice quiet and all the more fierce for the lack of volume.

Oh. *Oh.* He's flustered by me. Suddenly, the self-consciousness is completely gone.

He clears his throat. "I mean, you look great." He shakes his head as if he could dislodge the words he wants and let them fall out of his mouth. "Fine. You look fine. Are you ready to go?" He stands up suddenly and jams his hands into his pockets.

I rise more slowly, trying not to laugh at his discomfort. "Yes," I say. He's looking out the door to his balcony, then he shifts his gaze to the ceiling. It's clear he's avoiding me.

Smirking, I sashay past him, swinging my hips a little more than necessary. "You haven't seen me in a while. It's okay if you forgot how pretty I am," I tease. "But this one's on you."

"What does that mean?" he asks, his voice much steadier. If there's anything that could always get Lennon to calm down, it's teasing him. Glad to see that hasn't changed.

I raise my eyebrows pointedly. "You were the one who told me to bring this dress." I tap my chin, pretending to consider something. "In your defense, though, you've never actually seen me in it. Consider yourself warned."

Lennon lets out a grunting sort of sound. "Do you think your ego will fit through the door, or should I bust it open to make room?" And just like that, the air in the room has snapped back to normal.

I make a big show of studying the door. I spread my arms to measure it lengthwise, then step on my tip toes to see how tall it is. "Hmm." I face him and press my back to it, batting my eyelashes. "If yours fits, it should be fine."

He takes a few long strides toward me, pinning me to the spot with his hazel eyes. They're so fucking beautiful in person; there's even more liquid gold swimming in them than I remembered. I'm mesmerized as he locks them on me. When he's inches away, he leans down into my space and wraps his hand around the doorknob to my left.

"Glad to see you're feeling better," he practically whispers. His warm breath tickles my cheek. I have to fight to keep my eyelids from fluttering closed.

He straightens up after a moment and twists the doorknob. "Shall we?" he asks in an overly polite tone.

I guess two can play this game, because now I can't seem to control the butterflies in my stomach. I clear my throat and shake my head quickly. "Um, yeah," I say as I try to get my knees to stop wobbling so I can follow him out the door.

This trip is already shaping up to be more of an adventure than I thought it'd be.

***

Lennon pulls up to a small whitewashed building with a green sign that simply says *Tacos* in bold letters. There are mismatched tables and chairs on a giant patio with a view of the ocean far in the distance. Some of the tables are occupied, but not as many as I'd expect on a gorgeous day right in the middle of what would be considered the lunch rush back home.

"Believe it or not, this is the best place for tacos in the city," Lennon says.

I twist in my seat to face him. He's squinting out the dashboard at the restaurant as if he's suddenly second-guessing his choice of lunch venue.

"I love tacos," I reassure him.

His eyes shift to mine and bounce back and forth between them for a moment. "You and Devin took me out for tacos the last time I was in Michigan. You ordered fish ones. They were so bad, but you didn't want to be rude and take them back, so I did it for you."

I smile softly. I had forgotten that until just now, but the memory comes rushing back to me. "The second batch was still really bad." What

I don't mention is the sauce dripping down my chin that Lennon wiped away with his finger. He tasted it and immediately spit it out. Devin giggled like a maniac, so he hammed it up, taking drinks of water and spitting them back out. I was so grateful for the humor to take my mind off the way his calloused finger felt on the skin of my chin.

But from Lennon's smirk, it's obvious he remembers it as clearly as I do now. "I figured I'd show you what real fish tacos are supposed to taste like."

"From here?" I'm sure the tacos are great, but it doesn't look very well-kept.

"I told you—it's the best in the city. And besides, Noah wanted to wine and dine you at some five-star place, but I figured this was more your speed."

I hum. "I don't know whether to be offended that you don't think I'd enjoy a fancy lunch or admit that you're probably right."

Lennon chuckles, the sound so much richer and warmer in person than it is over the phone. It relaxes something in me I didn't even realize was tense.

"Everyone enjoys fancy lunches sometimes," he says, looking out at the restaurant again. "But Noah is... Well, he can be intense. And these sorts of meetings aren't typical for him, so I'm not really sure what he's got up his sleeve. I figured keeping it casual was the best way to keep *him* casual." He shrugs and shoots me an apologetic glance. "Not sure if it'll work."

Suddenly nervous, I run a hand through my hair, trying to re-tame the curls after the open-air ride here. "Thanks for looking out for me."

"Don't thank me yet." There's a dark edge to his voice that makes me turn to look at him. "Jessica will also be there, and she's kind of a wild card."

I flip the visor down and open the mirror to check myself. "A diva?" I run my tongue over my teeth to catch any errant lipstick stains, even though I don't see any.

Lennon hums in agreement. "And young."

I eye him sidelong. "And successful. A dangerous combination."

He nods silently, then reaches out to grab my hand. His warm palm presses into mine as his fingers squeeze the back of my hand reassuringly. "You look great. They just want to meet you. No big deal."

My eyes narrow. "You're kind of making it seem like a big deal."

"Probably a bigger deal for me than for you." His voice is quiet enough that I need to lean in to hear him. Which might be a mistake as that scent that is so distinctly *him* washes over me—one that smells ethereal. Like big open skies and white, puffy clouds. Between that and his hand still holding mine, the inside of the Jeep feels too small, and my skin feels too tight.

"How so?" I ask, my voice sounding much steadier than I feel.

He flashes his best smile. If I were standing, my knees would go weak at seeing it. "I want my new friends to like my old friend."

There it is. My way out of this trap of insanity and want I've been wound into. I keep getting assaulted by how everything about Lennon is perfect and magical and feels like home, even two thousand miles away from it.

I make an overexaggerated frown and rip my hand away from his to bring it to my chest. "Who are you calling old?"

He laughs again, but this time I'm prepared for it. I meet it with one of my own.

"Let's get some tacos, Songbird," he says before hopping out of his Jeep.

CHAPTER 10

LENNON

LARK IS NERVOUS. IF I didn't know her so well, I'd probably miss it because she's laughing and her voice is rich and smooth like really good coffee. But every so often, she pulls at her dress as if she could make it longer. She's crossed and uncrossed her feet at the ankles at least four times in the past five minutes. And she keeps flipping her hair away from her face, as if having it touch her cheek is a nuisance.

I didn't mean to be so early to this lunch. I'd say I misjudged midday traffic, but that's not the whole truth. Seeing Lark in that sundress completely threw me off. The apartment suddenly felt like it was closing in on me, and I needed to get out. One minute, I was minding my own business, scrolling aimlessly on my phone, and the next, she was *there*. Looking like *that*. And I couldn't breathe. Even my four-count breathing couldn't help claw me out of the tunnel vision I had when I looked at her.

She's always been gorgeous, but the past ten years have been kind to her in a way I hadn't expected. Her hips are just a little fuller. Her lips are slightly pinker. Her cheeks are more flushed. Her back—always straight and confident—is relaxed a bit in the way of a woman who knows she doesn't have to pull out any false bravado anymore.

The blue in her eyes is only deepened by the color of that dress. The sliver of ocean behind her glimmers as if in response to her. She looks like she was made to be here. Like this was always meant to be. She just got here, and I'm already dreading her leaving so much that I'm having a hard time concentrating on the story she's telling about Devin's graduation.

"Lennon!" A booming voice comes behind me, and as grateful as I am for other people to put some kind of buffer between me and whatever I'm feeling for my best friend right now, I'm also annoyed that they've broken off Lark's singsong storytelling voice.

I smile reassuringly at her as she folds her hands in her lap. She's probably clenching them there, and I wish I could take one and rub my thumb over her knuckles in reassurance like I used to do when she'd be waiting backstage before a show.

"You don't have to wait with me."

"I don't mind. Besides, who else is going to remind you not to bite your lip so you don't ruin your makeup?"

I shake my head quickly. I don't have time to reminisce. Noah is here, Lark is looking at me expectantly, and Jessica is almost assuredly going to be in rare form. I need to focus.

I twist around to wave Noah over, but what I see has me jumping out of my seat before I can think better of it. I hear Lark's chair scrape against the restaurant patio as she follows suit.

Jessica isn't going to be the only wild card at this lunch, though her skin-tight, sleeveless, red bodysuit, straight-legged jeans, and heels suggest she came to play.

They also brought along Silas Matthews, Lark's new counterpart.

He looks suave as always in a black shirt and gray jeans. His black hair is slicked back, and he's wearing dark aviator sunglasses. The man perpetually looks like a modern James Dean. I don't even want to know how much product it takes for him to get his hair to stay like that as he rides around with his convertible top down. I can sure smell it as he brushes right past me and invades Lark's space so thoroughly, I think she might need to take a step back.

She doesn't, though. She holds her ground, even as she has to crane her neck to look up at him. That's my girl.

"You must be Lark Caspian," Silas says. His voice is raspy in a *this is what I sound like in bed* kind of way. And vaguely Southern, though he's never told anyone where he grew up. He takes Lark's right hand between both of his and shuffles his body back slightly under the guise of appraising her.

It's not a competition. Of course it's not. That would be ridiculous. I don't need to compete with Silas Matthews. And I probably couldn't anyway, because despite his rebel-without-a-cause appearance, the man is undeniably and legitimately *nice*.

But I get no small amount of joy out of the fact that he made a clear power move by stepping into Lark's space and she didn't budge.

She smiles tightly up at him. "I am. And you are...?" Her eyes dart to mine, her eyebrows raised in question.

Without thinking, I clear my throat and step closer to place my hand on the small of Lark's back. I'm just as bad as he is, posturing like a caveman. Showing ownership over a woman who has her own damn wings and can fly wherever she wants.

Silas is still cupping her hand in his, but her face is turned toward me. Her eyebrows tick up another half inch, and the corners of her tight smile press down, as if she's trying to suppress a laugh. She knows exactly what I did, all right. At least she thinks it's funny.

"This is Silas Matthews. He'll be narrating the chapters in the male point of view in *Sizzling Secrets*," I say quietly.

"Ah." Lark turns her attention back to him, then deftly rotates her hand so their right palms meet. She shakes his hand in greeting, then lets go. "Nice to meet you."

"And this is Jessica Jordans, the author of the book," I say.

Jessica comes forward and throws her arms around Lark, who lets out a surprised "Oh." Jessica steps back, holding Lark by the biceps to get a good look at her.

"You are just *adorable*," she squeals. "Lennon, why didn't you tell me how *cute* she is?"

I grimace. I'm not sure if Jessica is being genuine or trying to diminish Lark in some way. My guess is the former, but it's never easy to tell with her.

"He probably didn't mention it because it's not relevant to audiobook recording," Lark says drily.

Jessica tips her head back and cackles, her long brown hair tipping over her shoulder and falling down her back. "Oh my *god*. She's funny, too!" She claps her hands in delight.

Lark's mouth spreads into a fake smile. Judging by that expression, she was definitely not trying to be funny.

I clear my throat and glance warily at Noah, who is hanging back. He's covering his mouth with his hand, and his brown eyes are twinkling. That asshole is amused by this.

"And this is Noah Baker, producer for Luminaudio." I gesture for him to join this motley crew.

He quickly gains control of his laughter and firmly shakes Lark's hand. "It's a pleasure to meet you, Lark. Thank you for coming. And for taking this on at the last minute."

"You're a life saver," Jessica breathes, her eyes wide.

"Of course. I'm excited, and I'm ready to get started." The smile she gives Noah is genuine, though more reserved than the ones she saves for me. I'm not surprised he makes her feel more at ease than the others. Noah is an extremely casual guy; he's dressed in chino shorts and a T-shirt like I am, and his hair and beard that are starting to edge more toward salt than pepper are well-maintained but not over-styled.

He nods once and surveys the group. "Great. Let's get some tacos, shall we?" His eyes land on me as he shoves his hands into his pockets. "Lennon, want to come inside and help me order?"

I scan over Jessica, Silas, and Lark. I don't want to leave her here with two people she just met, but Noah is probably asking me inside for a reason. Hopefully, it's to explain why Silas decided to show up.

"You okay here?" I ask Lark.

Her shoulders shake, but she doesn't break into a full out laugh. "Yeah, I think I can handle it," she says sarcastically.

"Okay." I nod. "We'll be right back, then," I say as I follow Noah into the restaurant.

Noah doesn't even let me say it. The second the door closes, he turns to me with his hands up. "He wanted to meet her. He heard her audition and was really impressed. We all were."

"Why was he listening to her audition?" I fight it, but a protectiveness edges my voice.

Noah scoffs. "Come on, Len. You know how this works. They have to sound good together. He was listening to see if he'd need to make any adjustments to his part, and that's when he decided meeting her would be a good idea. Since the opportunity presented itself."

I glance behind me at the closed door. "I just wish you would have texted me or something so I could have prepared her. She's nervous." And I won't admit it out loud, but I'm nervous, too. This whole situation is stoking some anxiety I haven't felt in a really long time.

"She has no reason to be. She's got the job. And probably more if she wants them," Noah says reassuringly.

"I know that." I run a hand through my hair. "I told her that, too, but she's..." I trail off and press my lip together in a tight line. I won't speak for her. I've already pulled enough weird-ass alpha moves today. "Just tread lightly, okay? She's only here for a few weeks to do this project, and then she's back to her professor gig in Michigan."

Even as I say it, a pang of regret hits me straight in the chest. I rub at it, as if that would make it go away. I'm on the verge of too many emotions today, and I suddenly wish I still saw my therapist regularly to work through some of this shit.

Noah tugs at his beard as he glances down to where my fingers are moving over my heart, then back to meet my gaze. "And to see you."

"What?"

"She's here to see you," he insists as we take a step forward in the line to order. When I frown at him, he continues. "I more or less watched you stitch your own heart back together after the last time you saw her. You think she didn't feel the same way?"

It had honestly never occurred to me. I thought I had hidden it better than that, but apparently not.

It doesn't matter. She might be here because we're friends, too, but so what? That's not what this meeting is about.

"Twenty-five years of friendship will do that, I suppose," I mutter, but it's nice that he saw it. It makes me feel better about how long we've been apart, that we've been able to mostly pick up where we left off. It gives me hope that whatever this weird tension or attraction is between us is just giddiness at our proximity. It'll wear off, and we can go back to being the way we've always been.

Noah studies me, his eyes narrowed. "Right," he says, then steps up to the counter to order.

The lunch starts surprisingly well, despite the awkward introductions. Lark is an absolute dream. In between bites of fish tacos and reassurances that they are, in fact, better than the ones she had in Michigan, she tells them story after story about her daughter, her job, her life back home. She talks about Devin, of course, but doesn't dwell on her. It's clear that wound is still raw. Then, she moves on to her boss, perfectly imitating his nasally voice and miming pushing glasses up her nose as she speaks. She affects her students uncannily as well, overexaggerating the know-it-all and the kid who she says did the absolute least he could do to get a C.

The whole table is in stiches. Her eyes practically glow with joy as she recounts event after event, feeding off their energy to make each story more ridiculous than the last.

I eat and watch silently, soaking up her light. This is her show. I want to let her be center stage.

"You can't make this shit up!" Jessica exclaims at the end of a story about how Lark's friend, Hannah, had asked Lark to be present during office hours and act as a timer for a student who made a habit of staying an entire hour just to talk about comic books.

"You really can't," Lark agrees.

Then, Jessica gasps. "You should write a book!" she exclaims and lays a manicured hand on my forearm. "Shouldn't she write a book, Len? It would be so funny."

And then she not only leaves her hand there, she rubs her thumb gently back and forth over my arm.

It's like shutting off a faucet. The mood at the table suddenly bottoms out. Lark goes still, conspicuously *not* looking at Jessica's hand. Which is still on my arm.

"Oh, I think I'll leave the writing to the experts." Lark's voice is flat and a bit sardonic. Like she isn't quite convinced Jessica fits in that category, and perhaps she should have left the writing to them herself.

Jessica doesn't flinch at the change in mood. The woman is completely oblivious. "Nonsense!" She leans forward, her hand pressing even further into my arm. "Any idiot can write a book, and you are such a good storyteller."

Noah eyes me from across the table, his face unreadable. Silas is looking at Lark with moon eyes, either unaware or willfully ignorant of the shift happening right in front of him.

Lark's lips curl into her fake smile again as she makes direct eye contact with Jessica. "I'm here to tell your story," she says in the smooth way of someone who is practiced at manipulating an audience. Her eyes meet mine as she continues. "Nothing more." Then, she gives Noah a soft expression, and that moment is over. "I'd love to talk about the process, if we can. What will be expected of me?"

Noah gladly takes the reins and launches into an explanation of the audiobook recording process, studio time, deadlines, pickups. He and Silas answer all of Lark's questions. Jessica chimes in with some notes here and there, and when she thinks no one is watching, she finds reasons to make side comments to me. Leaning in, brushing against my biceps, touching my arm again.

I try to shrug her off of me as much as I can, but she's either persistent or unaware. Or both. It occurs to me that she's always been like this, and I've always tolerated it. Liked it, even, if I'm being honest. I'm not one to shy away from the attention of a beautiful woman. But it's as if Lark is holding a magnifying glass to it, and now each touch feels like I'm burning as the sun is concentrated underneath it.

Much to my surprise, Silas never acts even remotely annoyed at having to walk Lark through everything like the absolute newbie she is. In fact, if I didn't know any better, I would think he was almost flirting with her, the way he flashes indulgent smiles and compliments her questions. The man acts as if there is an art to question-asking, when all Lark is after is communication.

Something primal and instinctive screams at me to tell him to back the fuck off. That she's not here for some greasy workplace fling—even as a sick part of me is curious if his hair stays that perfect while he's banging someone. And then my brain immediately short-circuits at the thought of him and Lark in bed together. My fingers involuntarily curl inward where they rest on either side of my now-empty basket of tacos.

Jessica lays a hand on top of mine as she leans in so only I can hear. "You okay?"

I would be if she'd stop touching me. If Silas would stop mooning over Lark. If Lark would just *look at me*, but she's avoiding my eye contact.

"Fine," I grind out, pulling my hand out from underneath hers and putting it in my lap. "I think the tacos are messing with my stomach."

"Really?" Lark asks skeptically. "We all ate the same kind, and the rest of us are fine."

Oh, *now* she wants to pay attention to me.

"Must have been the whiskey sours at the bar last night," Noah chimes in. "I was feeling pretty rough this morning, too."

I frown at him. We didn't go out last night. I went to bed early and barely slept because I was so excited Lark was going to be with me in less than twenty-four hours. It belatedly occurs to me that he's giving me an exit strategy. That he's watched this entire thing play out, has put some pieces together about the four of us, and knows exactly what has Lark acting all prim and proper and me acting like a Neanderthal.

"Yeah, that's probably it." I lean back in my chair. "Whiskey and tacos and sunshine don't mix."

Lark tilts her head, her fair eyebrows pinching together. "You seemed fine this morning."

I shrug. "Late-onset hangover, I guess."

She narrows her eyes and mumbles, "Pretty sure that's not a thing." She looks around at the other people at the table, balling up her napkin and tossing it on top of her empty basket. "But I've had a long day of traveling and seeing my daughter off to her next chapter."

Jessica gives a sympathetic pout, and Lark presses her lips up into a thin smile.

Noah stands. "Yes, of course. Thanks again, Lark. I think this is going to be amazing."

We all say our goodbyes and make our way to our respective vehicles. Silas gives us a little *beep-beep* as he pulls out of the parking lot. Lark beams at him and waves. I gape at her as she slides into the passenger side of the Jeep.

She notices me staring. "What?" she asks defensively. "He was nice."

I force my jaw closed, only to clench it as I start the car and pull out of my parking spot.

"You okay?" Lark asks after a while.

"Yeah," I say, not taking my eyes off the road. "Just a little under the weather." I pause, then risk a glance at her. She's staring at a fixed spot out into the distance. "You?"

"Hmm?" She blinks as if waking up from a trance. "I'm fine. Tired."

Those are the last words we speak for the entire evening. When we get back to the apartment, she excuses herself to her room and shuts the door. A few hours later, I decide to get some work done on another project before going to bed.

I stand outside her door, wanting desperately to knock and see if she wants to grab dinner. But I'm pretty sure I hear soft sobs coming from inside the room. It's so quiet that I can't be sure, but I decide not to bother her. She'll come out to talk when she's ready.

I make myself a couple of peanut-butter-and-jelly sandwiches. I leave the supplies on the counter for her if she wants one later, then I tiptoe to my room. But I make sure to leave it open a crack so she knows she can come talk to me if she wants.

CHAPTER 11

LARK

I told Lennon I'm fine.

I'm not fine.

I'm worried I made a huge mistake.

If I had stayed home, I'd be missing Devin even more than I already am, but at least I wouldn't have had to watch Lennon get pawed by the most gorgeous woman I've ever laid eyes on. I wouldn't have seen that flush creep up his neck every time her hand landed on top of him or the way he kept trying to catch my eye to shoot me an apologetic glance.

He's banging her. For sure. Casual acquaintances don't touch each other like that. And I don't care. I really don't. Except that he told me he wasn't, and we don't lie to each other. It was a promise we made in high school—and I thought we had kept ever since.

"It wasn't your best performance." Lennon looked sorry to have said it but shrugged in a way that said, What can you do?

"Don't hold back on my account." My voice was completely flat.

"I'm not going to lie to you," Lennon said earnestly. "I'd never lie to you, Lark. You're my best friend."

"I just can't get it right." I frowned, frustrated, and studied my shoes. I kicked a rock in the parking lot and watched it skitter a few feet. "I know this character is my age, but I don't understand her motivation. Why would she spread these rumors, knowing it could end in people's deaths?"

Lennon chuckled and shook his head like he was indulging me in some way. "That's because you're the best kind of person, and Abigail is the worst."

I looked up at him then. He had stepped closer without my realizing, and he took up all the available space in front of me. I could smell his scent, like big open skies. It was almost as if he brought it with him to landlocked Michigan all the way from all the beautiful places he and his parents lived before here.

"I can be mean," I protest, but it's half-hearted.

Lennon laughed, a sound as big as his body and those open skies he carried with him all the time. "No, you can't, Songbird." He met my gaze then. "It's my favorite thing about you." The gold in his eyes sparkled with amusement in the fluorescent light flooding the school parking lot, and suddenly, I felt as if I had been slapped across the face. I wanted him to see me as more than just nice. Something bigger and bolder, like he was to me then—something that took up as much space in his life as he took up in mine.

I couldn't hide the disdain in my voice when I responded, "Your favorite thing about me is that I'm nice?"

But his lips stayed curled to the side, and his hazel eyes remained pinned meaningfully on me in a way I didn't quite understand. "One of them," he said as he reached out and tucked a curl behind my ear.

I swallowed hard, unable to look away from him, and he seemed unable to move his fingers from my hair. The desire to push myself up onto my tip-

toes and meet his lips with mine came completely out of nowhere, washing over me so thoroughly, I would have been surprised to find I hadn't been doused with bucket of water.

But I was only sixteen. I hadn't ever felt that way about anyone outside of the boys my friends in middle school would tease me about. And even then, that was a desire borne more of peer pressure than anything else. This thing with Lennon in the parking lot of our high school after a long and grueling rehearsal was different. The newness of it was so overwhelming, I blinked. Just a few times, but my shock must have been so plainly written on my face, because Lennon dropped his hand to his thigh with a loud slap.

His voice was slightly over-loud as he said, with a confidence I certainly didn't reciprocate, "You'll figure it out. You always do."

I press the pads of my fingertips into my eyes, hard enough to hopefully wipe that memory from my brain and, with it, the lingering feel of his fingers on my hair after all these years. I'm not sure where that came from, but the sting of adolescent awkwardness scalds my chest just as harshly now as it did then. What was that, twenty-four years ago? You'd think I'd feel less like an idiot about a fleeting, hormonal moment of desire after all that time.

And yet my skin is still burning from the way he hugged me in the airport, his big hands curling around my shoulders and back, his chest hard and smooth underneath his soft shirt. Hannah's talking about "Hot Lennon" had rung, uninvited, in my ears, and I had foolishly let myself think that maybe she had a point. He was cute in high school in a completely unassuming, puppy-dog kind of way. He always looked lost, whether because he was worried about fitting in or because he wasn't ever quite used to his long limbs.

But over the years, he has really grown into himself. I remember thinking it when I saw him ten years ago, but now, at forty, he's even better. *Like a fine wine*, I think, then cringe at the cliché. But it's accurate.

He still has that boyish charm with his lopsided smirk and sandy-blond hair that flops over his forehead after he runs his hands through it. He's still larger than life, too, but now it's almost as if he knows it. He's grown into it, just like he's grown into those long limbs.

God, what is wrong with me? Lennon is my friend. That's *it*. Even if there had been some attraction there all those years ago, it was fleeting. Over before it even started. The result of confusing and overpowering teenage hormones, and nothing more.

And this is just my hormones, too. I'm sure of it. Almost-forty-year-olds can be hormonal, right? It's probably just been too long since I've had someone to share a bed with. I dated a bit when Devin was younger, though I never brought anyone home with me. That would have required a level of commitment I wasn't ready to give to anything besides my daughter and my job. And then there's no real dating during a pandemic. After that, it just felt pointless. Everything I needed was right in front of me. I was never lonely. Devin's bubbly laughter and firm hugs were the center of my universe, and Lennon and even Hannah were in a close orbit to fill the gaps of adult conversation.

My phone chimes, and I flip it over to see if it's Devin checking in. As if she were summoned by my melancholy retrospective through my nonexistent love life, Hannah's message lights up my screen.

> **Hannah:** You didn't tell me Silas fucking Matthews is your co-narrator.

> **Lark:** I didn't know until today. How did you know?

Hannah sends a screenshot of Jessica's social media. It's an announcement listing Silas and me as the narrators of the audiobook coming soon. It makes sense why I haven't seen that; I have zero social media presence to speak of.

> Lark: I still don't know why that's a big deal.

> Hannah: Are you kidding? That man is sexy AF.

> Lark: "Love looks not with the eyes, but with the mind."

An image of Silas plays out in my mind—all slicked-back hair and mysterious gray eyes. Full, pillowy lips, broad shoulders, narrow hips. The outline of muscular legs hugged by dark jeans. Come to think of it, he was very attentive to me at lunch, answering every question and laughing at every joke. I hadn't noticed because I was too consumed with Jessica as she got handsy with Lennon across the table, but if I had been less obtuse about it, I would have been flattered.

Another message from Hannah breaks through my thoughts.

> Hannah: Don't quote Midsummer Night's Dream at me. No one said anything about love. If I had looser morals, I'd write a book and make you introduce me so he could narrate it and then fuck me so hard I'd forget my own name.

> Lark: Gross.

> Hannah: A girl can dream.

> Lark: I didn't know who he was before today, but he seems very nice.

> Hannah: You've been there for less than a day, and you've already met!? You lucky bitch.

> Lark: Yep. Met Jessica, too. And their producer.

> Hannah: From your tone, I can guess how that went.

> Lark: Text messages don't have a tone.

> Hannah: Yours do.

I lay the phone face down on my chest and stare at the ceiling. She's needling me for information, but I'm not trying to get into this with her before I've sorted it out myself. Maybe if we were sitting in our empty office...

And just that unfinished thought stabs at my heart so hard it makes it difficult to breathe. The enormity of what I've done washes over me in a wave. I'm the mom, for crying out loud. The sensible, stable one. The one with the good job and health insurance who pays the mortgage on time every month and buys healthy groceries every week. Who drops her kid off at school every morning and cooks dinner with a carb, a protein, and a vegetable every night. I am not the kind of person who signs on for a job she's never done and flies halfway across the country on a whim.

Who am I even kidding? I don't belong here. I belong in Ann Arbor, in a tiny, one-windowed office sitting across from Hannah and complaining about our summer-term students. I certainly don't have the skills or knowledge to jump onto an audiobook project with a narrator people apparently swoon over.

And I absolutely do not belong in Lennon's guest room, inserting myself into his life and scowling at him every time a beautiful woman touches his arm.

I'm out of my depth here. I traded the loneliness of an empty apartment for another, worse kind. It's probably better if I face the music sooner than later and admit that I want Lennon to fill the hole Devin left behind, but he can't. No one can. When the center of your universe disappears, it creates a black hole, not a new galaxy.

Another message dings, and I flip it over to see a picture of Devin and Molly, arms slung over each other's shoulders and a giant, Gothic-looking building behind them. Their eyes are blocked by sunglasses, but their smiles are brilliant. Young and beautiful. Bold, daring. Happy.

All things I am not. Not anymore.

That's about when the tears start in earnest, conflicting emotions pounding over me like ocean waves, so powerful that they leave nothing left for me to do but ride them. Happiness for Devin, pride in having raised such an incredible and fearless kid, sadness that it took everything I had left in me to do it. Nostalgia for her goofy, giggly laughter, for a time when I was the one smiling brilliantly next to her in selfies. Anger at Richard for starting a new life on the other side of the country and leaving us high and dry, but gratitude I got to have her all to myself most of the time. Maybe even a little resentment at Lennon for getting to live out his twenties and thirties without any of this weight pulling him down. But nostalgia for him, too. For the way we used to love each other in the uncomplicated way of teenagers without all this baggage.

My main goal in raising Devin was that she never had any of this weighing her down. And looking at her smiling face, it would seem I succeeded. But now what? She'll still need me, of course, but she's out in the world now. Where does that leave me?

I wipe away the tears long enough to type back a quick message. Something sensible about having fun and being safe. Then I flip over, my back to my phone, and let all of it roll over me. Normally, I'd call Lennon and talk it all through with him. It occurs to me that he's right there, on the other side of the wall. That this would be even better than a phone call because he'd fold me into his arms and let me cry it out and help pick me back up when it passes. And it'd feel so *good* to let him.

But I can't do that. I can't risk any of these confusing feelings about him resurfacing. I'll just sleep them off. I'm sure it's all just shock at seeing him again after so long a time, and in the morning, things will look different.

At least that's what I mumble softly as I cry myself to sleep.

Chapter 12

Lennon

Every four years, our high school would put on a big Shakespeare production. It was huge, and the older of the two drama teachers was the one to direct it. It was the only show he directed, and you'd think it was like working with Steven Spielberg the way the other kids talked about it.

Not being from the area, I had no idea what any of this meant, but the show came up our junior year. When the director announced that it was going to be *A Midsummer Night's Dream*, everyone went absolutely wild. Speculations abounded about literally everything. The staging and costumes, who would be best suited for which role, whether or not they would use music or sing the songs in the play, who they'd hire to do blocking, which person's parent would be in charge of set design. But one thing everyone was absolutely sure about was that Lark was a shoo-in for fierce, independent Hermia.

Lark was a triple threat. She could sing, dance, and act. She could play whatever part she wanted, and she did not want to play Hermia.

But she also wasn't going to make waves. That wasn't in her nature. Every time someone brought it up, she'd smile politely and say she'd be happy to be cast at all, no matter the role.

Which was bullshit, obviously.

When the cast list went up, she hung back with me instead of pushing her way through the throng of students wanting to see who was playing what part. I didn't have any skin in the game, aside from wanting Lark to get the part she was hoping for. We stood back there, fingers threaded together between us, Lark gripping my hand with a silent plea to anchor her, no matter what.

Like some kind of eighties John Hughes movie, the crowd of teenagers hushed. One by one, they started to turn and look for her. When they spotted her standing at the back of the crowd, they fell silent.

"Is it that bad?" she asked, her voice light and teasing. But I could feel her hand trembling in mine.

"You're Helena," one of the freshmen said up front.

Lark visibly relaxed, and her smile turned genuine. That was the part she wanted. The lovesick, witty, skeptical woman. Not the bold, free-spirited one. She thought Hermia was too one-dimensional, and Helena would give her an experience to learn from.

That was Lark. Always learning.

But what keeps me up into the wee hours of the morning isn't a walk down memory lane. It's the image of sixteen-year-old Lark dressed in a Grecian-style costume, standing on a stage littered with so much glitter that I'm sure they never fully got rid of it. She's leaning against a makeshift pillar wound with ivy and brightly colored flowers. She closes her eyes and takes a deep breath, pinching her eyebrows together as she recites:

O weary night, O long and tedious night,
Abate thy hours! Shine, comforts, from the east
That I may back to Athens by daylight,
From these that my poor company detest.
And sleep, that sometimes shuts up sorrow's eye,
Steal me awhile from mine own company.

I don't know why my mind goes there, but something about that lunch today didn't feel right. Lark hiding in her room and not coming out feels even worse. I wanted so desperately for her to fold herself seamlessly into my life here that I never stopped to think about what might happen if she didn't instantly fall in love with the sunshine and the ocean like I did when I first came out here for college.

I'm too much in my head about it, when all I want to do is sleep and try again in the morning. I'll explain about Jessica, support Lark in whatever decision she wants to make about Silas's clear interest, pray she wants to stay and not throw in the towel early to head back to Michigan.

The problem is I don't sleep. Not much. Lark is right there, and she's crying. A big part of me expects her to come out and talk to me. But by midnight, she hasn't emerged from her room, which is about the time I decide I need to let sleep steal me away, and I fall in and out of something like repeatedly being dropped into the middle of a dream and yanked back out again before it can conclude.

Visions form behind my eyelids—Lark coming up behind me at that first day of Drama Club, Lark kicking rocks in a parking lot, Lark leaving Richard and me alone on a park bench so we can get to know each other, and Richard telling me it would be better for her if I left, Lark smiling out at me from her phone screen, Lark and Richard at their wedding, Lark and Devin holding hands and skipping through rows of blueberry bushes on a summer day in Michigan, Lark the day she told me Richard was moving to New York with a look of determination that she could do this on her own, Lark waiting for her suitcase at LAX and tucking a strand of hair behind her ear, Lark staring aimlessly out of the passenger seat of my Jeep on the way home from lunch.

And through it all is the never-ending strain of her seductive voice:

We don't have much time before someone comes looking for us, so I make quick work of the buttons on the fly of his jeans. I reach my hand into them, circling it around the smooth, hard length...

Every time, I'm jolted awake before she can finish that sentence.

Lark has always consumed most of my waking hours, even when she wasn't here. I'd see something she'd like and text her or land an awesome job and call her to celebrate. For as long as I've known her, nothing that has happened to me has felt real until I've told her about it.

But now, she's occupying my dreams, too. And to make matters worse, I wake up from every one of those dreams with a hard-on and a desire I haven't felt since I was a teenager. The kind that painfully eats away at you, eroding your willpower bit by tiny bit.

At around five in the morning, I decide that I'd rather see Lark's actual face than another dream version of her, so I roll out of bed and quickly throw on one of my many threadbare USC T-shirts and some sweatpants. I open the door to my room quietly in case Lark is still asleep and walk barefoot into the living space.

My heart bottoms out when I pass the open door to her bedroom. The room looks, frankly, untouched. Her bed is crisply made. I can't see her suitcase anywhere. More important than any of that, Lark isn't in it. A quick glance at the living room tells me she's not out there, either. The bathroom door is open and the lights are off, so she's not in there.

Did she...leave?

I lodge my fingers in my hair, gripping at the strands and using the sensation to distract me from the panic slithering its way up my stomach and squeezing my heart. It's a sensation I'm deeply familiar with—an anxiety that would arise every time I woke up to find my parents gone with no idea where they went or when they'd be back, and one that revisits me sometimes when things start to feel beyond my control. But I haven't felt that in a long time. Years and therapy healed most of those wounds, though it would seem some are still lurking below the surface.

Breathing in and out as deeply and slowly as I can, I try to get the edge of my adrenaline to soften. No luck. I scrape the dust off my checklist of things I'd do to make myself at least functional when I used to feel like this. *Deep breathing.* No help. *Close my eyes and think of something happy.* I try that, but it's no surprise that Lark's face is front and center. Shaking my head violently, I snap my eyes open. That made it worse. *Call Lark.* Well, I can't fucking do that, can I, because she's supposed to be here and she's not.

I tug even harder at my hair, trying to at least feel something other than this. Somewhere, a faucet drips, and the sound of it grates on my already-frayed nerves.

Okay, Lennon. Get it together, I tell myself. *Deal in facts only, not worst-case scenarios. What do you know?*

Yesterday did not go as planned, but was she that upset with me that she'd just up and leave? Without saying goodbye? No, that's not like her. She was always the one who stuck around, no matter what. Who saw me for who I was—a lost boy needing somewhere to belong, a lost man searching for connection and never really finding it—and was never scared away.

She has to be somewhere.

I force my feet to continue on their way to the kitchen, even though they'd rather stay rooted to the floor. The peanut-butter-and-jelly supplies are still on the counter where I left them, and now I don't even know if she ate anything. I'm the world's shittiest host. I didn't plan for any of this.

Coffee. My brain is in a fog, and coffee will at least help me clear it. I fill the tank, grab a pod, and push the button to start the machine. Which is about when I see movement on my balcony out of the corner of my eye.

Lark is sitting outside in one of the giant outdoor armchairs. She's made herself a little nest with a blanket and some pillows that she must have found in the hall closet. Her short blonde hair is mussed slightly, and her back is to me as she stretches her arms wide, then curls up again, tucking them under the blankets on her lap.

I hadn't seen her in my panic. I assumed the worst, and my brain on two nights of very little sleep took it from there.

Lark would never just up and leave. I don't know why I feared she would. My parents would—and have. Used to anyway, when I was young. I woke up alone in my house sometimes with a note to go check in with a neighbor who had a similarly aged kid. They liked to party. Or "network," as they called it, which may have been true to some extent. Dad was always looking for the next big job that could change our lives. Mom was always looking for something exciting to do. Eventually, they came back, but it was the same thing every time. I'd panic, force myself to pour some cereal and eat it, and go to the neighbors' house to hang out for the day. The neighbors never seemed to mind. They liked having me around to play with their kids, but I never let myself get too attached.

Dad would find a different job soon enough or Mom would want to see somewhere new, and the friendship would be over.

As I got older and was able to be by myself, I'd stay and try to read a book until they came home but would usually end up flipping the pages without registering any of the words. They brought Daisy home with them after one such evening at a party that turned into the whole night and the entire next day. Just came back after an entire day gone with the dog as an apology, or maybe as a makeshift babysitter. It's hard to say.

Eventually, I had Lark, too. She suggested once that we notify some authority, but she must have seen the dread in my face when I insisted she not tell anyone. Children's Protective Services could take me away, and once I found her, I couldn't imagine being anywhere she wasn't. So I'd call her, and she'd come over with a paper cup in each hand—coffee for me, tea for her—and we'd sit together on my back patio watching Daisy chase rabbits while we waited for my parents to show up.

It only takes a few minutes for my coffee to brew. I set it aside and use the machine to make tea for her. With a mug in each hand, I cross the living room to the sliding door. I set one of the mugs down to open the door, then walk outside. I put her tea on the small table in front of her and cup mine in my hands against the slight chill in the morning air as I take a seat in the other armchair.

"Thanks," she says, but she doesn't look at me. Her eyes remain fixed on the sliver of horizon between the buildings.

I hum and sip my coffee. It burns my tongue a little, but I welcome it. It feels better than the numbness I was experiencing inside. "I'd ask if you slept well, but it's five in the morning, so probably not."

She shakes her head. "You?"

"Same."

Her blue eyes slide to me then, glancing down to my bare feet and up to my bed head. She huffs a small laugh. "What's your excuse?"

"You," I say without thinking.

Her eyebrows lift in question, but I haven't had enough coffee to explain that away. I take another sip. She doesn't push it; she just sighs and turns back to the horizon.

The silence between us is charged but easy. Something's coming, but it's not going to wreck us. That's impossible. But it does stretch for a few moments. I drink about half of my coffee and Lark starts on her tea before she speaks.

"I'm not sure I belong here." Her voice is small, unsure. It's unclear whether the heartstring that snaps at that is because of her words or because of the way she says them as if she's defeated. She sounds like a woman who has tried to talk herself into something one more time than she's tried to talk herself out of it.

I want to jump out of my seat and get on my knees and beg her to stay. I already thought she left once this morning, and it sent me into a spiral. If she actually left now after I've had only one day with her, I'd be inconsolable. But I try to keep my words as measured as possible. "What do you mean?"

She swallows some tea, then fidgets with the tea bag as she speaks. "This isn't me, Lennon. I don't make impulsive decisions to fly to LA and sign on to do a job I have absolutely no qualifications for. No matter how much I've missed you." Her gaze meets mine as her voice cracks on the last sentence.

Fuck, I've missed her, too. It's easy to ignore when life gets busy and we talk every day anyway, and I probably should admit that a big part of me was avoiding seeing her to also avoid the necessity of parting again. But having her next to me right now is a million times better than talking on the phone, even if things are fraught between us in a way neither of us seems to be able to explain.

She drops her gaze back to the mug in her hand. "And I don't want to burden you."

I set my cup down and take hers from her to do the same. I hold her hands in mine as I lean forward. They're warm from the mug but also clammy. She's nervous again. The desire to take away this pain of hers and make it all better is a constant beacon, but there isn't much I can do.

I run my thumb back and forth over her knuckles. Her eyes track the movement for a second before she closes her eyes. She looks pained. Heavy. Older, suddenly.

"What's going on here?" I ask, not changing the rhythm of my thumb tracing the back of her hand.

"I don't know. What if I'm not any good at this?"

"The audiobook? Lark, you're going to be amazing. Noah, Silas, and Jessica are already obsessed with you. Or were you not at the same lunch I was at yesterday?"

She huffs, then opens her eyes and pins me with a serious gaze. I know what's coming before she even says it.

"Jessica was obsessed with one of us yesterday. I don't think it was me."

"I'm not sleeping with her. I told you that."

Her lips form a thin line, and she ticks an eyebrow toward the sky. "It wouldn't bother me if you were. You're allowed to have women in your life. I just want to know before I get knee-deep in this project."

I squeeze her hands. "I wouldn't lie to you."

She softens at that. "I know. I'm..." She trails off and looks upward to the sky again. "I don't know what's going on with me. I'm sad, Lennon. I'm out of my depth, and I miss my kid."

I stand and motion for her to scoot over. There's barely enough room on the armchair for both of us, so I pull her halfway into my lap and wrap my arms around her. She rests her head on my shoulder and sighs. For a moment, I think she might start crying, but she doesn't. Maybe she's all out of tears for now.

I steal a kiss on top of her head. It's probably wildly inappropriate, but I can't help myself. She feels so good in my arms. Satisfying, like the piece to a jigsaw puzzle I thought had been missing and suddenly found under a couch cushion.

"You're a good mom," I say into her hair. "Devin is a testament to that. She's the best kid, and she feels safe to explore the world because you made sure she's been safe her whole life."

"Shit." Lark sniffles. "I had literally *just* stopped crying, you asshole."

She doesn't mean it. It's just how she is—deflecting with a joke or a taunt. I'm glad she's back at it. It feels much more normal than the deep introspection.

I squeeze her tighter, not quite ready to tease her back yet. "You carried her for eighteen years. Let me carry you for a few weeks. Stay here, be as sad as you want. We'll do some fun stuff, drink some good wine, you'll be brave and try something new. We'll be together. It'll be great."

She wipes her nose with the back of her hand and shifts so she's sitting sideways on the armchair, her legs spread over my lap and her head still on my shoulder. "Okay."

And then, even though I know it might be a death sentence given the words on repeat throughout my dreams last night, I ask, "Do you want to practice before you start recording tomorrow?"

She chuckles, the sound vibrating against and through me, all the way to the tips of my toes. "You mean run lines like we used to do in high school?"

Yep. This is a terrible idea, but like toothpaste out of the tube, there's no going back now. I'd do this and a lot more for her, just to hear that laugh again. "Something like that."

"You think you could help?" she asks skeptically.

I scoff, offended. "I've engineered, like, hundreds of these things. Yes, I think I can help."

She tips her face up to mine. We are so close together that I can feel her warm breath on my skin. It smells of tannins and lemon.

"My bad." She nestles her head into the space between my neck and shoulder. "I'd be grateful for the help. Thank you."

We sit there in silence for a long while before I ask, "Why did you come out here? Just to think?"

"I wanted to watch the sunrise."

I hum as I roll my lips together and bite them to hide a snicker. She must sense it, though, because she looks up at me again.

"What?"

"Nothing," I insist. I nod in the direction she's been facing. "That's west."

She doesn't move. "Oh."

And then, because I can't help myself, I say, "Out here, we watch the sun *set* mostly."

"Mm-hmm," she hums, each note a short staccato. She's annoyed with herself, probably, but I can sense the humor coursing through her, too.

"Because it's the West Coast," I add through a chuckle.

She smacks my arm. "I got it, you dick."

"I think you're confusing me with your ex-husband."

She barks out a laugh. Her head pops off my shoulder, and she looks at me, incredulous. "Lennon Samuel Hollis. Stop."

I roll my eyes dramatically. "Okay, okay."

Her body shakes with restrained laughter as she rests her head back on my shoulder. I smile out over her at the brightening sky and the buildings beyond the balcony. Eventually, she settles, and she lets me hold her in a comfortable silence as the sky goes from navy to pink to a bright royal blue. I watch as the sun starts weaving its way through her hair, twisting it into gold fibers that tickle my cheek in the morning breeze.

Once the sun has broken over the top of my building, she unfurls herself and stretches her neck one way, then the other. "I don't know," she says on a breath, her voice airy and content. "This might be the West Coast, but that was the best sunrise I've seen in a while."

She stands and takes both our empty mugs with her inside, but I linger on the balcony for another few minutes wishing I could hold her for a little longer.

CHAPTER 13

LARK

I VAGUELY REMEMBER LENNON coming in from the balcony, saying he was going to grab a quick shower, and then disappearing into his bedroom. I had every intention of also showering—and bringing my clothes with me this time—but I flop onto his couch for a minute.

The next thing I know, Lennon's voice is whispering into my ear, low and rumbling. Sensual, like a lover might talk in the stolen hours of early morning. "Hey, Songbird."

I bury myself into something, which I hazily start to realize is a throw pillow on Lennon's couch. The moan that escapes me is only half-voluntarily.

Lennon chuckles. The sound of it pings through me, and suddenly, I'm alive. My eyes pop open, and he's there. His sharp jaw dotted with sandy stubble, his equally fair hair falling casually over his forehead. Boyish dimples on either side of an indulgent smirk. Hazel eyes with flecks of gold.

"How long was I out?" I ask, rubbing my eyes and hoping that when I open them, he'll look marginally less attractive.

No such luck. If anything, the light catches an even better angle when he shifts back onto his heels from his crouch in front of me. It throws his sharp features in an even starker relief.

"It's two," he says remorsefully. "I wanted to wake you a few times, but you seemed so tired this morning."

I groan and roll to my back. "This feels like jet lag."

"I mean, you are on a three-hour time difference," he says, trying to be helpful.

"And going on two nights with no sleep," I add. "I'm sorry. This isn't the start to this trip I wanted."

He takes my hand in his, our palms flush against one another. "You're not going to believe this," he says as he studies our hands coupled together over my stomach, "but the only thing that matters to me is that you're here."

I sigh up at the ceiling. "How did ten years pass between our last visit and now?"

He settles in closer, resting his elbow on the cushion next to my hip. "My parents moved. Again. So when I traveled, I had to see them most of the time." I don't miss the bitter edge to his voice, and I give his hand a squeeze. He squeezes back. "Richard left, Devin had a lot more going on, and when you traveled, you had to take her to him. Money was tight for both of us."

I huff at that. "That's an understatement."

"Toss in a pandemic that caused a crisis in the airline industry, and here we are, I guess." It sounds like he's dodging something, but I'm too tired to press him.

"I should have made it a priority as soon as I could," I say to the ceiling.

"We both should have," he agrees quickly. "You're not alone in that, so don't go feeling all guilty."

I eye him sidelong. "You're right. If anything, it's mostly your fault. You're the single, childfree one."

He nods solemnly. "I'm free as a bird."

"The irony," I say drily.

Lennon hums, then pauses for a moment as we both smile at each other like idiots. "So, listen. I know you need to practice before tomorrow, but I want to show off a bit first. Can I take you out?"

I chew on my lip as I study him. "Out where?"

He shrugs, but he's got a giant grin on his face that makes me suspicious. "I didn't intend to surprise you, but now I feel like I should."

"What? No. Just tell me."

He shakes his head, still smiling. "Dress casual."

***

About two hours later, we've gotten a bottle of pinot noir, a giant charcuterie plate, some lavender almonds Lennon insists I try, and a box of dark chocolate truffles from a hip-looking wine bar in downtown Santa Monica. They package everything up while we wait, and Lennon carries the bag to his Jeep where he sets it carefully on top of the blanket and two hoodies he brought.

"We can't drink on the beach, so the wine is for later," he says apologetically as he starts the car and pulls out of his parking space.

"Is that where we're going?" I ask. "How unique."

He spares me a glance as we pull out into traffic. "You can't come out here and not go to the beach. We won't walk the pier. Unless you want to."

"This is your show. I'm merely along for the ride."

He nods once, decisively. "We'll save the pier for another day when we have more time. It's iconic, if a bit cliché."

"Should I have brought my swimsuit?" I don't tell him I only have the one from Hannah, and I haven't even tried it on yet.

"It's always a little cold to swim," he says as he pulls into a parking spot on the sand. Then, he turns to face me in his seat with a shit-eating grin. "We're going to watch a proper sunset."

I narrow my eyes at him. "I'm never going to live it down, am I?"

"Nope." He jumps out of the Jeep and makes his way to the back to get the supplies.

"Tell me you don't have a kid who has woken up at five in the morning every day since she was in utero without telling me." I swing my legs out of the Jeep and hop to the ground.

"What do you mean?"

"I mean, I am a sunrise person. I'm up every morning before the actual crack of dawn." I take the blanket and wrap it into a bundle so I can carry it easily. "You are a sunset person, sleeping in as long as your heart desires and staying awake until well after the sun disappears. We live very different lives, my friend."

"Well," he says, tossing a book my way. A quick glance tells me it's my copy of *Sizzling Secrets*. I tuck it between the blanket and my body as he continues. "This sunset is going to rock your world."

"We'll see," I say skeptically.

"Completely upend everything you thought you knew about the rotation of the Earth," he carries on lightheartedly as we make our way toward the water.

"Pretty sure the Earth keeps rotating, and that's all anyone needs to know about it." I keep my tone dry even as the blue expanse of the ocean right in front of me takes my breath away.

"It might even be a religious experience."

"I kind of doubt a sunset has that kind of power."

Lennon stops in what looks like an arbitrary place and drops the bag of food to the ground. "This is a good spot."

I take in our surroundings. People in various states of dress walk around. Kids squeal as they dip their toes into the cold water and run back to their parents. A sand-volleyball game is in progress a few yards away. In the distance, the Santa Monica Pier stretches out into the water. The giant Ferris wheel rotates, the yellow-and-red basket seats swaying gently. "What makes this a good spot?"

Lennon works to spread the blanket out on top of the sand. He walks around it, tugging at the corners until it lays how he wants. "I can sense that you're skeptical. I suppose you'll just have to trust me."

He motions for me to sit. I fold my legs underneath me and drop to the blanket. He starts taking boxes out of the bag from the wine bar and preparing our spread of food. When I try to help, he swats me away. "Relax. Let me do this for you." His hazel eyes are so intensely focused on me that the cool, salty air blowing off the ocean isn't enough to cool me down.

"What am I supposed to do, then?" I ask weakly.

He smirks and shrugs. "Whatever you want. People watch. Look at the ocean and contemplate life. Read your book." He winks, and it sends a shiver up my spine. Luckily, he's turned back to his preparations, so he doesn't see me tremble from head to toe.

It doesn't take long for him to set up the spread of food. It looks delicious—several cured meats, blocks of white and yellow cheeses, olives, grapes, and a little pot of honey. He rips off a small piece of a baguette and hands it to me. I top mine with some meat and cheese and honey and take a bite, moaning as the salty sweet taste hits my tongue.

I catch him watching me, and my cheeks heat. "Sorry," I mutter. "I haven't eaten anything in a while."

He takes a bite and chews carefully as he looks out at the ocean. I watch his Adam's apple as it bobs against his swallow. The surprising and completely inappropriate urge to lick his throat to see if it's salty, too, crashes into me out of nowhere.

I turn away quickly and follow his gaze. The shimmering water lapping at the shore calms my heart. The rhythm of it is almost hypnotic, calling to me like a siren. Without thinking too much about how ridiculous I'll look, I kick off my sandals and roll up my jeans before jumping up and running toward the water. When I reach the very edge of the tide, I slow to a stop. My toes just kiss the edge of the water as it laps in and out of the sand.

"Wimp." Lennon's taunt comes from right behind me, and before I get a chance to face him, his arms circle my waist and lift me off the ground. He easily throws me over his shoulder in a fireman carry and runs out into the ocean.

I squeal in delight as he turns me this way and that. Salty water splashes my face and touches the tips of my hair as it hangs behind him. His laugh is a booming sound. Bigger than the ocean. Larger than life.

The only thing grander might be my love for him. It pushes against the seams that have haphazardly stitched me together over the years, bursts out of my pores, and explodes from me. It feels like sunshine. Like joy. Like finally coming home.

"Get ready for it," he warns, and before I can ask what I'm supposed to be getting ready for, he sets me down in the water. It licks my ankles and soaks the cuff of my jeans. And it's *freezing*.

"Holy shit." I'm breathless, from the shock of him carrying me, from the explosion of emotions, from the cold ocean water on my bare feet.

He reaches down and splashes me. I throw my hands out in front of me with another laughing shriek. "It's invigorating, right?"

"Something like that." I splash him back.

He laughs heartily as the water turns his sage-green shirt darker where it lands. "You gotta jump in, though. Standing on the sidelines doesn't have the same effect."

I fold my arms and kick water at him this time. "Sounds like a very pointed metaphor."

Lennon tips a shoulder up. "It probably is."

"Well, aren't we full of clichés today?"

His only response is to twist his mouth into an unamused thin line and splash me again.

"Stop!" I yell, laughing and putting my hands up to ward off the spray of water. "I get it. Message received."

"Good. Now can we get out of this fucking cold water and eat, please?"

I throw my arms wide and tip my face to the sun. Its warmth loosens the tight strings inside my chest, and my face stretches into a smile. The tang of the sea air stings my lungs as I breathe it in. "Yeah," I say. "Let's eat."

We spend the next hour or so munching on meat and cheese and chatting about mostly unimportant things. The nerves I had about starting to record tomorrow fade and are replaced with an old, familiar confidence I haven't felt in a long time. It's going to be fine. Whether it's because of Lennon's demonstration in the ocean earlier or because of his general presence or because of the sun shining on my back as I lay on my stomach, I can sense it now.

Eventually, we fall into a companionable silence, which is novel for us. Being silent on the phone usually means the conversation is over, and we hang up. But the luxury of being silent in person seems special as Lennon lies on his back with his hands clasped over his chest just a few feet away from me.

Unwilling to break the silence, I pick up the book and start reading. It's a different sensation, reading it and no longer being consumed by nerves. I can actually enjoy it.

Or at least, I try. It isn't long before I snort loudly, and Lennon rolls his head to squint at me, one eye closed.

"What?" he asks, amused.

I don't look up from the page. "Nothing. Sorry."

He tips his head back to the sky and closes his eyes again, but it only takes a few minutes before another sound of disbelief makes its way up my throat.

"It's not that bad," Lennon says without looking at me.

"It's not that." I flip back a few pages and find what I'm looking for. "I know you insisted you don't want to sleep with her—"

"I don't." He still doesn't look at me.

"Right. Fine. But it's pretty clear that's one-sided."

"What do you mean?" he asks, his voice edged with disbelief.

I flip back a few more pages, confirming what I've already seen clearly throughout the entire book. "Oh, come on. Marcus is you, Lennon."

He faces me again, then, shading his eyes against what's left of the sun. "You're going to have to be more specific."

I pin him with a skeptical look. "Sandy hair, backward baseball hat, chino shorts..."

"You're describing half the people on this beach."

"'His biceps ripple around me as his arms encircle me. I run a long finger over the tattoo of a mountainous outdoor scene on his shoulder,'" I quote. "Come on."

Lennon cranes his neck to look at the tattoo of an outdoor scene on his shoulder, then tips his head back to the sky and closes his eyes, the picture of relaxation. "Still could be anyone."

Exasperated, I flip forward a few pages. "'I lick my way up his thigh to the birthmark just above his right hip bone.'" In a flash, I reach out and lift his shirt up a few inches, exposing the birthmark there. "Lennon. Don't lie to me. How does she even know this is here?"

"Same way you do." He tugs his shirt back into place without looking at me. "It's California. We swim."

"I didn't know you were close enough to go swimming together."

"We aren't." He rolls his head to face me again. A piece of hair falls over his forehead, making his mischievous grin even more boyish. "We met at a party."

He doesn't offer any more information, so I ask slowly, "A party where you slept with her?"

The skin around Lennon's eyes crinkles as he chuckles. The sound is low and deep, almost ominous. "For someone who says they're not bothered by this, you sure seem bothered by it." When I only blink at him in response, he huffs. "A pool party. She had told me she was drafting a novel then, so she must have seen my birthmark and used it as inspiration." He waggles his eyebrows. "I am very inspiring."

I roll my eyes. "You're right. This probably isn't about you. Marcus's ego isn't nearly as big as yours."

We smile, watching each other for a moment before I go back to reading silently. But now that I've started this, I can't seem to stop. "Okay," I exclaim. "'Marcus grips my knees, forcing my legs open further,'" I read. "'The heat of his gaze burns into my core as he circles himself and pumps a few times. "Such a pretty pussy, Gia. I'm going to fuck it so hard until you come." His voice is gravelly with desire, and I gush.'" I cringe at that last part. I'm not an expert in every woman's arousal, but I've certainly never gushed anything from anywhere unless I was very ill.

As I'm busy blinking away my disbelief, Lennon turns over onto his side and props his head up on his fist. "See, that's how you know beyond a shadow of a doubt she might be fantasizing about me, but she doesn't have any experience with the real thing," he says softly. He's close enough that his breath tickles my ear.

"Oh no?" I ask quietly. Maybe it's the sunshine or dipping my toes in the cold ocean or the dizzy feeling I have at the close proximity to Lennon's body. Whatever it is, it's making me bold. "That's not what you'd do, if given the chance?"

His hazel eyes darken, and I must be drunk on sunshine, because I could swear they dip to my mouth before returning quickly to meet my gaze.

Is he...thinking about me while we talk about bad smut on a blanket at the beach?

That can't be right.

But his voice goes raspy and low when he says, "No, Songbird. First of all, I'd never refer to anyone's 'pussy.' It's crass, which some people like, but I prefer more nuance. I wouldn't force their legs open, either."

I swallow hard, the combination of his intense eye contact and his sultry voice making me giddy. "You wouldn't?" Even I'm surprised at how measured my voice is when I feel like I might implode.

Lennon shakes his head slowly, his eyes never leaving mine. "I wouldn't need to. She'd lie on the bed, and I'd start at her ankles, kissing slowly up her gorgeous calves. Her breaths would grow shorter with anticipation as I worked my way over her knee, and those pretty legs would fall open all on their own."

He shifts slightly so his foot is pressed against mine, the sand stuck to his skin deliciously scraping against mine. I'm not even sure if he notices he's done it, but my entire focus zeroes in on the warmth of him against my foot. It takes a great deal of control to keep my own breathing even.

"Oh," I whisper.

A corner of Lennon's mouth tips up ever so slightly. "And I'd never touch myself."

"Why not?" Even though I might combust from the inside out, I have to know.

That corner pulls up even further. *He's enjoying this*, I vaguely register. Well, fuck. I am, too.

"That would imply that my pleasure takes precedence, which is just rude, don't you think?"

My already tenuous grasp on this conversation is slipping quickly. "I don't know…" I try to remain skeptical. "I think it's okay for you to enjoy yourself."

Did I just say that? I'd be mortified if I weren't so turned on.

This time, it's unmistakable when Lennon's gaze dips to my mouth. "I'd enjoy myself, Lark." Did he just say my name? While looking at my lips like he wants to drag them through his teeth? Surely, I'm imagining it. "Don't you worry about that. But it's my job as a lover to take my time. Make sure she's satisfied." The way he says the word is positively decadent. I want to crawl out of my skin and into that word and live there for all eternity. "And then"—he leans closer—"I'd make sure she's satisfied again."

His eyes linger on me, driving the point home, before he rolls to his back, clasping his hands over his chest and closing his eyes as if he didn't just completely upend my entire day and make me question everything I thought I knew about sex and seduction…and him.

"And that's how you know," he says nonchalantly.

"Know what?" I squeak out.

"That she's not basing her work on anything real. Because if she was, that smut would be a lot better."

It's a joke. I should laugh. I should make another crack about his giant ego. But I can't manage anything but a shudder that works its way up from where his foot had been resting against mine, over my legs, and up my spine.

"Cold?" he asks, glancing at me.

"Yeah," is all I can manage. I sit up and fold my legs underneath me again so I can rub life into my suddenly leaden arms.

He gets up, too, and slides one of the hoodies over my head. It's his, so it's not only giant but it smells just like him. I certainly don't need him to seep inside me any more than he already has, but I tuck my hands inside the large sleeves and bring them to my nose. I inhale deeply with the hope that it'll calm me down, but the big open smell of him only serves to stoke the embers Lennon's words left behind.

I'm able to get a grip on my libido before the sun sets. He was right; it's unbelievable. The sky explodes in shocks of oranges and pinks, dark palm trees silhouetted against the watercolor sky. The Ferris wheel on the pier lights up with colors that match. The ocean refracts and reflects everything, sparkling and waving in and out as the sun dips into it once and for all.

But it's not a religious experience. It doesn't make me question what I know about the Earth's rotation.

No, that comes later. In my bed, with my hand between my legs and my face buried in a pillow so Lennon can't hear my breathy moans as I think about what his kisses might feel like on my inner thighs.

CHAPTER 14

LENNON

"I THOUGHT I MIGHT find you here." Noah's muffled voice cuts through my music just before he appears over me. I take my earbuds out and wince as the hard rock I had been ruining my eardrums with becomes a tinny sound I'm sure we can both hear. I tap my phone to turn it off and look up at him under the barbell that's on the rack above my head.

"Spot me?" I ask. He steps closer to my head and gets into position. I lift the barbell, grunting at the weight I've loaded it with. I lower it slowly toward my chest, then exhale in a whoosh as I press it up again. I make it about six reps before I have to rack the weight.

Noah eyes the plates I've stacked on either side of the barbell, and I can see him adding them up in his head. "Are you punishing yourself for something specific or just in general?" he asks as I sit up and rest my forearms on my knees.

My chest rises and falls quickly. I pull up the neck of my sleeveless shirt to wipe my face and grab my water bottle, shooting him a sidelong glance. He's in his normal weekday workwear—a button-up shirt and jeans—so he clearly walked over here during a break in recording. This morning, I set up everything at the studio and then turned it over to Noah's intern and got out of there as fast as I could. On a big project like this, I should probably be manning the recording booth, but there's no way I could listen to Lark read the same words she was taunting me with on the beach last night in real time. Noah had agreed to let the intern handle it since I'm doing the final edits, so I ran a few errands to kill some time.

Unfortunately, it didn't kill nearly enough, and even my deep-breathing exercises didn't take the edge off. So, I walked to the gym and decided the best way to stop thinking about her flushed cheeks and soft, parted lips as I completely and thoroughly crossed a line last night was to load up as much weight as I could.

I take a quick drink from my water bottle and wipe my mouth with the back of my hand. "How's Lark doing?"

I know full well I'm avoiding his question. The truth is, since high school, Lark has always been one of the first people I think about when I wake up, and the last person I think about before falling asleep. When she started dating Richard, I tamped down those feelings. Or at least, I thought I did. Until last night. I am probably punishing myself for how far I let myself go. What was I thinking, whispering about the type of lover I am? And I won't even let myself pretend I was speaking generally. Her sea-salted ankles were calling to me as I talked about kissing the insides of them all the way up to her inner thighs...

"She's a fucking natural." Noah thankfully saves me from that train of thought. His grin is about a mile wide, and he ticks an eyebrow up. "You could come back to listen."

I shake my head and take another sip of my water. The part of me that knows she's just playing a character is not strong enough to drown out the part that is aroused by listening to Lark moan out full passages about a man's cock and what it can do for her. I'm going to have to figure out how to make this editing process as clinical as possible, and fast. Jessica will need a sample of the first few chapters to approve, which means I'll need to edit them for her this week. But that is a bridge I have not figured out how to cross yet, and I'm not trying to make it worse by hearing any of this before I've got my shit together.

Just the thought of having to start edits on this book has my stomach doing flips. I jump up and start unloading my weights from the barbell and organizing them to avoid thinking about it.

"It'd mess her up if I were there," I say simply.

Noah's nostrils flare and his beard twitches as if he finds that funny. "Sure." He sits on the bench I had been occupying. "And it has nothing to do with whatever was going on at lunch the other day, right?"

"I thought it went well, all things considered," I say, but it sounds weak even to me. I slide two of the plates on the rack and go back for the others.

He barks out an incredulous laugh. "Right. Which is why I had to pretend you had a hangover from some drinks we never had." He tilts his head. "What's going on, Lennon? Did you just now realize your best friend who is living with you for the summer is actually a talented, smart, gorgeous woman? I can't imagine you haven't noticed before now." He gives me a pointed look, and I'm reminded of what he said at lunch about watching me stitch myself back up ten years ago.

Am I that easy to read? Does Lark see it written plainly on my face like Noah does? I yank another plate off the barbell with more force than necessary.

I can't talk about this right now. Voicing any of it will make it real, and it's not. It can't be. She's my best friend and my favorite person in the world. That's all we've ever been, and after twenty-five years, it's all we can ever be. Full stop.

"Is she ready for me to come get her?" I grind out as I return the last of the weights to the rack. "She hasn't texted."

Noah doesn't razz me for my second change in subject of the conversation. Instead, he looks like he's hiding something as he stands and straightens his spine. "Uh, no." He shoves his hands into his pockets. I know before he says anything that this isn't going to be good. "She's actually recording a bit with Silas."

I stretch my arm across my chest so he can't see my hands shaking. "Why would she be recording with him?"

Noah makes a humming sound in the back of his throat. He winces and scratches the side of his head. "Well, Jessica called this morning talking a mile a minute about duet narration and how hot it is right now—"

"And you thought tossing the new kid a challenge would be fun." I walk past him to the cables where I fiddle with attachments and weights before starting tricep push-downs.

"That's just it." He leans forward, eyes wide. "She's new, but I think that's working in her favor. She doesn't know what to expect from a project like this, so she's flexible. We got Silas in a booth and let them just start fucking around with some of the dialogue. It's magic, man."

Of course it is. Everything Lark does is magical. This was never going to be any different.

I drop the weights and shake out my arms. "So, you're here to ask me if I'm willing to edit a duet."

It's a significantly more difficult project. I have to make sure both voices sound good together, edit out any weird pauses, and sift through more hours of recording because, inevitably, there will be more takes when two people are playing off each other. It's nothing I haven't done before, but it's not insignificant.

Not to mention I'll need to figure out how to not only listen to Lark's sensual voice but Silas's response to it. Just the thought makes my stomach bottom out. I start another set of push-downs, working faster this time.

Noah studies me, his tongue working on the inside of his cheek as he thinks. "We can find someone else if this is going to be an issue," he says slowly. "But we are willing to pay you double."

My hands slip and the weights drop with a sharp clang. "Double?" That would certainly go a long way toward alleviating my roommate issues.

"Yeah," Noah says on a chuckle. "For whatever reason, this book keeps climbing the charts. The audio is already projected to do really well, and making it a duet—"

"With Silas, no less. You're going to make this money back in a week."

"Pretty much. But there's clearly something going on here"—he circles his hand in the general direction of my chest—"so if you can't, it's really okay. We'll find someone else."

"No, I can do it," I insist with a confidence I definitely do not feel. At the very least, I wouldn't want to throw Lark for another loop by having her work with a different editor. This weird desire will fade. I'm sure of it. And worst case, if it doesn't, I can set it aside to do this for her.

Her tear-stained face coming through my phone screen flashes in front of me. Talking about her life slipping away, wondering how forty crept up on her while she was busy doing a bunch of things she never thought she'd have to do.

She saved me all those years ago by dragging my sorry ass into that Drama Club meeting. And then she kept showing up when I needed her most. The least I can do is do this for her.

Noah is still scrutinizing me as I start another set. "I'm not going to argue with you. You're the best I've worked with, and I want you on this project. But if you need to talk..."

"I'm fine." There's that false confidence again.

"Okay, then." He checks his watch. "They should be done in an hour or two. I'll, uh...leave you to it."

I give him a curt nod and stretch out my arms again, but I can feel his eyes on me for another moment before the door to the gym closes behind him.

***

I finish my lift, then take my time showering in the locker room before I make my way back to the studio to pick up Lark. When I get to the door, I pause, looking through the window. Noah is there, working on something in the corner of the room, but the first thing I really see is Lark and Silas outside of the booths, chatting. He leans in to say something to her, and her face breaks out into a grin. Her shoulders shake as if she's giggling, then she looks down. Her long eyelashes brush her cheeks, flushed a pretty pink.

She's practically vibrating. It's obvious even from here. The relief I feel at seeing clearly that she must have had a great day is quickly overshadowed by white-hot jealousy when Silas tips his body even closer to hers and says something softly into her ear. Lark's smile turns shy, and her shoulders turn inward in a bashful way. She tips her blue eyes up to his, and they look at each other for a beat.

Holy shit. They're flirting.

And I know—I *know*—I should let them. Lark hasn't dated a ton of men since Richard, but they've ranged from dead ends to downright shitty. She deserves someone like Silas, with his Southern charm and his perfect hair and his tight T-shirts and his raspy voice.

But my brain isn't driving right now, so I push open the door as hard as I can without seeming like a caveman coming to club this guy and take his woman out of here.

"Hey, Songbird." It's a shameless use of my nickname for her. I might not knock Silas out, but I will stake a claim by reminding him I have a nickname-level relationship with her and he doesn't.

It only takes a quarter of a heartbeat for Lark's entire body to light up in my presence. It's so instantaneous that it takes me far longer to process her body language than it does for her to show it. Her spine straightens, and she bounces to the tips of her toes as her eyes go round and her grin grows wide.

I'm the one who makes her look like that, I realize. And I like it far too much.

"Hey!" she exclaims. She sounds girlish in her excitement, like she used to after a really great rehearsal when everything clicked and she was riding a high. "Oh my god. I cannot wait to tell you about today. Let me get my stuff, and we can head home, okay?"

Home, I think dully as she goes into the back room to gather her things. Could this be her home? Can I even dare to hope for such a thing?

But I don't have time to dwell on it, because Silas comes forward to shake my hand in greeting. "Lennon. I'm glad you're here. I wanted to ask you something."

"Sure," I say distractedly.

"Lark. She's single?"

Everything stops, like a record scratching to a halt. "What?"

"I was thinking of asking her out." He looks toward the door she disappeared behind and runs a hand through his hair. It doesn't move.

Noah clears his throat loudly and pointedly from the other side of the room.

I cough a few times, trying to dislodge whatever just landed in my throat. "Oh," I manage, then cough again. "Sorry. Right. Yes. She's single."

Silas smirks as he watches me try to collect myself. "You okay?"

No. "Yeah. Worked hard at the gym is all."

"Okay," he says, clearly skeptical. "I wanted to take her to a nice dinner or something, if you think she'd be interested."

I hope not. "I don't want to speak for her. But she's only here for a few months," I warn. I say it to deter him, but the reminder sends a sadness through me that sags my shoulders and steals my breath.

"Really?" Silas frowns at the door to the back room. "Interesting."

Thankfully, Lark comes bounding out just then. "Ready?" she asks, breathless and full of joy.

Her happiness is contagious. It always has been. It fills me from the inside out and takes the edge off these tumultuous feelings that have been at war all day.

I offer her my arm, and she takes it. Little bursts of sunlight tingle in the crook of my elbow where she touches me.

"Ready," I tell her. We toss a wave to Silas on our way out, and I try very hard to ignore the knowing glance Noah throws my way as we make our way into the bright, sunny afternoon.

CHAPTER 15

LARK

OVER THE NEXT WEEK, we quickly fall into a routine. Lennon, to my complete surprise, is awake every morning before me and has a mug of tea and a bagel waiting on the counter as soon as I emerge from my bedroom. He never once mentions our antics on the beach, so I don't either. By midweek, it's as if it never happened, and it fully verifies my assumption that it was simply our proximity that had me all hot and bothered when I first got here. Now we can get back to being best friends.

On Friday morning, Lennon eyes me over his coffee. I am, of course, conveniently taking a giant bite of my bagel when I notice him watching me. I try to make it a smaller bite at the last minute, which only has the effect of causing a bit of cream cheese to plop onto my plate.

Good thing Lennon isn't under any pretense of me being cool.

"Let's go out tonight," he says softly, his voice full of amusement.

I try to scoop up the cream cheese with another piece of my bagel. It keeps falling off and back onto the plate. "It's a wonder you want to take me anywhere, what with all this grace and coordination." I give up and wipe the cream cheese with my finger to re-deposit it onto my bagel.

He shakes his head slightly and places his mug carefully on the counter. "You don't even know how gorgeous you are, Songbird." His hazel eyes stay trained on his mug as he says it, but it doesn't matter. The words move through me and lodge themselves in my heart all the same.

My gaze lingers on his sharp jawline, his pre-shave stubble catching the overhead light above the counter. There are grays hidden in there that I hadn't seen before, but it only makes him more attractive. Distinguished, in a way. Confident. Not for the first time since I arrived, I'm struck by how kind the years he's spent in the Los Angeles sunshine have been to him. I'm so happy he has found a place where he feels like he belongs. It was always something I worried about with him. When he chose USC for his undergrad, it felt like he was running from something and that he'd be doomed to roam the Earth forever. But he didn't. He loved it here so much that he stayed, and the rest is history.

One side of his mouth lifts as he watches me watching him. With anyone else, this moment would be awkward, but it's Lennon. We've watched each other for years. Decades, even.

"What?" he asks.

"Just thinking that you're not so bad to look at yourself," I tease.

He runs a hand through his hair in a mock-sultry move. "If you think this is nice, wait until we go out tonight. I'll dress pretty just for you."

"There's that ego," I mumble into my mug. He kicks me lightly under the counter, and I laugh. "Fine. Let's take our old asses out somewhere cool and celebrate the last weekend of my thirties."

"If you're going to get old, you might as well have fun doing it." He winks at me, and it makes my insides flip over themselves.

Proximity. That's all it is.

I stand to deposit my now-empty mug into the sink and move away from him to get ready for the day.

***

Recording is going really well. Noah keeps telling me I'm a natural after listening to the raw recordings, and I keep reminding him that I have spent a long time studying—and teaching—acting technique. But it's nice to hear, considering how little faith my department chair, Carl, had in me last we spoke.

Silas and I have an undeniable chemistry, too. Even I can feel it. Voicing this book with him feels electric, like something long dormant inside me is waking up and stretching its under-used muscles. It's so fun to banter back and forth in the voices of these characters, even if it is taking longer than we anticipated to get takes we are both happy with.

So, I suppose I shouldn't be surprised when we leave our booths on Friday afternoon and he asks me to hang back. Noah's brown eyes bounce between the two of us for a second before he excuses himself to upload the audio files to the server for Lennon to get started on this weekend.

The air between Silas and me goes still as he bites his lip with a shyness that doesn't seem like him at all. It's not disingenuous, exactly, but it doesn't feel characteristic of him, either.

And that's about when I understand what's going on here. If only I picked up on it a beat earlier, because I would have made some excuse about why I couldn't stay and saved him from what comes out of his mouth.

"I'd really love to take you out to dinner, if you're available."

Hannah wasn't wrong when she said Silas is hot. He is incredibly good-looking in a dark, suave, put-together way. And he's very kind, or at least, he has been to me as he patiently walks me through a lot of the recording process that a more seasoned narrator would already be familiar with.

And even though it has been ages since I've been on a proper date—or gotten properly laid, for that matter—I can't help but feel that it's not a great idea. At the very least, Lennon hasn't brought anyone home since I've been here, so I can return the favor.

"Oh," I say as I take a deep breath. "That's so nice. But this summer is just a temporary thing. I have a kid, and she just went to college, and... I'm not really here to date, you know?" I want to crawl into a hole and sleep for fifteen years after bumbling through that. Could I be any more awkward?

Silas, to his credit, smiles softly. "Fair enough." He shrugs. "You're just so captivating, Lark. I had to shoot my shot." He doesn't say it like he's trying to persuade me. They're just facts: I'm captivating. He had to try.

Now I feel bad for some inexplicable reason. "Well, I mean...Lennon and I are going out tonight? It's the last weekend before my birthday—"

"Happy birthday," he says, his voice deep and raspy. Sexy, but it doesn't give me goose bumps like Lennon's suggestive murmur as he talked about how he'd coax a woman to open her thighs...

Now I'm all thrown off, and my mouth seems to be working without the full attention of my brain. "Thanks. I'm not really sure what he's planning, but I haven't seen much of the city so—"

Just then, Jessica bursts through the door, bouncing in on a cloud of perfume with her dark hair pulled back into a sleek ponytail and a white shirt tucked into skin-tight jeans. "There you are! My two favorite people." She must notice how close Silas is to me, because she stops in her tracks and waggles a red-painted fingernail between us. "Oh, what is going on here?" she asks suggestively.

I laugh nervously and take a step back. "We just finished recording for the day. I think you're really going to like it."

She waves this away. "I already love it. Did I interrupt something else, though?" Her eyebrows shoot up her head.

Silas, ever amused, clears his throat. "Lark was telling me that she and Lennon are going out to celebrate her birthday tonight."

"No, it's not—" I start, but Jessica interrupts me with a clap of her hands.

"Oh! I know the perfect place."

Noah re-enters the room, shouldering his messenger bag and jingling his keys. He stops when he sees the three of us.

"I think Lennon had something in mind," I say feebly.

"Whatever he had planned, this is better," Jessica insists. "I'll text him." She starts tapping her phone, her long nails clicking against the screen in rapid fire.

"He's probably right outside—"

"Done!" She pockets her phone.

God, he is going to kill me. I can't imagine this is at all what he had in mind. I blow out a puff of air and turn to Noah. "I guess we're all celebrating my birthday tonight. You in?"

Noah rolls his lips together and bites down as if he could prevent himself from cackling. When he's past the point of outright laughter, he smiles at me, teasing. "I wouldn't miss it."

"Great." I try not to sound sarcastic when I say it, but Noah snorts anyway. "I'll...uh...see you all later, I guess." I wave quickly and get out of that building as fast as I can.

Sure enough, Lennon is waiting at the curb in his Jeep, looking at his phone. When I climb in, he turns his face slowly to me. "You invited Jessica and Silas to..." He checks his phone again to verify. "The Velvet Mirage?"

The look I give him must accurately convey my confusion and horror at what happened inside, because he throws his head back and laughs.

"I didn't mean to," I protest. "Silas asked me out—"

"He what?" Lennon asks, his laughter abruptly dying. "Shit, I didn't think he'd actually do it."

My eyes go wide. "You knew?" I notice the three of them behind the window of the front door, coming our way. "Drive, please. I don't think they need to hear this."

He obliges, pulling out into the street and driving away from the studio. Once we round the corner, I turn to him.

"Spill," I demand.

"He asked me the other day if you were single. I told him you were." Lennon shrugs, staring hard out the windshield. "I guess he thought it was a green light."

I fold my arms over my seat belt. "And you didn't think to mention it to me?"

"I didn't want to...get your hopes up?" he guesses.

"More like warn me," I correct. "If I'd had notice, I wouldn't have panicked."

Lennon smirks. "What do you mean you panicked?"

"It's been a while since someone has asked me out," I say in my defense.

"I asked you out this very morning," he reminds me.

I roll my eyes. "Not like that," I insist, but I don't miss the way his lips pull into a tight line. "Anyway, I felt bad turning him down, so I mentioned we were going out and..."

"And Jessica walked in, they both invited themselves, so you asked Noah, too," he finishes for me.

"That's pretty much how it went, yes." I screw up my face in apology. "I'm sorry. I was caught off guard."

Lennon reaches a big hand over to squeeze my knee reassuringly. "It's not a problem, Songbird. It'll be fun."

"Will it?" I grumble.

He chuckles. "It will. But I hope you brought something to wear to go out dancing."

I slowly turn to face him. "What does that mean?"

He doesn't tell me, though. He just smirks to himself as he watches the road pass us by.

***

"What the fuck do people wear to go dancing?" I prop my phone against the wall on the dresser in my bedroom so Hannah can see the options I've lined up on my bed. I frown at all of them as she hums.

"Hello to you, too. How's it going? How's Silas?"

I dip my chin, giving her an exasperated look. "Silas is the one who got me into this mess in the first place. We are not fans of Silas today." I hear Lennon's shower turn on and figure I have about fifteen minutes before he comes out and hears everything I'm saying, so I need her to get down to business.

"There is definitely more to that story, but I can see you're distressed. Show me what we're working with." She's trying very hard not to laugh.

"I'm too old to go out dancing," I mumble, holding up a black T-shirt and flowery maxi skirt.

"You're only as old as you feel. That's not bad, but maybe a little casual. What else?"

I hold up denim shorts and a black tank top.

She scrunches her nose. "Do you have anything that isn't black?"

"Don't people wear black to dance clubs?" I ask.

"Old people, maybe," she jokes. "I'm kidding! Black doesn't really suit you, princess. What about that skirt over there?" She points behind me to where a denim miniskirt is draped over the armchair in the corner.

"That wasn't one of the options," I tell her.

"Yeah, well, your options all suck. Hold it up. Do you have a tank top?"

"Aside from the black one?" I hold the skirt in front of my waist and look around to the clothes tossed onto the bed. "I have this one, but it's meant to be an undershirt."

"That's how you know it's perfect for a dance club." Hannah bounces her eyebrows up and down.

"I swear to god, if you're fucking with me—"

"I'm not!" She laughs. "Strappy heels?"

"Black ones." I tick up an eyebrow in the direction of the phone.

She hums, tilting her head. "Maybe the black top, then. With a necklace."

I sigh, rummaging through my suitcase to find my bag of accessories. "Gold or silver?"

"With your skin tone? Gold, definitely. Put it on and let me see."

By the time I've gotten Hannah's stamp of approval on my outfit and given her the basic rundown of how I found myself in this mess of an evening while doing my makeup, I can hear Lennon banging drawers in his room. She tells me to text her later and hangs up. I give myself a once-over in the full-length mirror on the door and send up a quick prayer that Lennon doesn't get all weird about this skirt like he did the sundress the other day. That would only be awkward, and I don't know how much more awkwardness I can take today.

The good news is that when Lennon's hazel eyes do a once-over on my outfit, he doesn't say much.

The bad news is that as soon as he comes out of his room, my mouth goes dry. His sandy hair is styled, but not overly so. I can tell he combed some product through it because his waves look more refined than they usually do. He's wearing a navy dress shirt, the top few buttons open and the sleeves rolled up to expose his corded forearms and the tattoo of a compass that stretches almost from his right elbow to his wrist and wraps around his entire forearm. His stone-washed jeans sit low on his trim hips, and his feet are still bare, which is somehow sexier than any shoes he could accent the outfit with.

"You look nice," is about all I can manage.

He smirks, pushing his sleeves up a bit further over his elbows. "You think so?"

"Yeah," I say, forcing an air of nonchalance. "You know. For someone who's forty."

Lennon huffs. "You have four more days to make that joke. Better make good use of it."

"I plan to," I assure him, though the butterflies in my stomach are still doing flips as we both put on our shoes and leave for the club.

When we walk up to the Velvet Mirage, the pounding bass from the loud music is spilling out onto the sidewalk. Jessica insisted we give her name at the door, which we do, and we're let right in.

"I didn't know she was famous," I yell over the music as we climb the stairs to the rooftop bar. Hopefully it'll be a little quieter up there.

"She isn't. She just knows a lot of people," Lennon shouts back. "Which isn't the same thing," he clarifies.

When a familiar song starts playing, a wave of people comes down the stairs, pushing both of us to the side. Lennon reaches out a hand to grab mine, squeezing it as he pushes through them like a fish swimming upstream. Eventually, we're spit out of a door and onto the roof, where the bass still vibrates, but it's quiet enough that we can talk without yelling.

"I think I am too old for this," I mutter so only he can hear. Jessica, who is already at a table with Noah and Silas, waves to us from across the rooftop.

Lennon laughs softly, slowing his pace so we can have a few extra moments. "We don't have to stay long. Say the word, and we'll leave."

I hum quietly. "Do we need a safe word?"

That stops him completely. His gaze meets mine, intense and dark. "Do you want one?" His voice is low and suggestive, and it knocks something loose in my head. Desire rises in me like a hot, scalding thing, so tangible it takes my breath away. The need for him—to feel him pressed against me, pushing me to the edge but knowing I can say the word and he'll back off—solidifies in my belly. There's no ignoring this or explaining it away. It's him and me locked in a gaze I can't read and am too afraid of losing him to try.

I blink a few times and swallow thickly. "Um, no. I think I'll be okay." What a goddamned lie. There is no part of me that feels okay. I only feel off balance and on edge, dangerously close to tipping over into uncharted territory with no way back.

Lennon's throat works against his own swallow, and I dare to wonder if he's feeling this, too. It's so palpable to me that I can't imagine he isn't. But it's been twenty-five years. If he ever wanted me as much as I want him now, surely it would have come up.

He squeezes my hand again. I had forgotten he was still holding it. It snaps me out of my haze enough to nod and separate myself from him to continue my way to the table.

Jessica greets me with a kiss on either cheek. Silas gives me a one-armed hug, and Noah smiles warmly from across the table. A waitress comes by and deposits a drink in front of each of us.

"I hope you don't mind," Jessica chirps. "I ordered for you. First round's on me. The mojitos here are to die for." She nudges me in the side, then leans over me to talk to Lennon. "And a whiskey sour for you, of course."

"Whiskey sour?" he asks, taking a sip and puckering his lips.

Jessica looks between him and Noah. "Yeah, you said you had been drinking them the other night, so I thought that's what you'd want."

Noah laughs quietly into his glass, shaking his head. Lennon takes another sip and does a better job of hiding his distaste. "Right. Thanks, Jess."

She beams at him. "No problem! Now, birthday girl, tell us some more stories about your life in the Midwest."

Three mojitos and at least ten stories later, I need a break. Noah left one drink ago, the lucky bastard, excusing himself with something about going home before his kids' bedtime. For some reason, we stayed, and the exhaustion of being so constantly in the limelight has thoroughly hit me. There's too much residual adrenaline coursing through me.

As a crowd of people push their way through the doors to the rooftop, and a familiar beat pulses in their wake. I gasp and turn excitedly to Lennon. "I love this song. Let's dance."

He downs the rest of his whiskey sour, which he sure is drinking slowly, and smiles down at me. "Funny, I didn't think you'd actually want to dance tonight."

I shrug. "When in Rome." And when I've had three drinks and enough pent-up sexual tension to last me the next forty years of my life. I stand quickly, ignoring Silas studying me and Jessica giggling. "I'm going. You don't have to come if you don't want." I turn on my heel and walk into the club.

I'm immediately swallowed by a mass of bodies, most of them swaying to the beat. I join in, and only a few seconds later, a warm arm wraps itself around my belly, pressing me into a hard chest at my back.

Inhaling deeply, I close my eyes and lean backward into him. I'd know that smell anywhere. Big blue skies and crisp mountains and pine. *Home.* The word pulses vaguely in time with the beat of the music, with the sway of Lennon's body with mine.

He reaches down for my hip and spins me to face him. One of his powerful thighs slides between mine, and his hand drifts dangerously close to my ass as he presses me closer. My nipples pebble through my thin shirt as they brush against the hard edges of his chest. He must not have shaved today, because the course hairs of his stubble scrape against my cheek as he leans in to speak into my ear. "I'll always dance with you, Lark."

My skirt rides up as we move together, the motion at once the innocent dancing of two friends and the sensual grinding of two people wanting more. The only thing separating his thigh from my pulsing core are a few layers of thin fabric, and I reach up to circle my arms around his neck. The mojitos are either making me bold or stupid. Maybe both. But every cell in my body has been replaced by desire, and I'm tenuously holding myself back by the last few, thin threads of reason I possess.

A rumble rises in his chest. I feel it more than hear it, but it's unmistakable. I pull my head back from where it was pressed close to his neck to meet his gaze. It's open and honest and focused solely on me, even as our bodies keep swaying to the beat. It sucks out all the air that was left in this hot, sticky room as his hand dips even lower on my back. His other hand cups my jaw, and his thumb drags over my bottom lip. The rough pad of his finger feels so good just there. Like he's strumming a satisfying chord. I undeniably want him to replace it with his mouth.

Fuck, I am going to explode. I thought moving myself to the dance floor would help me work out some of this pent-up energy. But my body is sighing in relief at finally having him so close to me, even as my mind is screaming at me to back the fuck up before I ruin our friendship forever.

"Water," I yell over the music. He, thankfully, drops his hand from my jaw and leans in closer. "I need water. And the bathroom," I add. "I'll be back."

I don't wait for a response from him before pushing my way through the crowds and to the bathroom first, where I know he won't follow me. I need a second to breathe, to *think*, and so I lean against the wall outside of the bathrooms, trying to knock some sense into myself by lightly banging the back of my head into it.

Up until now, I could explain this away. Our proximity after so long apart. My libido in overdrive after an epic dry spell and while consumed with narrating straight-up smut every day. A bit of a harmless crush I've probably always harbored for him rearing its head at me. But every time, it has been the same thought that has doused me in cold water: We are friends, and I can't risk that changing. If my impulsive decision to come out here is any indication, I need him. With Devin gone, he's all I have.

Not to mention that I've haven't been sure that these feelings are reciprocated, but there isn't any doubt now. Not after feeling the pad of his thumb graze roughly against my lips. My tongue darts out to taste the place he touched, and it's just as salty as it has been in my dreams lately, which sends another wave of desire through me.

The door to the men's room opens, and Silas emerges shaking out his wet hands. "Oh, hey, Lark. Are you okay?"

My anguish must be plainly written on my face, because he looks very concerned and crosses the hallway quickly to come to my side.

"I'm fine," I assure him before he can reach out and touch me, which it looks like he might do. "Just...hot."

Understatement of the century.

"It is really warm in here," he confirms. He looks at me for a moment longer, then takes in a quick breath. "You know, you could have just told me you and Lennon are seeing each other."

"What?" I reel back, breathless again. "We're not."

Silas purses his lips and glances over my shoulder to the dance floor, then back to me again. "You're not?"

I shake my head vigorously, but it makes the room spin, so I stop. "No. We're just really good friends."

He tilts his head and frowns. "If you say so. See you back out there?"

"I think I might find Lennon and head out, actually. But this was really fun. I'll see you Monday?"

Nodding once, he walks past me and makes his way out of the hallway to be swallowed by the crowd.

I quickly use the restroom to give myself an extra minute to calm down, and when I emerge again, Lennon is waiting for me.

"You were gone for a while," he says. "I was starting to get worried."

I give him my best casual half smile. "Worried I got swept off my feet to dance with another man?" I try to joke, but it falls flat. Lennon doesn't say anything to that, so I clear my throat. "Can we go? I'm kind of over this place."

His features soften, and he looks almost relieved. "Yeah, me, too. Let's get out of here."

Those are the last words we say to each other for the whole ride home. I wrack my brain trying to find something to say, but it all either dies on the tip of my tongue or is rejected by my common sense before it gets there. By the set of his shoulders and the ticks in his jaw, he seems to be struggling with the same thing. About five minutes into the drive, I give up and settle into being grateful for the cool breeze that flutters against my hair and ripples against my skin.

Once inside, I kick off my shoes and cross the few steps to my room. Against my better judgment, I stop in the doorway and turn around. Lennon has his palms pressed into the edge of the kitchen countertop, his head dangling between his shoulders. His muscles pop against his dark shirt as he grips the counter. He looks utterly defeated, and it snaps my last thread of reason into place. Ignoring this isn't getting us anywhere. We're going to have to talk about it sooner or later. Might as well be now.

"What are we doing here?" I ask softly.

He doesn't lift his head. "I don't know," he admits. And there's something so heartbreaking in the curve of his shoulders and the anguish in his voice that I know, right then and there, that whatever we've been tiptoeing around has to stop. He'll never admit that losing someone close to him scares him shitless. That his parents' neglect has fucked him up in so many ways. He'd just jump right into this—whatever it is—if I wanted it, for no other reason than to make me happy.

Can I dare to hope he wants me, too? Does it even matter? He'd spiral when I inevitably leave at the end of the summer. It's my responsibility as his best friend to make sure that doesn't happen.

"I love you, Lennon." My voice cracks when I say it, and his head snaps up at the sound. "You're my best friend. I can't lose that." Except that I'd try. I'd do anything to have him near me like he was on the dance floor again. My body sways forward an inch, like a sunflower pointing its face to the sun.

But I plant my feet and try to convey as much gravity in my gaze as I can. For him. For us.

"I can't either," he says thickly, though it sounds like he's trying to persuade himself more than inform me.

"Okay, then." My gaze drops to the floor as I search for more words, but there aren't any. "Good night," I say to the tile at his feet.

"Good night, Lark," he whispers as I step into my room and close the door softly behind me.

I replay the conversation in my head at least ten times before sleep finally takes me. By the time it does, I'm not sure if what I heard in his voice was determination or disappointment.

CHAPTER 16

LENNON

Marcus drags his palm up my inner thigh, rumpling my skirt as he does so. The others can't see us because his hands are hidden under the table, but the idea that they could discover what we're doing is thrilling. I slide forward on my chair, hoping to guide his hand to the tops of my thighs, wanting him to find out that I left my panties at home tonight. But he just chuckles softly and pinches me, silently warning me to be a good girl if I want any more from him.

I'D LOVE TO SAY I've become inundated with Lark's sultry voice coming through my headphones, but I don't think it's possible. Especially after I almost kissed her a few nights ago.

Every rational part of me knows I should admit it was a mistake to let her body grind against mine on the dance floor. To revel in her warm thighs wrapped around mine. To drag my thumb over her soft, pink lips. But I can't. It didn't feel like a mistake, and it still doesn't. It felt more like my body was exhaling in relief. The desire to do it again is still there, barely held at bay by her words.

I love you, Lennon.

You're my best friend.

I can't lose that.

Why the fuck didn't I finish what I started, cross that room, and kiss her? Why didn't I tell her I love her, too? I do. Of course I do. I always have, even if I've never actually said it aloud. The words have always felt like a poor substitute for what I feel for her. They're not enough to encompass all she is.

She's everything.

I do what I can to make it through the three hours it takes me to edit the first two chapters—including, but not limited to, referring to her as Jane in my head and taking a break for a very cold shower. Except cold showers are awful, so I quickly turn it warm and rub my hand against my perpetual hard-on as the water rushes over me. She's at the studio anyway, and I tell myself I'm just taking the edge off.

It doesn't even feel wrong, touching myself and thinking of her. It feels right all the way down into my soul. There was a missing piece there that I had ignored for so long. A Lark-shaped piece. And now that she's here, I never want her to leave. I want her here with me, to touch her and find out if her berry-colored lips are as soft they felt under my thumb.

I finish fast. Way faster than is reasonable for a man of my age and experience. It's surprising but also not. Lark has me in a chokehold, and I'm not sure what to do about it. If she had asked me to kiss her on Friday night, I wouldn't have thought twice. I would have crossed the room and kissed her until she forgot her own name. But she didn't. She told me she couldn't lose our friendship, and she sounded broken when she said it.

It's hard to admit, but she was right. We've been everything to each other over the years. Everything but that, I guess. If we tried being together in that way and she decided to go back to Michigan at the end of the summer anyway, it would ruin me.

And that's assuming I could even figure out how to be in an actual relationship in the first place. I've often thought I might be broken in that regard. The longest relationship I've ever had was with a woman I dated for a few months after I graduated. Lark knows that, too. She knows everything about me. She's probably just saving herself.

That thought stings, but I can't even blame her for it. She deserves someone stable, which is ultimately why I never said much about Richard when they were together, despite him being as boring as they come. And also probably why I didn't deck him in the face when he told me it'd be better for Lark if I left. Deep down, I believed he was right. I might have remained in LA for twenty years, but I've only put down as many roots as I absolutely had to. No girlfriend, no family. I don't even own property. On paper, I'm a flight risk. And Lark is as constant and steadfast as they come.

I shut off the water and dry myself with a towel. Back to work, I suppose.

***

On Wednesday morning, I don't wait for Lark to wake up. Instead, I tiptoe into her room with a cupcake, a candle, and a lighter. I crouch down next to her bed so my face is level with hers. Her eyes are still closed, but I suspect by the twitch of her mouth that she's indulging me.

"Good morning, birthday girl," I say softly.

She groans, but it's tinged with laughter. "Go away."

"If you don't open your eyes, I'm going to sing," I warn.

One eye opens. "You're going to sing either way," she says when she sees the cupcake.

"You got me there." I carefully light the tiny birthday candle.

"That's absolutely a fire hazard."

"I'll sing fast," I promise. I launch into the same ridiculous rendition of the birthday song I've sung for her every year since we met, but it still has her laughing so hard she's holding her belly and tears are peeking out the corners of her eyes. When she blows out the candle, her breath grazes my cheek. When she smiles, her whole face lights up.

Her phone rings from where it lays on the nightstand. She grabs it quickly, then winces in apology. "It's Devin," she says.

"Better take it, then." I stand up from my crouch, my knees popping as I do. "But we're going out for your birthday tonight, for real. Just us." I glare at her playfully as I back out of her room.

"Oh my god," she groans as she taps her phone.

"Don't invite Silas," I say from the other side of the threshold.

"Don't eat my cupcake!" she calls as I shut the door to give her some privacy.

***

I make it through the audiobook edits faster and with less of a hard-on than the past few days. Things are looking up, I suppose, though it could be because these chapters are more plot and less erotica. It's naive, but I have a vague hope that I might be able to get through this project in one piece.

When I pick up Lark from the studio, she's as effervescent as usual. Things have been going well, and it has been such a privilege to watch her come back out of the shell she found herself in these past few years.

"So, where are we going?" she asks as soon as I pull away from the studio.

I smile slyly. "I was thinking of seeing a show."

She straightens in her seat and leans toward me. Her sunshine-and-citrus scent wafts in my direction on a breeze. "What show?" she asks, clearly elated.

I laugh heartily. "I wasn't going to tell you..."

Lark pushes her bottom lip out into a pout. She clasps her hands under her chin and makes her eyes go wide. "But it's my birthday," she pleads. "Tell me!"

"That's not fair. I don't stand a chance when you make that face."

"Which is why I don't use it unless I really need to. Power and responsibility and all that. Come on, tell me," she begs again.

I sigh good-naturedly and glance at her before turning my attention back to the road. "Shakespeare in the Park."

At that, Lark goes absolutely giddy. She claps her hands and bounces like a schoolgirl, and I can't help but be delighted to have made her so happy.

"What show are they doing?"

This was the big surprise. "You're not going to believe it," I say slowly, "but they're doing *A Midsummer Night's Dream* this season."

Lark gasps. "I love *A Midsummer Night's Dream*," she whispers.

"I know."

"We did it in high school."

"Did you think I could ever forget?"

She studies me thoughtfully, chewing on her lip. Then, she shakes her head. "I don't suppose you could."

I don't know if I realized how ingrained my memories of her are into my psyche until she got here, but now I can't unsee it. She's as much a part of me as my own DNA. And yet I still want more. Even though it's unfair of me to ask more of her than she's already given, I still want it. I want to go back to that dance floor and press my lips to hers before she has a chance to tell me it's a bad idea. To prove to her that it's not.

We both sit in silence for a minute before I try to break whatever moment we're having. "Do you think you could still do all the lines?"

She sits back in her seat and laughs. "I could totally still do all the lines. But I promise I won't. That would be insufferable."

Even though I told myself I wouldn't, even though I know it's a terrible idea, I reach over and grab her hand. She smiles her brilliant smile up at me.

Nothing she does could ever be insufferable.

***

We arrive at the park early. There's a stage with a tall green set decorated in fairy lights at the end of a grassy field. I spread out a blanket as close as I can and unload the snacks I packed earlier to bring with us.

"You did not bring a cake," Lark groans when she sees it. "How embarrassing."

"It's just a little cake," I insist. "And it's not every day you turn—"

Lark's blue eyes narrow, and she juts out the bottom of her jaw.

"Twenty-nine?" I ask.

She smiles, appeased. "Good man."

I drag the picnic basket in front of me to hide what her praise does below my waist under the guise of unloading more stuff.

We eat and chat as we wait for the show to start, and it's so easy. Everything with her is refreshingly simple. Even wanting her has been effortless, if not uncomplicated. But being here with her tonight, lying on a blanket in the grass snacking on almonds and cheese, laughing and joking like old times...it's perfect.

And when the show starts, we settle in to enjoy it, though I probably spend more time watching her than the stage. When Helena enters, Lark lights up. She doesn't recite the lines, but her lips move almost imperceptibly in time with Helena's words.

Toward the end of the fifth act, I slide a packet of tissues next to her hand. She glances at it, then looks at me, her brow furrowed.

"You always cry at live theater," I whisper.

"It's a comedy," she murmurs back.

"Doesn't matter." I flash a knowing grin.

And sure enough, when Puck starts his epilogue with "If we shadows have offended..." Lark sniffles and takes a tissue from my hand.

"It was just so beautiful," she says, gazing longingly at the stage as the actors take their bows.

"I know," I reply. But I'm not looking at the stage.

I'm looking at her.

CHAPTER 17

LARK

FOR THE REST OF the week, I oscillate between delirious happiness and a giddiness I haven't felt since the last time I was onstage. Narrating this audiobook has opened a door in my mind. It has reminded me how much I love acting, and while I don't know if I'd take on a project with as much erotic content as Jessica's book again, I start to think I might try to figure out how to do this from home in the very near future.

I had been a little worried about how Silas and I would interact after I more or less rejected him. It happens all the time where actors date—or don't—and it messes up the chemistry between them. But Silas is nothing if not professional, and we fall right back into our easy rapport as we knock out the middle chapters much faster than the early ones.

Lennon seems to have gone back to normal after whatever that was last Friday night, too. Or at least, he's doing a good job of pretending it never happened. He doesn't bring it up, and neither do I. The idea of kissing him seems to be buried between us, even if I lie awake most nights thinking of the pad of his thumb pressed against my bottom lip.

I'm thinking about it now, in fact, as I pour butter over air-popped popcorn. I sprinkle in a little salt, too, and that reminds me of the saltiness of his skin. I only got a little taste, and admittedly, I want more as I pop a well-seasoned piece of popcorn into my mouth.

It's just forbidden fruit, I tell myself. The only reason I want it is because I can't have it.

Lennon's broad hands land on my hips as he gently moves me to the side so he can get to a drawer I'm blocking. I gasp and jump out of his way, almost knocking over the entire bowl of popcorn in the process.

He chuckles. "Sorry, Songbird. I said your name, like, three times, but you were in your own world."

"Oh." Nervous laughter tumbles out of me, and I can't control it. "My bad."

He opens the drawer and rummages around a bit before closing it and opening another. "You okay?"

"Yeah," I say with more confidence, even though the feeling of his hands on my hips lingers. "Just concentrating."

"Popcorn does require a lot of concentration." He finally finds the corkscrew he was looking for. Wiggling it at me in triumph, he moves to the other side of the counter to open the bottle of wine we bought when we went to the beach.

I cock my hip and rest my hand on it. "I will have you know that I take popcorn-making very seriously."

His eyebrow ticks up as he twists the corkscrew into the bottle. "It would seem so." After a little effort on his part, the cork comes free of the bottle with a pop. He pulls down a couple of wineglasses from an overhead cabinet and pours us each one.

I stir the butter into the popcorn and taste it again, then add more salt. Lennon takes a drink of his wine and hums. "It's good," he declares, handing me my glass.

My eyes flutter closed as bring it to my nose and inhale deeply. "Smells like berries." I take another sniff. "And smoke." I sip it and hum my approval.

"I didn't know I was in the presence of a sommelier," Lennon teases.

I huff a laugh, balancing the wineglass in one hand and the giant bowl of popcorn in the other. "Just a connoisseur. Wine tastings are, like, a rite of passage in the mom world."

"Have you heard from Devin?"

Sighing, I follow him to the couch. "She texted me this morning that they made it to Lucerne. She sent a couple of gorgeous pictures of the mountains. I sent back a picture of the ocean, and she said she was jealous. I suspect she was just trying to make me feel better."

Lennon has already cued up the movie—something artsy and award-winning that I'm sure I don't have the attention span for, based on my spaciness in the kitchen. He flops onto a cushion at the far end, lifting his right arm so it rests on the back of the couch. I pause, still holding the popcorn and my wine, trying to rewrite physics to make more space on the couch. There isn't much room to sit if I'm not going to be touching him, and I fear that any contact I make might be dangerous.

We've watched movies and cuddled together thousands of times, I remind myself. *It's fine.*

He starts the movie and looks up at me, smiling expectantly, so I settle into the crook of his arm anyway. If I sit at the other end of the couch like a sensible woman would, he'd know something is off.

It's not hard to ease into him. I fit here, my legs stretched out length-wise on the seat of the couch, my head resting back against his chest. His heartbeat is strong and steady. It whooshes under me, louder than the movie.

We sip wine and munch on handfuls of popcorn, but I can't concentrate on the screen. Not with Lennon's heart so close to my head. Not with his blue-sky scent overtaking my senses. Not with his arm stretched out behind me, his shirt sleeve riding up, and his tattoos taunting me like they have since I got here.

Lennon is singularly focused on the television, but my attention wanders to his arm. He didn't start getting tattoos until he was in his late twenties. He'd send me pictures of things he wanted to ink and then pictures of the finished product. It fascinated me. I used to spend a lot of stolen moments between Devin's dance classes and school drop-offs looking at the way pieces of his body changed with art and time.

This particular tattoo is the outdoor scene that has been plaguing my thoughts. Jessica's character has a similar tattoo. I always have to bite the inside of my cheek so I don't laugh about it as I'm recording, but if she was writing about Lennon's tattoo, she hasn't done it justice. It's beautiful and intricate, circling all the way around his biceps and up his shoulder. I have seen pictures of it, of course, but in person, it's stunning. I hadn't realized it went all the way around the inside of his arm, or it hadn't registered as important. Or maybe he's added to it since I saw it last. But now all I want to do is touch it. Trace the soft skin with my fingertips. Let some of the ink metaphorically bleed into my psyche, to shore me up for the inevitable stretch of time where I won't see him again.

Just when I'm about to chastise myself for thinking about this yet again, he shifts forward to get another handful of popcorn. The sleeve of his shirt lifts up a little more, and something there catches my eye in the flickering light of the television. Two birds, flying above the trees, crests on their heads and black stripes on their faces.

Larks. The dim realization dawns on me like a soft stage light. He tattooed larks onto his arm.

When did he do that? He never told me.

I don't even think then. I reach out and trace them lightly with my fingers. Lennon sucks in a breath, but I don't stop. His skin here is so soft, and these birds...

"When...?" My voice comes out as a whisper.

"Ten years ago." His is rough and restrained. "After I saw you. Right when I got back. It..." He trails off and swallows audibly. I don't dare tear my eyes away from the birds on his arm to look at him lest it causes him to stop talking. I barely even breathe.

"It hurt, leaving you. It always hurts, but it was worse that time. Maybe a part of me sensed it'd be so long before I saw you again. Spending time with you and Devin... She's such a cool kid, so much like you. It felt like..." He coughs, then runs a hand through his hair. "It felt like being part of a family. I almost packed up everything here and came back. But I didn't know how that would make you feel, having me hanging around. You and Devin had a great thing going by then..."

My brain must have shut off or short circuited, because I lean forward and lightly brush my lips over the birds on his arm. Even though I know it's wrong. I know I shouldn't. But I do it anyway. It's featherlight, but I can taste his skin. Clean and salty and smooth.

Lennon's head tips back, and he moans. It's an almost feral sound, low and full of pent-up desire and bad decisions.

I spring to my feet. "Shit," I breathe, and I walk straight out the sliding door to the balcony. I close it behind me and lean against the railing. I can't look at him, or I might make a terrible mistake.

My mind is going a mile a minute, looping around and around the fact that he has larks permanently tattooed onto his arm. That could be a normal thing that best friends do, right? If I were someone who had a habit of getting tattoos, I'd get one for him. And yet that sound he made when I kissed them didn't sound at all friendly.

I shake my head violently, still gasping for air. If I can just get a handle on my breathing...

The door slides open behind me. My heart skips a few beats. What did I think was going to happen? He was going to just sit there and continue on with his movie while I hyperventilated on his balcony after kissing his arm?

"Lark." His voice pierces through the cool night air, deep and weighted with something. Grief? Longing? Without looking at his expression, all I know is that the word falls quickly, lodging itself in my gut like a bullet, and it hurts almost as much.

What was I thinking, kissing his arm? He's my best friend. The man who held me as I cried when I realized my acting career was over before it began. Who spent endless summer nights in college gazing at the stars and telling me stories about what they looked like over the ocean. Who dragged me out of my own self-pity and into the brave new world of audiobook recording. Who makes me happy. I need him. But I had to go cross that line—the line that *I* drew.

"I'm sorry," I say out into the space between his building and the next one. "That was inappropriate."

"Lark, look at me."

No way in hell can I look at him, I think, even as my body turns around.

His frame fills the doorway, and his chest rises and falls with labored breaths. He looks anguished. Wounded, almost. I suddenly want nothing more than to crash into him. Taste him again. Take away whatever he's feeling and replace it with something better.

Instead, I grip the banister behind me to keep me in place. "Those are larks. On your arm."

He nods once. "They are."

LOVE OUT LOUD 161

"For me?"

"Would you believe me if I told you I just like the way they look?" He smirks, but it quickly falls. "Of course they're for you."

It's such a soft, tender admission. He leans forward as he says it, as if that could make the words hit home more than they already have. It's unnecessary. They've already burrowed their way into my soul and taken root there.

"Why?" I breathe.

He runs a hand through his sandy hair again and blows out a puff of air. He looks up to the sky, clutching at the strands on his head, the birds on his arm on full display. He must have done this motion a hundred times since I've been here. I don't know how I possibly missed them.

"Why not, Lark? You're everything to me. You have been since we were fifteen. I was nothing until you dragged me into that Drama Club meeting. I have tattoos of things that mean far less to me than you. You're my favorite person. You're my best friend."

"Oh." I don't know what I was expecting. An admission of desire? A declaration of love? Twenty-five years of friendship and he's never once told me he loves me. Just that I'm his favorite or his best. I kind of thought it had become a sort of joke—one of those things you keep saying because you've always said it, that ends up meaning more than an *I love you*. But maybe not. Maybe I'm the only one feeling these warring emotions, and I'm imagining him reciprocating any of it.

Like being part of a family, he said. Not being a lover. That's reserved for other women. I've been a fool to think otherwise. Suddenly, I'm embarrassed to have brought it up when we got home from the club last week. He probably thought I had lost my mind.

He drops his hand to his side, and it smacks his leg. The sound is loud in the quiet night, and I jump back into focus.

"I'm not doing a good job of this," he mutters. "I don't want to screw this up."

"Screw what up?"

He crosses the balcony to stand in front of me, and it's so fast, I'm caught off guard. He's in my space again, invading my senses. I'm sure my knuckles are white from gripping the banister. He lays his palms on my hands, gently loosening my fingers and clasping them between us.

He holds both my hands in one of his and brings the other up to cup my jaw. "You said you couldn't lose me, and I don't want that, either," he says softly, his hazel eyes searching mine in the darkness. "But if I told you that feeling your lips on my arm just now snapped something inside me I thought I could control, would you run away and never talk to me again?"

I shake my head slowly, unable to take my eyes off him. "Not possible."

"If I said I've been in a spiral of wanting you ever since I heard your audition, would that freak you out?"

It takes barely a second to process what he's saying, but when I do, my breath whooshes out of me. He wants me. I haven't been making it up.

"Only since then?" I tease, trying to break some of the tension between us, even as I have to fight to focus with his thumb tracing a delicate line against my cheekbone. It's not that I don't think we can handle the strain, but that I know we don't have to.

He laughs quietly. "I've probably been living in denial."

"I'm not someone you bring home from the bar for a night." I don't know what makes me say it, and I try not to cringe as soon as it's out of my mouth. Aside from some playful jealousy at his freedom, I've never taken issue with his parade of women, but that's also not me. It might crush me to finally have his lips on mine and know in a few weeks he was on to the next thing.

He shakes his head. "If I wanted to psychoanalyze that, I'd probably say none of them ever stuck because I was waiting for you."

"We're friends."

"We're more than friends," he counters, leaning closer to rest his forehead against mine. "We've been a million things to each other over the years. Why not this, too?" His pleading voice shifts something between us, and the ache to kiss him balloons inside me, expanding and rising until it takes up all the available space.

"We're friends first." I open my eyes to meet his again, hoping to drive the point deeper.

He nods and inhales deeply as if to drink in the air we share between us. "First and always."

And then, like he can't hold off for one more second, his lips are on mine. Warm and sweet. Soft and careful. Exploring. Sure, but tentative lest one of us makes a wrong move.

It hardly feels real. I'm kissing Lennon, and it feels *good*. Somehow I know this is exactly what I've always wanted but have never let myself admit for fear of losing him and shattering my heart into a million pieces.

His tongue teases at my mouth, and I open to draw him in. That's when something else changes. He steps closer, pressing my back against the railing and his body into mine. He tastes like salt and wine, but under that is a flavor so distinctly Lennon. I haven't ever tasted it before, but I'd know it anywhere.

"Songbird," he whispers against my skin as he lowers his mouth to my neck, pressing a hot line of kisses down to my collarbone. A moan escapes me, lifting up into the night like a prayer: *Please let me keep all of him. Just like this.*

I weave my fingers into his hair, tugging so he'll look at me. His eyes are hooded and dark, his lips bee-stung and swollen. I lift my face to his again, unable to stay away. Needing more. More of his taste, more of his chest rising and falling against mine, more of the railing biting against my back.

Our tongues dance together, teasing and exploring. A strand of hair gets caught between us. He palms the side of my head, pushing my hair out of the way in a move that seems both practiced and special as he winds the strands of it around his fingers.

I don't know who breaks the kiss. Maybe we both sense the need to come up for air as we separate, our breathing ragged and loud.

"Is this... Are we...okay?" I ask.

His lopsided grin could singlehandedly light up the night. "I don't think I've ever been more okay than I am right now."

My returning smile feels love-drunk and woozy, like my face can't quite do what I'm asking it to. "Good."

He dips his lips to mine again, then parts too quickly. "I don't know how we spent twenty-five years *not* doing that."

My laughter starts quiet but quickly takes flight on the night air. His joins mine, low and rumbling but no less joyful. His eyes glitter in the ambient light from the building across the way as he tucks my hair behind my ear and studies me.

I can sense the moment is over, even though he hasn't separated his body from mine. "I hope it doesn't take another twenty-five years to do it again." My voice tips up like a question.

Lennon shakes his head, his eyes never leaving mine. "I'm just getting started. Getting my feet wet, if you will."

I smirk, cocking an eyebrow. "What happened to jumping in?"

He laughs incredulously. "I'd say that was a pretty huge jump."

I shrug a shoulder, taunting. "I mean, we're not in the deep end or anything."

"Not yet," he says, his voice suddenly dripping with a sultry promise that sends a shiver up my spine. Lennon's eyes gleam.

"I want to ask you to spend the night with me or something," I say tentatively, but he shakes his head.

"Soon." He takes a step back and reaches around to take my hand from his neck. He weaves his fingers through mine. "I don't..." He trails off and brings my knuckles to his lips. They're warm against my hands, which I'm just now realizing are chilled from the night air. "I want to do this right, Lark. Let me." His face is open and earnest, the sharp edges of it softening.

I nod, squeezing his hand and leaning into his shoulder. Truthfully, I'd let him do anything right now. But he's right. So instead of cracking that joke, I silently lead him back inside. We settle on the couch again to finish the movie, a little closer and a little lighter. Every so often, he nuzzles my hair or presses a kiss to the top of my head, and I trace my fingers along his shoulder like I've longed to do since I got here.

When the movie is over, we laugh as he walks me to my door. He lingers, kissing me again.

"I'll see you in the morning," he promises against my lips. And then, as if it takes a great effort, he leaves me and goes into his bedroom, closing the door softly behind him.

I fall asleep quickly, my hand pressed against my mouth, as if I could keep the feeling of Lennon's lips with me long into the night.

CHAPTER 18

LENNON

I AWAKE IN A haze, a warm kind of comfort settling my heart and soul. I don't know why I feel so relaxed and content, but I burrow into my pillows to try to keep this feeling going for just a little while longer.

It only takes another minute or so for my senses to fully power up and, with them, my memory. My eyes fly open.

I kissed Lark.

I *kissed* Lark.

I kissed *Lark*.

Doesn't matter how many ways I say it to myself, it happened. I draw my lips around my tongue so I can taste them, and sure enough, she's lingering there. She tastes like she feels—all buttery sweetness and nostalgia, citrus and sunshine.

I fell asleep to a montage of memories of her, and the one thread running through all of them was a vague understanding that I've wanted to kiss her since even before I could even name the feeling.

It was worth the wait.

And she's still here.

The anticipation of seeing her this morning has me jumping out of bed and quickly pulling on a shirt and gym shorts so I can burst through the door. I feel like a kid with a crush who's excited at even just the possibility he might lay eyes on her. Actually, I feel like I used to in those early days after just having met Lark at Drama Club—bounding to school early in hopes of seeing her before classes started, hanging around late for a few extra minutes with her before she headed home.

She's already sitting in the kitchen when I burst through the door, her hands cupped around a mug. Her expression brightens when she sees me, though I can tell she's been gnawing at her bottom lip and there's still a crease between her eyebrows as if she had been frowning.

"Please don't say it was a mistake," I blurt out. The urge to slink back into my room and hide for the rest of the day slams into me, and if it weren't for the way she rolls her gorgeous lips between her teeth to bite back a laugh, I probably would have.

"I don't think it was a mistake." She's calm, but her voice is edged with humor. "But I guess I don't have to ask how you feel about it."

Before my sleep- and lust-addled brain can even register that I've moved, I cross the room and pull her up and into my arms. She doesn't hesitate to lift her face to me, and our lips meet in a deep kiss.

When I was a teenager, my mom had these fancy measuring spoons that had a tongue-and-groove pattern on the handles. They also had magnets, so if you put one near the other, they'd snap together with a satisfying click. I fidgeted with those things often, especially when my parents were gone. Lark and I would sit at the table in silence, and I would pull the spoons apart and snap them back together over and over again.

The way Lark fits with me reminds me of those measuring spoons. Her body meets mine with the same satisfying snap, and mine turns concave to mold around the curve of her breasts, the swell of her hips.

And yet it's not enough. I ache for her to be closer, to give me more, even though she has given me everything that matters for the past twenty-five years.

Lark Caspian is mine, and I'm never letting her go.

A thud sounds several times at the door, then again. I try to swim up through my consciousness and back to reality as I reluctantly part my lips from hers.

"Expecting someone?" Lark's voice is husky and sensual. It draws me back in. I've waited twenty-five years for this. Whoever is at the door can wait another minute.

Unfortunately, the pounding pulls me right back out. I slump forward with a frustrated growl. A musical giggle rises up out of Lark's throat. I want to know what that sound tastes like and swallow it. I want to make it mine.

The knocking comes again, more impatient this time, so I untangle my hand from Lark's hair and pull open the front door.

I immediately wish I hadn't. Because standing just on the other side of the threshold are my parents.

My mother is standing with her arms outstretched like she's expecting a hug. My dad is grinning like a fool. Both of their expressions falter when I cannot so much as muster up a hello, let alone whatever fake exclamation of joy they were expecting.

They don't drop in on me often, but it has happened a handful of times over the past few years—usually when they're on their way somewhere else. A wind carries them in for a few hours, then out again. And every time, it dredges up old emotions and leaves me wrestling with them for days. Will they stay this time? Do I want them to? How long before I see them again?

I sense Lark behind me before I feel her hand on my back, warm and reassuring. "Sage. Arlo. What a nice surprise!"

Mom's eyes light up, and she turns her still-outstretched arms in Lark's direction. "Lark! Baby! I had no idea you'd be here, too." She brings Lark into a tight hug and sways her back and forth. I finally wrap my head around the situation enough to shake my dad's hand and motion him into the apartment. Much to my chagrin, he picks up a duffel bag that had been sitting off to the side and drags that in with him.

"Oh, this is so wonderful," my mom is saying as she and Lark join us in the living room. "We haven't seen you in ages. Are you living in California now? How is that little girl of yours? Is she here, too?"

Ever the actress, Lark pastes on a high-wattage smile as she lowers herself gracefully to the armchair, leaving my dad and me to the couch. My mom folds her legs underneath her and sits on the floor, her preferred way to sit in any company.

"She's not so little anymore," Lark singsongs. "I saw her off to college a few weeks ago."

Mom gasps. "No. I can't believe she's all grown up! Is she at college in Los Angeles? Is that why you're here?" Her questioning gaze bounces back and forth between the two of us, but I'm still having trouble processing the fact that they're here—and that I was kissing Lark before they arrived.

My mouth opens and closes a few times. Lark must be able to tell that I'm floundering, because she jumps right in. "No, she's headed to NYU. I'm here because I'm recording an audiobook this summer. Lennon is working on it, too."

The sound of my mother's hands clapping in glee is finally enough to break me free of the mental calculations I've been trying to do to figure out how long they're likely to stay. Based on the size of the duffel bag my dad dropped inside the door, my guess is not long. And the part of me that is still fifteen and overjoyed to see them is at war with the part of me that is forty and jaded and wishes they'd never come. Not to mention the giant part of me that just wants to get back to kissing Lark.

"What brings you two here?" My voice sounds strangled, even to me. Out of the corner of my eye, I see Lark's head snap to me, but I avoid her gaze and, instead, focus on my dad.

"Oh, just passing through," he says. That fifteen-year-old part of me withers. They'll stay an hour or so and then be on their merry way.

"Where are you headed this time?" I try to keep the bitterness out of my voice. I really do. But it sneaks in nonetheless.

If my parents hear it, though, they don't let on. My mom looks up at my dad with a dreamy gaze from where she's sitting on the floor. My dad looks back at her indulgently.

"We're on our way up the coast. The plan is to spend the rest of the summer working in wine country, then continue on to Oregon for the fall," he says.

"What's in Oregon?" Lark asks politely.

Dad's face splits into a grin. "Golf."

"Since when do you golf?" I ask, frowning.

"Since never!" he exclaims. "But I guess no one is a golfer until they try it, so I might as well give it a shot."

Mom nods emphatically, her eyes wide and her eyebrows raised. I glance at Lark, but she's already looking at me. The corners of her mouth pull down as if to say he has a point.

No one is part of Drama Club until they come to a meeting.

I blink rapidly to dispel the memory, but maybe she's right. Maybe Dad does have a point. I guess I just kind of always wish they'd try to be part of something permanent instead of looking for the next something to try.

"How long are you in town for?" Lark asks. "Can you join us for lunch?"

I can't tell if she really wants them to stay or if she's faking it, but she just clasps her hands in her lap and smiles sweetly, waiting for their response. Dad winces as if he's getting ready to apologize, but Mom looks up at him again, this time pleading.

"Oh, I think we can stay for lunch, right, Arlo?"

Dad scrunches up his face. "I wanted to get back on the road before it gets dark."

Mom laughs. "It's a good thing lunch is well before sunset, then."

What my mom wants, my mom gets. Dad has always done anything to make her happy, including moving me halfway across the country multiple times during my school-age years. It was because of this that I went straight to her during my junior year when I caught wind that they were planning another move. I begged her to let me stay. I told her I could stay with Lark if they couldn't stick around, even though Lark's family hadn't offered.

I didn't even tell Lark. I couldn't bear to. I just started pulling away like I always did when I figured out we were leaving. I never forgave myself for that, either. It's a core memory now, seared into my mind.

"What's going on with you?" There was an angry edge to her voice, but she seemed concerned more than anything else.

"What do you mean?" I evaded. She must have known I was avoiding answering her, because she pursed her lips, cocked an eyebrow, and glared silently at me. Even though I knew she was angry, she was so cute when she did that. I was overcome with the urge to cup the back of her head and bring my lips to her forehead.

"You've been distant," she says finally, saving me from the embarrassment that would surely have come if I had let myself kiss her.

I shrugged. "Sorry. Things are just...weird." That, at least, was the truth. I was so upset about the possibility of moving again that I had made some mistakes, and I wasn't sure how to make up for them.

Lark covered my hand with hers, intertwining her delicate fingers with my lanky ones. She squeezed, looking up from where she was seated on the couch next to me. "You can tell me anything. You know that, right?"

Anything? Like how my heart beat faster at the mere thought of her? Like how I thought far too often about what her pink lips tasted like? Like how I had wanted to ask her on a proper date for years?

I didn't know what it was. Maybe the set of her jaw or the earnestness in her eyes, but I felt courageous then. I opened my mouth to say something like that, but what came out instead was a quiet, "I know."

She stayed silent for another beat, studying me. Then, she sighed and looked off into space. "Richard asked me out," she said, her gaze not meeting mine.

It was like a knife in the gut. Four simple words, and the air was knocked out of me. "Are you going to go out with him?" I managed to choke out.

If she noticed my struggle, she didn't let on. She shrugged and said, "Might as well, I guess."

I nodded slowly. Richard was an okay guy. Not my favorite person in the world, but he seemed pretty decent. He'd probably go to college and get a job in finance or something boring and stable. Lark deserved someone like that. Not a drifter like me.

"I'm thinking of applying to colleges on the West Coast," I blurted out for no reason other than to change the subject. I hadn't really been thinking about it with any seriousness, but there it was. Out in the open.

Lark hummed distractedly. "That makes sense for you, I think," she said. She smiled up at me, the expression completely changing her face, and the breath was knocked out of me again. "Maybe I could come visit you."

Lark's hand landing gently on my back brings me out of the memory and into the present. My parents are looking around the living room, and Lark is eyeing me with concern. I excuse myself to change into some actual clothes and get a handle on my emotions, then we spend the next hour or so chatting, until my dad pointedly mentions some golf tournament he wouldn't mind watching now that they're somewhere with a television.

I turn it on, then go to the kitchen to make myself more coffee. Lark joins me after a few minutes, standing close enough that the heat of her body seeps into my skin. She places her hand over mine where it rests on the counter. I stare at her still-delicate fingers as they thread through mine and squeeze. The motion is familiar; it's the same thing she's always done when she knows I'm upset.

"This can't be easy," she says softly.

I nod, swallowing audibly. "Yeah." I look down at her, and her brows are pinched with concern. "Just threw me for a loop. I'll be fine."

Her hand remains on mine as she watches me for a moment, probably knowing I'm full of shit but not willing to make me admit it while they're still here. She leans into me slightly. Her presence steadies me, reminds me that they'll leave but she won't.

Except she will. She's only got another few weeks here while she wraps up recording, and then she's back to her life in Michigan. The realization hits me like a ton of bricks and throws me completely off-center. For a few hours, I was able to live in denial, thinking there was some way we could be together like I'm sure now that we were always meant to be. But now I have more questions than answers, and I have to power through time with my parents before I can ask any of them.

I shift my gaze to the coffee, which has long since finished brewing. The nutty scent of it fills the air, and it suddenly seems like a sour smell. "I'm struggling," I say quietly.

"I'm here," she whispers as she gives my hand another squeeze.

My brain screams the obvious and most pressing question at me: *Yeah, but for how long?*

But I don't want her to see any of this, and I certainly don't need my parents involved in my mental turmoil, either. Not now. Not when things were just getting good.

I smile down at her reassuringly, putting my anxieties away for later. "You're my favorite person in the world, Songbird."

She beams up at me, and for a second, it feels like everything might be all right after all.

CHAPTER 19

LARK

LUNCH GOES WELL, ALL things considered. Before we go, I ask Lennon if he wants to spend time with them alone. He drags his knuckles down my jaw and says, "I think I'd rather have you there."

Sage tells us she's given up meat, and Arlo rolls his eyes good-naturedly. We take them to a cute vegan place down the street from Lennon's apartment. We spend a couple of hours there talking and catching up, and whatever tension Lennon was clearly experiencing when they first got there seems to dissipate.

I love watching him talk to his parents, and I take a back seat to their conversation so they can have time to catch up. With them around, he turns into the boy I loved in high school—all sheepish grins and casual sarcasm. And even though they have always been misguided about the time their son wants to spend with them, his parents clearly adore him. Sage gets misty-eyed on the walk back to the apartment, and Lennon slings his arm around her shoulders to hold her as Arlo and I shuffle along behind them on the sidewalk.

They don't want to come up again, so I give them big hugs and pinch Lennon's arm in reassurance before excusing myself back into his apartment. I wanted to give them some time alone to say goodbye without being an awkward observer, but Lennon doesn't come back. He texts me that he's going for a walk, so I settle in with *Sizzling Secrets* to review the chapters we have coming up for the next week.

As usually happens, I end up spread out in the living room with five different highlighters and even more pens in coordinating colors. When I first started, Noah gave me a printout of the pages so I didn't have to hold the book, so there are sheets of paper fanned out all around me. It's an organized sort of chaos, but it works for me.

The thing I love most about narrating this audiobook is the ability to play multiple characters. Marcus and Gia get the most page time, obviously, but Gia has other friends who require slightly varied voices. It's fun to take on these different characters, but it also takes a lot of prep work if I'm going to get it right without a million takes. The result is often pages that look like a unicorn threw up rainbow highlights on them, with each character's dialogue marked in a different color and margin notes about tone and voice scratched all over the page.

But the passages I have the most difficulty with are the ones that require intimacy. Noah and Silas have both made it a point to tell me—multiple times—that my handling of the sexier chapters is great, and I believe them because I've worked hard to make sure my narration reflects the scene. Doesn't mean it doesn't require a ton of work beforehand.

And now that I've kissed Lennon, I'm having an extra hard time with it. When Marcus is trailing kisses down Gia's neck, feeling her pulse under his lips, I can't help but remember what Lennon's lips felt like doing the same last night. When Marcus says, *I want to hear you scream my name*, I can't help but wonder if Lennon would also want that or if he'd prefer his name on a desperate moan or a breathy exhale. When Gia insists she'll *make his cock fit*, I chew on the end of one of my pens and think about the hard length of Lennon's desire pressed to my aching core.

This new shift in our relationship is thrilling and unexpected. It's not that I've never entertained the idea of sleeping with him. Of course I have. There was a time during our sophomore year in high school that I was desperate for him to kiss me, even if I couldn't admit it to anyone but myself at the time. And I'm not living in a cave. All through our thirties, I watched as his muscles grew more toned and as ink filled in some of the expanse of his skin. I may have made a habit of scoffing any time Hannah referred to "Hot Lennon," but I never disagreed. It's just that he's always been so much more than hot to me. He's sweet and kind and funny. Steadfast and loyal. The one I want to tell everything, and the one I want to sit with while we say nothing at all. My best friend. My best *everything*.

I grimace when I come back to reality and see that my pen cap has been chewed beyond repair. The sun is just visible above the neighboring building, so I check my phone. No messages, and it's well past four o'clock. Lennon has been gone for over two hours, which seems a little strange.

No sooner do I open our message thread and start typing than the door swings open. But my relief is short-lived. He hangs back, his hand on the doorknob, his shoulders slumped and eyes bloodshot. The smell of weed hits me next, which is about when I register the wide-eyed apology on his face.

"I ran into some friends." He doesn't move from the open doorway, almost as if he's waiting for me to kick him out of his own apartment.

Which I'd never do. All I've ever wanted is to be there for him, and that hasn't changed. But this isn't the first time this has happened, and that didn't end well for us, either.

I stood on Lennon's porch with my tea in one hand and coffee in the other. Muffled voices came from behind the door, which was weird. He texted me about an hour ago that he'd woken up alone, which has always been my cue to come hang out with him.

When the door did finally fly open, Lennon was there, all gangly limbs and pearly-white smile. Only, his smile was dazed and his normally clear, hazel eyes were clouded, the gold in them turned brassy.

And he didn't smell like himself, either. I wrinkled my nose when a skunky, earthy smell wafted out to me. I'd smelled weed before, of course, but not on Lennon. My first thought was that something must've been really wrong. My second was that the director of the fall play, Mr. Jensen, had a zero-tolerance policy for drugs and alcohol, and if he found out Lennon was smoking, he'd kick him off the show.

"Oh, hey, Songbird," he said, as if he hadn't been expecting me.

"Is that Lark?" a voice came from inside. I peeked around Lennon to see Liam Mann and Vincent Kristo, two seniors who had made a name for themselves for always knowing where the next big party was going to be. Apparently they also knew where to get pot.

"Hi, guys," I said drily. "I'm, uh... I just wanted to drop off Lennon's coffee." I shoved his cup into his chest, and a bit of it sloshed out the top onto his gray shirt.

He looked down at it, then back up to me, his brow furrowing. "You can come in," he said softy, as if he didn't want the others to hear him.

I bit back the bitter taste of disappointment. "I can't be around that stuff." I wasn't going to judge him for something he felt he needed, but I wasn't going to risk being kicked off the show, either.

Lennon nodded, and he took the coffee from my outstretched hand. "I shouldn't have..." He swallowed hard, kicking a toe against the threshold of the open door. "I didn't want to bother you."

"You could never bother me, Lennon. I love you," I whispered, not wanting to embarrass him in front of his new friends.

His eyes cleared at that, and they met mine for a second before falling back to the floor. "I'll call you later."

"Yeah." It was all I could muster before I turned on my heel and left him to it. I didn't look back even as the driveway stretched out impossibly long in front of me. By the time I hit the sidewalk and dared to check behind me, the door was closed.

I didn't want to cry over something as silly as my friend hanging out with someone else. But I also thought that if he could make new friends, I could, too. A boy in my stats class had given me his number the other day, but I had been too shy to do anything with it but put it in my wallet.

As soon as I got home, I pulled it out and ran my thumb over the name on the torn sheet of paper: Richard Novak. With shaking fingers, I dialed the number.

Just like I told Lennon then, when he finally called me days later to clear the air, I don't have a problem with pot. I only wanted him to let me in instead of using it to dull his emotions. I still do. And now he's still hanging in the doorway of his apartment, looking like he's not sure if he should be outside or inside. And I'm still sitting in the middle of a rainbow of papers on the floor of his living room, wishing he'd tell me what's going on in his head.

He needs me, I realize. He's looking for permission.

"Are you going to stand there all night, or should I make us some dinner?" I keep my voice carefully unbothered, even as my stomach roils with nerves about what anxiety he's probably dealing with and what I can do to help.

Lennon huffs, and a little of the tension that had been bracketing his mouth relaxes. His gaze drops to the ground as he shuts the door behind him and falls back against it as if he can't hold himself up anymore. "I'm sorry, Lark."

I stand, shaking my head, and close the distance between us. I reach up to cup his jaw, letting his sandy stubble scrape against my palm. He closes his eyes and leans into it.

"I don't deserve you," he says, his voice raspy. He turns his head to place a kiss against my palm.

"And yet here I am," I quip.

He winks an eye open and laughs heartily. "Did you mention something about dinner? I'm pretty hungry."

I tick an eyebrow up. "I bet you are," I intone.

He huffs again, then leans in to kiss my forehead. "I'll just...shower?"

"I'll get started on some food," I say.

I cook while Lennon freshens up. When he emerges, his eyes are far less red, and as he folds me into a tight hug, he's back to smelling like big blue skies. We eat and chat. I'm careful not to bring up his parents or his state when he came back to the apartment. He'll talk when he's ready. But when we're standing outside my bedroom door and he hasn't once brought it up, I can't help but wonder if he's pulling away from me like he did when we were kids. It feels particularly cruel, when I've finally gotten a taste of him, to stare down a life where I can't do it again.

We spend a few moments silently studying each other, perhaps each waiting for the other to make a move. Eventually, he leans in to kiss my cheek, then disappears into his bedroom. I get ready for bed, then spend a good hour or so tossing and turning, unable to quiet my mind enough to settle.

My door opens, and Lennon's dark silhouette fills the doorway. "Can I..." He trails off, and even in the sliver of light coming through the curtains, I can see his biceps rippling as he runs a frustrated hand through his hair. "I understand if you want to sleep."

"I'm not sleeping." I scoot over to make space for him and fold the comforter back. He wastes no time climbing in and looping his arm around me, drawing me close to his side. I rest my cheek in the crook of his shoulder, half on his chest so I can feel his heartbeat, strong and steady beneath me.

"I don't want to be alone," he says into the air between us.

"I'm here." I squeeze impossibly closer to him. "I'm always here."

He bends his neck so he can kiss the top of my head. "I know." He's silent for a moment before he continues, "I still get so anxious about them when they show up like that."

"And when they leave," I suggest gently.

He nods. "It's stupid. I'm not a kid anymore."

"Doesn't matter," I insist, not wanting to let on that I was also a little surprised at his reaction to them earlier. He'd be ashamed if I admitted that, and that's the last thing he needs. "You were a kid when they would randomly disappear. Makes sense those feelings would come back up when you're reminded of them."

"I should never have stopped seeing my therapist," he mutters. "I thought I had some ways to work through that anxiety, but seeing them here with you..."

He doesn't finish that sentence, so I say, "I don't want to make it worse for you by being here."

His arm tightens around my shoulders. His other hand lands on my chin, tilting it up so his lips can meet mine. "You only make things better, Songbird." He kisses me again, as if once weren't enough. "Seeing you and them together brought up some shit I regret."

"Like what?"

"Like getting stoned instead of telling you how I felt back in high school."

"Hmm," I hum. "So you went and got stoned again instead of telling me how you feel?"

"It's not a perfect system," he jokes. He scrubs his free hand over his face. "I'm sorry. I wanted to feel something different while I sorted out whatever was going on in my head."

"You don't have to apologize to me. I don't have a problem with weed, Lennon. You're acting like I've never smoked and you're ruining my virginal sensibilities by coming home high."

He peers down at me in the darkness, his eyes gleaming in the dim light. "We're going to come back to that piece of information."

I lightly smack his chest. "I have no doubt. But I need you to understand that I'm here. I'm not going anywhere, and I've got twenty-five years of friendship to prove it."

He faces the ceiling again, and my head rises and falls on his chest as he sighs deeply. "But you are leaving," he whispers, almost as if he can't bear to say it aloud.

Guilt crashes into me like a wrecking ball, because he's right. I am. And until now I hadn't thought past the next kiss and the ache to have his body next to mine. I know he didn't mean it to make me feel bad. And I know he knows me going back to Michigan isn't the same as his parents coming and going on a whim. Though in the haze of his anxiety, that probably doesn't matter as much as the sheer fact that I'm physically here now and in a few weeks, I won't be.

"Come back with me." I hadn't thought about it before, but I'm suddenly desperate to have him there. To make him coffee and share breakfast before I head off to teach my classes, to kiss him deeply when I come home.

As if he can read my mind, he kisses me. It's long and languid, and our tongues tease each other. "The only thing good about that place is you," he says into my lips.

I pull back as the unspoken end of that sentence hits me: *And that's not enough.*

I blink a few times against a rising tide of uncertainty. I'm sure he didn't mean it like that. He just loves it here. He always has. And I can't blame him; I love it here, too.

"We'll figure it out," I say with much more certainty than I feel. "Unless..." I trail off, the suggestion almost too painful to give voice to. "Unless you don't want to try?"

Lennon rolls out so he's on his side, facing me. Our heads rest on the same pillow, our noses almost touching. His breath smells like minty toothpaste and a lingering earthiness that isn't at all unpleasant. "I thought about that," he admits. "While I was out today. I figured it'd probably be easier for both of us if we cut our losses and walked away before one or both of our hearts got really broken."

My stomach bottoms out, and I chew at my bottom lip. "Oh," I say, and I can't keep the disappointment from dripping from the word.

Lennon tucks a piece of hair behind my ear and tilts my chin so I have to look at him. The sliver of light from behind the curtains casts a silvery glow over his features. His eyes are warm, and they crinkle at the edges. "And then I got back here and saw you and your notes all spread out on the floor, taking over my life and my space. You're so fucking beautiful, Lark. I want you to take over. I want you in every way, in every aspect of my life." He smirks. "Fuck easy."

A relieved laugh bubbles out of me, too loud in the quiet night. "Fuck easy," I repeat.

He leans in and catches my nervous laughter with a kiss. This one is different than the others, at once more intense and more caring. I open for him, letting him taste me, swallowing his moans and soaking up the soft noises he makes.

His hands land on my hips, the warmth of them seeping through my pajama shorts. He hooks my leg over his hip and pulls me closer to him. My nipples pebble under my shirt as he squeezes me into his chest.

"Can I..." His hand gently grazes the underside of my breast.

I arch into him. "Yes," I breathe, and in a beat, his hand cups the swell of it. Our eyes meet in the dark. We can both sense it, being on the edge of something new. The air between us is charged with need, the ache of it a physical, tangible thing.

And then, because I can't hold back any longer, I push him onto his back and climb on top of him as he watches me, his jaw slack and his eyes sparkling, in the second before I jump in and lose myself in his body.

Chapter 20

Lennon

I CAN'T BELIEVE I almost walked away from this. Having Lark in my arms, her body covering me in the moment before her kiss turns almost wild with desire feels more right than anything I've ever experienced.

She's mine, and I'm hers. It's the way it has always been, only we'd been too young or too far apart or too convinced we'd fuck it up to admit it.

And when our lips finally meet again, her golden hair falling in a curtain around my face to shield us from the rest of the world, I silently resolve to not waste a single minute more without her. Whatever it looks like for us, wherever we are. We can figure all that out later. Right now, she's here. Squeezing me with her glorious thighs, angling her head this way and that, breathy moans escaping between kisses as she rolls her hips on top of me.

I cup her breasts with both hands, feeling her nipples tighten underneath her shirt. Lark pulls back until she's sitting upright, her eyes hooded as she toys with the hem. She shimmies it up just enough for me to catch a glimpse of her belly button, her skin shimmering in the dim light of the room. I want to touch every inch of her I've never been able to before, and I suddenly realize I can. That the soft part of her lips and the trembling in her hands as they lift her shirt higher is permission.

I skate my hands down the curves of her sides until they meet her skin. It's even softer than it looks.

The way she's looking at me now—her blue eyes glinting in the light of the moon and wetting her swollen lips with her tongue—is downright sinful. She's no longer my best friend as she straddles me in my guest bedroom. I've said it over and over that she's my everything, but right now she's *more* than everything.

"Lark." I dig the tips of my fingers into her, marking her. I want all of it. Every piece of her I've always wanted but was never able to have. "Show me more. Please."

She drags her bottom lip through her teeth, and I resolve to drag it through mine as soon as she gives it back to me. "Okay," she whispers. Slowly, so slowly, she inches her shirt up over the expanse of her torso until the swell of the undersides of her breasts are just visible. I'm barely breathing, anchoring myself into her with my tightening grip on her skin.

She finally peels the shirt over her head, and I'm rewarded for my patience with a perfect view of her smooth skin and tight, pink nipples. I drink in the sight of her. She's better than anything I could have ever imagined.

I press a hand to her back to bring her down to me so I can draw one of those gorgeous nipples into my mouth. I flick it with my tongue, and she moans, so I do it again. Her hips roll against mine, and her fingers find their way into my hair. She grabs on tight and tugs me closer. I wrap my arms around her and flip us so she's under me, which earns me a squeal and a musical giggle.

"Your turn," she breathes. "Show me."

I smirk. "It's only fair." Maybe a little overeager, I grab my shirt by the back of the neck and pull it off in one quick motion. I remain on my knees between her legs and let her eyes roam over me, hoping she likes what she sees.

Her elegant fingers climb up over the ridges of my abdomen, leaving goose bumps in their wake. She trails her fingers along the ink on my stomach—a random design I thought looked cool—up to my chest where the scene from my shoulder continues. It ends in a sunset just below my collarbone. Under that, in scrawling script, reads: *Love looks not with the eyes, but with the mind*. Lark squints to read the text, then gasps, her wide eyes finding mine. I clutch her hand to my skin, pressing her palm over the words.

When I had the quote from *Midsummer* tattooed, I convinced myself it was because high school Drama Club had meant so much to me. It had given me a place to belong, something to look forward to. Now it's clear to me that I had been fooling myself. It was invariably about her.

"You've always been everything to me, Songbird. Always." Maybe I've never been able to say out loud that I love her, but I can admit this. I hope she reads my love for her in those words. I pray she can see it in my gaze.

Her eyes shine. I kiss each one in turn, licking her salty tears from my lips. I continue on a trail down her neck and over her torso to the waistband of her shorts. She sucks in a breath as I hook my fingers around it and pull them off, casting them aside.

"Shit, Lark. You're..." I swallow hard. "God, you're beautiful." Turning my head, I kiss one of her inner thighs, then the other, and her legs widen a fraction. They shake with tension or need—I can't tell which—but that won't do. I want her relaxed and enjoying herself. I scoot down on the bed and hold her foot in my hand, leaning in to kiss the inside of her ankle. I made a promise that day on the beach, and I intend to fulfill it.

"Lennon," she sighs as I make my way up one, then the other. I drag my hand up the outside of her stunning legs as my tongue works its way up the inside. Her legs go slack under my ministrations, and they part easily for me. I settle in between her thighs, but not before flashing an *I told you so* smile up at her. She laughs easily, her gaze lust-drunk as she threads her fingers through my hair again and angles her hips just slightly.

I purse my lips and gently blow on her entrance. Her entire body shivers, and her grip on my hair tightens. I allow my lips to lightly graze the hair between her thighs. "I can't wait to find out what you taste like," I say. "Can I?"

"I..." She trails off and shifts her torso. "Yes, but... It's been a while."

On her moan, I lick up her center, lapping up her arousal. She tastes like she feels—warm and light. Her wetness slides down my chin as I flick her clit with my tongue. Her hips buck erratically, like she's not sure what to do with herself. I press my hand to her lower abdomen, keeping her where I want her as I continue to drink her in.

Her hands slide up to cup her breasts. I glance at her, and she's angled to watch me as she rolls and pinches her nipples between her fingertips. Desperate to explore inside of her, I press a finger to her entrance. I'm only able to get one knuckle in before I feel her walls squeeze around it.

"Relax," I implore her. "It's just me."

She huffs a breathy laugh. "That's kind of the problem. I don't know what you're thinking. Is this weird?"

I kiss the inside of her thigh again. "Oh," she sighs as I curl my finger upward, finding that ridge just inside her and stroking it. "Oh," she says again. "Fuck."

"I'm thinking that you're perfect," I say before dragging my tongue over her clit again. She relaxes fully underneath me. I add another finger, and she cries out. "That this was worth the wait." I taste her again and hum my approval. "And that you taste like sunshine feels."

She sucks in a breath. "Lennon, I..."

"Come for me, Lark. I want to taste that, too." I suck gently on her clit, and her chest starts rising and falling in rapid gasps. It doesn't take long before her entire body is shuddering, her walls squeezing against my fingers. I work for a little longer, drawing pleasure out of her in waves. When she sinks into the mattress on an exhale, I withdraw my fingers and use my wrist to wipe my mouth.

She raises herself up to grab the back of my neck and pull me down. Her tongue darts out. "Mmm," she hums. "Sunshine. I could see that."

Fuck, that's hot. I growl as I claim her mouth with mine, kissing her until she's needy and panting and I can barely stand the hardness of my cock straining against my shorts. Lark slips a hand inside them to circle it around me. My forehead drops to the space between her shoulder and neck.

"I know you have condoms around here somewhere," she teases.

It takes a second for me to register what she's saying, and as I hop off the bed and run into my room to quickly one. I pause briefly before turning around and grabbing a few more. When I rush back into the room to the sound of her laughter, I have the distinct sense of feeling the same way I remember from my first time with a woman. Needy and giddy and *ready*.

Lark kneels at the edge of the bed in front of where I'm standing. Her gaze drops to my cock, and she licks her lips. "I need you, Lennon. Please."

I cup her jaw, soaking in her warmth. "You have me, Lark." I make quick work of the condom and join her on the bed. She lies beneath me, and I hover over her again as her nails scrape along my back. Shuddering, I line myself up with her. In one thrust, I slide inside. She sucks in a breath, and her nails dig even harder into my back as her eyes flutter closed.

I go still. "Are you okay?"

"Ohmygodyes." She exhales it all in one, frantic word. "More. I need more."

"Happily," I say as I draw out and in again, further this time. Her softness meets my hardness, opening for me, taking me. After a few slow thrusts her breathing picks up, little moans and pleas escaping her with each movement. Her hips meet mine, driving me further in. Her perfect breasts bounce as I work harder, reaching a hand between us to stroke her still-sensitive clit.

She's even more beautiful in the ambient light of the room than any other time I've seen her, her hair mussed and her body writhing. Even in the dimness, I can tell her cheeks are flushed. I draw her bottom lip through my teeth, and she clutches desperately at my back. When she arches into me, I know she's close, and I've never wanted anything more than I want to feel her come on me.

I grit my teeth, trying to hold on just a little longer. "I need you to come again for me," I whisper into her skin. "I know you can."

"Mm-hmm," she grinds out. "I'm so close."

I increase the pace of the circles I'm making between her legs, and she cries out, the waves of her release clutching me, drawing me in. In two more thrusts, I'm following her.

When we both come to, our breaths slowing and our eyes opening, we find each other. She grins, and I can't help but answer her smile with one of my own as I pull out of her and flop onto the bed.

"That was..." I trail off, idly scratching my stomach. "Wow."

"Yeah." She giggles into her pillow. When she faces me, I kiss her forehead and excuse myself to take care of the condom as quickly as I can.

As I climb underneath the covers again, she's on her stomach, watching me with her face turned outward and her hands tucked underneath the pillow. I graze my fingers over the soft expanse of her back. "Can I stay here tonight?"

"I'd be sad if you didn't." A look of uncertainty crosses over her features as she chews on her bottom lip. "Are we... I mean..."

I remove one of her hands from under her pillow so I can hold it between us. "I'm yours if you want me."

She watches as our fingers intertwine, the cream of the pillow contrasting our shadowed hands. "I can't imagine not having you or you not having me."

"Good." I kiss her forehead, and she closes her eyes.

It doesn't take long for her breathing to deepen, but I lie awake for longer, watching her relax into a deep sleep. It's been a long time since I've allowed myself to want anything with the ferocity that I want to keep Lark here with me. Things in my life are rarely permanent, and her presence here is no exception.

Richard was probably right all those years ago. She deserves something stable, especially now that she's worked so hard to get it and can finally enjoy the fruits of her labor.

But Richard was wrong, too. He tried to keep her tied down. I want her to be free to choose, even if I want her choice to be to stay with me. Maybe I could go to Michigan with her, like she suggested. It would mean feeling landlocked and bored, but at least I'd have her.

We'll figure it out. She had sounded so full of hope, so sure. Maybe she's right. Maybe we can. We've remained long-distance best friends for almost two decades—surely that's the hard part, right?

She shifts in her sleep, her leg hooking over mine as she snuggles in close to me. Her contented sigh tickles the hairs on my chest. That's all it takes to persuade me to worry about this later. For now, she's here, and

I make a silent promise to myself to soak up every minute before we have to figure out what's next.

CHAPTER 21

LARK

"WHAT ARE THESE?" I'M standing in the doorway that separates Lennon's en suite bathroom from his bedroom wearing nothing but one of his giant USC T-shirts and dangling from my outstretched hand a pair of tortoiseshell glasses that had been sitting on the counter next to the sink. It's early Sunday evening, and we've spent all day in bed, having switched rooms because his is so much bigger. We explored each other's bodies over and over again and finally came up for air about an hour ago to order food.

Lennon is sitting—gloriously shirtless—against the headboard. He leans his head forward and squints, confirming my suspicions that these are, in fact, his and he hasn't been wearing them.

"I would think that should be obvious," he says drily. "They're glasses."

They sway back and forth in my hand. "But are they *your* glasses?"

His squint turns into a narrowed gaze directed at me. Or, depending on how bad his eyesight actually is, in my general direction.

"Yes." The word is curt and leaves no room to further broach the subject.

Too bad that's not enough for me. I cross to the bed and climb up so I'm straddling him. He watches me with and amused lift of an eyebrow as I place the glasses on his face. "Are you resisting them because your failing eyesight is a signal of your mortality?" I tease.

"No." By the quiver in his voice, I can tell he's trying to hide a laugh.

"Is it because you think they make you look old?" I tilt my head and make a show of studying him. "Because I am here to say, definitively, that they make you look distinguished."

"Every man's dream," he intones.

"*Distinguished* is professor-speak for *super sexy*," I explain.

His hands land on my hips, and he holds me in place as he lifts his. "Well, Professor Caspian, in that case..." The man is insatiable.

I tip my head back and laugh, and he uses it as an excuse to kiss my throat. These little touches are as natural as breathing. We've fallen into them as easily as if we've been together in this way for years, and my insides go a little gooey. As much as I like it, though, I still haven't gotten an answer.

"Seriously." I lean back slightly so I can look at him again. "You should wear them, if for no other reason than to be able to fully see how good I look."

"Songbird, I've been fully seeing how good you look for over twenty years. Trust me when I say I don't need the glasses for that."

I cross my arms and don't miss the way his eyes dip to my chest and drag their way almost reluctantly back up to my face. "Okay, fine," I say, pretending his compliment and subsequent gaze didn't just heat the room by ten degrees. "So why don't you wear them?"

He sighs and falls back against the headboard with a dull thud. "I put them on once, and I didn't like what I saw."

"I'll refer you to my aforementioned comment about you looking distinguished."

He chuckles and rolls his eyes. "No. I mean, I looked in the mirror and I could see myself. Clearly. Suddenly, there were all these lines and wrinkles I had no idea were there before. So, I stopped wearing them." He lifts a shoulder in a half shrug. "I don't really need them anyway. They're barely a prescription."

I blink a few times, trying to process what he just said. "You do know the wrinkles are there whether you can see them or not."

"If a tree falls in the forest and no one's there to hear it, does it still make a sound?"

I raise my eyebrows and blink at him again. "Yes." I take the glasses off him and fold them to carefully set them on the nightstand. "And besides, I'm here, and I can see them." I kiss the crinkly lines at one corner of his eye, then the other. "And I like them." Then, I kiss the lines bracketing each corner of his mouth, followed by the strong line of his jaw.

"There aren't any lines there," he insists.

"Oh, no?" I nip at his jaw, then smooth my tongue over the spot. "I thought I saw one."

Lennon mumbles something incoherent, even as his fingers dig into my skin.

"You can't be expected to look like a teenager for your entire life." I kiss the other side of his jaw for good measure.

"Says the woman who has fifteen bottles of potions lined up in my guest bathroom." He's being sarcastic, but it's a gentle prod. I pull back so I can see his full face. He's searching mine, his gaze snagging on places I know have those same lines he's so worried about.

"I don't look like I did in high school, either." Not just in my face, but in my fuller hips and deflated breasts. It's unfair those two can't be the other way around.

Lennon takes my chin between his thumb and forefinger. He turns my face this way and that, inspecting and squinting and humming thoughtfully until I fall into him in a fit of giggles.

"You look better than you did in high school," he proclaims.

I run a hand over the swell of his biceps. "You do, too," I say quietly.

He tilts my chin up so I'm looking at him again and smirks. "Even better that now I've had the added benefit of seeing you naked, which teenage me would be very jealous of. And I would very much like to see it again."

"Okay." I eye the glasses still sitting on the nightstand. "But you're going to put those on for me."

He frowns, the crease between his eyebrows deepening. "Why?"

I flash him a wicked smile as I pull the shirt off me and toss it aside. "Because I like them."

It only takes a second for him to snatch the glasses off the nightstand and put them back on. "Say no more." He kisses me deeply, effectively silencing any more teasing I might have come up with.

***

"Hey," Lennon's exasperated voice floats in from the living room on Monday morning. "Five till we leave."

"Thank you, five," I call back almost automatically as I dip the wand in my mascara and start quickly swiping at my lashes. It's his fault I'm late, since he was the one who woke me up by running his hands over my skin and kissing me. And when his lips met mine, what was I supposed to do but let him devour me again?

I watch in the mirror as a slow smile spreads across my face at the memory. It's not like I was an unwilling participant, so maybe I'm just as much to blame.

Lennon's face appears over my shoulder, a flush creeping up his neck and his lust-addled gaze trained on me.

My smile turns into a smirk as I tick an eyebrow up and meet his eyes in the mirror. "Oh, you liked that, did you?"

"A little too much, I think." He steps up behind me and wraps his arms around my middle, kissing my neck and letting me feel exactly how much he liked my theater talk.

I reach up to run my hand through his hair, holding him close to me and tilting my neck to give him better access. "What happened to leaving in five?"

His teeth scrape against my pulse, then he licks the spot to soothe the sting. "We're coming back to this," he practically growls into my skin.

Our gazes meet in the mirror, his hazel eyes dark and full of desire and my blue ones bright and happy. "Is that a promise?" I ask.

He nods, then lingers there as if he wants to say something else. But ultimately, the only thing he says is "We'd better go," before he pinches my side affectionately and walks out of the bathroom.

Lennon holds my hand the entire way to the studio. Even though we've held hands a million times over the years, this feels different. It's more meaningful, more noticeable. Before, I was hardly aware of when his thumb would brush across my knuckles. Now every slight shift registers, either with a shock of need up my entire arm or a vague worry about whether or not he's comfortable.

This budding relationship between us is so new. And now that we're outside the safety of his apartment, I'm not quite sure how to act. Do we tell Noah and the others or let them realize it themselves? Or do we not bother because I still don't know what's going to happen once I finish recording this audiobook? Do I tell Devin? Would it be weird for her? I never got serious with anyone when she was younger because I was always worried about how it would affect her. Would I still risk breaking her heart if things didn't work out with Lennon, or is she old enough to understand? She loves Lennon so much...would he still be part of her life if he wasn't part of mine?

Is there a world in which I'd survive if Lennon was no longer my best friend? Is that what's going to happen if I decide to leave Los Angeles and go back home at the end of this thing?

I've been chewing my lip for so long that I can taste the iron tang of blood by the time Lennon pulls up to the studio entrance. I lick it away quickly and paste a smile on my face before I turn to him.

He's still holding my hand, and he doesn't let go even when he parks the Jeep. He gives it a squeeze. "You look like your brain is working on overdrive, Songbird."

"Hmm?"

"You were pretty deep in thought over there." His tone is light, but his soft eyes suggest he's concerned.

He's already been so anxious about his parents, and we've barely been together for two days. I can't burden him with any of this yet, even though he'd be the first person I'd confide my worries in if I were falling for a different man. I decide to open the door just a crack. The other bridges are ones we can cross when we come to them.

"I don't really know how to act in public. Do I kiss you now, knowing whoever is in there can see us and is probably watching? Do we pretend everything is normal for a while longer while we adjust to...whatever we're doing?" I shrug helplessly.

He watches his thumb brush back and forth over my hand. "What are we doing?" he asks quietly.

"Calling you my boyfriend feels trite and juvenile, if that's what you're asking," I say honestly. "But I also don't know if that's really what you want. Or maybe you want to keep up your bachelor ways? I wouldn't blame you." This is going off the rails, and fast. I let out a frustrated grumble. "This is not how I wanted to have this conversation."

Lennon brings my hand to his lips and kisses it as he meets my gaze. It's a motion he's made a million times over the years, only it's different now. Softer. Surer. Hungrier. "Whatever you want to call me, I'm yours. I told you that. And if you want to shout it from the rooftops, I'll shout with you. If you want me to be your dirty little secret for a while, I'm on board with that, too." He winks.

I roll my eyes, but I'm grateful for his humor. It makes me much less worried. Maybe we don't need to take this too seriously. Maybe we can just have fun and enjoy each other without planning every single move.

"Is this about Devin?" he asks gently. Of course he sees right through to the heart of the issue. He's known me too long for me to give him half-truths and get away with it.

"Among other things," I admit.

"How about this?" He kisses my hand again, then brushes his lips softly against mine. "You're done recording in, what, two weeks?"

"And then pickups."

"Okay, three, give or take. Let's give it until then. Enjoy it. See what happens without putting it in a pressure cooker right away, and let you focus on getting this recording done."

I look upward and nod. "I do like to focus."

"You joke, but you forget I've known you for a long time." He ticks up a sandy eyebrow and pins me with a look. "So I am well aware of your tunnel vision at the end of projects like this."

I grumble because he's not wrong. "Fine."

"You get to focus. We get to do more of what we've been doing all weekend." His hazel eyes dip to my mouth as he drags the thumb of his free hand over my bottom lip again, as if he could live between the pillows of my lips and be happy there.

A breathy laugh escapes around his thumb, and his eyes make their way to mine again. "There's no script, Songbird," he says softly. "We get to make it up, however we're comfortable."

Improv. I can do improv. "Okay," I say, much more balanced now than I was a few minutes ago. Lennon always could steady me, even as he needed me to do the same for him. Our friendship has always been a beautiful give-and-take. And that familiar flush creeps up my cheeks when I think of the new kind of give-and-take we've been engaging in all weekend.

My phone rings loudly from my purse, and I start. I fumble through the bag and pull it out to see Devin's name at the top of the screen. Lennon peers over the minimal space between us and sees it, then kisses my forehead quickly before I jump out of the Jeep.

"See you in a few hours," he says.

I wave as I answer the phone before it can go to voicemail. "Hi, kiddo!" Even I cringe at how overly excited I sound. I've was so engrossed in Lennon in the bubble of his bed that bursting so unexpectedly out of it makes it necessary to recalibrate how I interact with people in the outside world.

Devin giggles, and the sound fills me up. "Hi, Mom. I just wanted to call to let you know I landed in New York. Dad's picking me up soon."

"Oh, good." I should have remembered she was landing today, but I lost track of time somewhere between the sixth and seventh time Lennon's lips met mine. Mom-guilt gnaws at me, even though I know it makes no difference to her whether or not I remember her schedule to the minute. "How was the flight?"

"Fine." She sighs, and I can hear how tired she is. "I think I might sleep for days."

Laughing, I start to make my way toward the door of the studio. I can make out Noah through the window, and it looks like he sees me. I hold up a finger, and he nods. "I know the feeling."

"How's LA?" she asks. "Is the recording going well?"

"It's great. I'm having a lot of fun."

"*Good*." She emphasizes the word hard. "You deserve it."

I rub at the center of my chest as my heart swells almost painfully. Just hearing her voice is a stark reminder of how much I already miss her. "Thanks, honey," I manage to choke out around the sudden swell of emotion.

"How's Lennon? Is he treating you well? Showing you a good time?"

I bark out a laugh at the double entendre she wasn't even aware of. "He's been a perfect gentleman." It's not entirely a lie, even though it feels strange keeping this huge thing from her. Lennon was right, though. We can make our own rules, and we'll tell Devin when we're ready.

"Awesome. Oh, I see Dad's car. I'll call you later?"

"Sure. Have fun. Send everyone my love."

We say our goodbyes. I take an extra minute to collect myself before entering the studio. Noah is there, along with his intern. They're both wearing headphones, and Silas isn't anywhere to be seen. When the door shuts behind me, Noah nods once and removes his headphones.

"Hey," I say. "Sorry I'm late. Lennon and I had to work some stuff out, and then my kid called..."

One of Noah's bushy, dark eyebrows raises as his beard twitches into a smirk. Oh, he definitely saw Lennon and me in the Jeep, then.

Luckily, he's professional about it. "No worries. I should have texted you. Silas is recording an audition for another project right now, so you have a few minutes to warm up." He trails off and his smirk widens. "If you need to."

Well, he was professional for a second anyway.

"Great. Perfect. I'll just...do that, then." Something about Noah's smirk is throwing me off again. I drop my bag onto a nearby chair and move toward my booth.

"Hey, Lark," Noah says before I can pull the door open.

"Yeah?"

"I promised Lennon I wouldn't overwhelm you, but I have a few projects I think you'd be great for, if you were interested in continuing on. Jessica is working on her second book, too. She's already said she'd love to have you on board for that audio. Given how hard it was to cast this one, it would be great for everyone if you wanted to do it." His arms are folded over his chest and he's clearly trying to adopt a casual air, but his wide eyes and clenched jaw suggest he's very excited about these possibilities.

I'd be lying to myself if I said I wasn't thrilled. It's every actress's dream to be offered another gig at the end of one. And a not-so-small part of me knows that this is a way forward for Lennon and me. That is, if I want to stay. Which would mean giving up everything I worked for back home.

No. I shake my head to clear it. We agreed not to make any decisions about anything for the next couple of weeks. But even if I don't stay here, this is probably something I can do back in Michigan. Who knows, maybe Carl would see it as good experience and let me teach some higher-level classes. I'd be a fool not to think about this, and I probably should separate it from Lennon. It's my career, after all, and doesn't need to have anything to do with him. If it came to that.

"Um," I say. "I'm definitely interested. Can I think about it for a few days? I need to figure out what's going on back home."

"Sure," Noah says quickly. "Of course. These aren't starting until after we wrap this one, so take your time. I just wanted to put it on your radar. I thought maybe..." He trails off and snaps his mouth shut.

I tilt my head and raise my eyebrows. "Maybe what?"

He glances over my shoulder to where Lennon and I sat in his Jeep a few minutes ago. "Nothing. The offers are on the table—that's all."

I nod. "Thank you," I say as I enter my booth.

Silas is on the other side of the window between the booths. I can't hear him yet, but he pauses and smiles at me, giving me a thumbs-up. Noah must have told him, too. It's sweet that he's happy for me. I flash him the same gesture before he goes back to the script in front of him.

My phone pings with an email. With everything this morning, I forgot to silence it before I came into the studio, so I quickly pull it from my pocket to do so, but the name on the email notification makes me pause.

From: Carl Stanton <cstanton@arborhillscc.org>

To: Lark Caspian <lcaspian@arborhillscc.org>

Subject: Next term classes

Hello Lark,

I'm writing because your audiobook work this summer is making quite the splash among the faculty here. We are all so excited to hear it. Given the buzz around your work—and the fact that we are having a difficult time replacing Monique—I wanted to revisit our previous conversation about you teaching some of the upper-level courses next term on a trial basis. Think about it! Let's meet when you get back.

Carl Stanton

Theater Department Chair, Arbor Hills Community College

It takes a few read-throughs before what he's saying clicks. I didn't even know he was aware I was recording this summer. Everything happened so fast, and with Devin leaving on top of it all, I hadn't had a chance to say much to anyone. Not to mention that I didn't want to get ahead of myself before it released in case it didn't turn out as well as I'd hoped. But he knows, and he's already impressed enough to offer me a trial run teaching some more rigorous classes. This is good. This is *really* good.

I have actual options, which I haven't been able to say since undergrad. Live here and keep doing this work that has sparked a joy in me I thought was long gone. Go back to Ann Arbor and work to progress in the career I fought so hard for. Stay with Lennon, try to drag him with me, or leave him behind. And even though I know making these decisions won't be easy, I'm not dreading them. It's as if the whole big open sky is mine.

For the first time in a long time, I feel free.

CHAPTER 22

LENNON

QUIET MORNINGS, DOING SIMPLE things for Lark while the sunlight warms the apartment and she bustles around, clinking bottles and clattering hair products in the bathroom, are a privilege. I stare down at my bare feet, tan against the white of the kitchen tile, wondering how many days like this we could have had if I had gone back to her like I wanted to ten years ago.

I had surprised her. She was turning thirty and caring for an eight-year-old Devin mostly by herself. Her divorce from Richard had just been finalized the month prior, and he was headed to New York. His job was ultimately the nail in the coffin. She didn't want to leave Michigan, and he was being transferred to New York. Their divorce was amicable; they both knew it was over long before they finally called it, and they had been separated for most of the year before filing for divorce. But Lark fought hard to keep Devin with her. In the end, Richard agreed it was best for her to stay with Lark during the school year and visit for a few weeks over the summer and on some holidays. That way she wouldn't have to adjust to a new school or have to try to fly back and forth too often and miss time with her friends.

Lark had been bound and determined to make sure Devin's life was as normal as possible, but I know she struggled with being the single parent in a sea of couples at school functions. Even before she and Richard finally split, she was the one taking her daughter to classes, cheering her on at science fairs, meeting her teachers, and all the other typical parent things one does. Knowing what I know now, I don't like Richard, and I think he could have done more, but Lark was always jumping in. She liked being the default parent, I think, and Richard was happy to let her.

But it was a lot to shoulder. I could see all of it weighing on her, even over the phone. So I thought surprising her for her thirtieth birthday would give her a lift. I wanted her to know there were people who cared about her enough to make her feel special on her birthday. I arranged for a dinner with her parents, got on a plane, and took a cab to her townhouse.

She opened the door wearing a fluffy robe and what looked like clown makeup, her hair a bird's nest of butterfly clips. There was glitter *everywhere*. I gripped the handle of my suitcase, scanned her up and down, bit my lip against a giant grin, and said, "Surprise."

She slammed the door in my face.

I couldn't stop laughing. It had been a long time since I had laughed that hard, and that was when I knew I made the right decision coming out to see her.

When the door opened again and a string-bean version of Devin—her dark hair in twin braids over each shoulder, a gap in her teeth, and her long skinny legs poking out of shorts that looked like she had almost grown out of them—was the one pulling it open, that's when I realized how much I had missed.

I never told Lark that even with Devin's dress-up makeup on, she was stunning. I should have. Instead, I spent a supremely normal weekend with them. They let me in on their routines: blueberry pancakes on Saturday morning, sitting on lounge chairs at the community pool and chatting while Devin splashed around with her friends, eating grilled cheese and baby carrots for lunch and ice cream for dinner. But the moments I loved the most were the ones where we sat face-to-face, leaning against the back of the couch, mugs of steaming tea and coffee between us, talking in the early mornings while Devin slept.

"What's wrong, Songbird?" I asked.

Lark's eyes remained unfocused as she stared out the window, her legs curled up underneath her and her hands cupping the mug of tea resting on top of her knees. "I wish I never married him," she said quietly. Her gaze snapped to mine, her blue eyes wide with worry. "I would never wish I didn't have Devin, you know? But Richard..."

Anyone who knew them could see they were a bad match from the start, but I didn't say that. That wasn't what she needed.

I rubbed her bare foot gently with my hand. "I know what you meant."

She tilted her head thoughtfully, her eyes bouncing back and forth between mine as if trying to gauge my reaction before she added, "I can't help but think of all the things I could have had if he and I hadn't spent eight years trying to make it work."

I shake my head as if to wake myself from the foggy memory. At the time, I remember wishing she had been talking about me, but I never asked. We carried on with our normal weekend, and I got on that plane back to LA with a giant hole where Lark had been.

I didn't tell anyone. Noah knew I was off, and he knew where I had been but didn't say much about it. After a week of ambling around my apartment, my roommate at the time invited me to go to the beach with some of his buddies. We drank some beers, smoked a bit. We had a great night, and even though I sat there, looking up at the stars and wishing Lark could be there with me or that I could point out some of the different constellations to Devin, I knew I wasn't leaving LA. Lark and I were worlds apart.

The next week, I got those little larks added to my tattoo. I wanted them on the inside of my arm, closest to my heart. The quote from *Midsummer* had been there for years already—it was the first tattoo I had gotten in college. Those birds, though...they were just for her.

Maybe we could have made up the physical distance somehow back then, but emotionally, she was so vulnerable. I had seen it in those moments on the couch. She let me in when Devin couldn't see. I didn't want to show up like a lost puppy, knowing she'd open her heart to me but never knowing if she had been truly ready to.

But when she walks up behind me and wraps her arms around my middle, it sure feels like she's ready. It feels like I'm ready. Maybe I thought I was before, but now I can't imagine living another minute without her next to me.

"I got an interesting email the other day," she says into my back.

I dip her tea bag in and out of the water. "Oh yeah?" I ask. She lets go of me, and I turn around to hand her the mug. The edge of the counter bites into the skin of my lower back as I fold my arms and give her my attention.

She sips her tea, looking into the mug as if it holds some kind of answer for her. "Yeah. From Carl. My boss at Arbor Hills?"

I nod, silently watching as she fiddles with the tag on the tea bag. She creases it between her fingers and runs a fingernail over the edge.

"He said they're having a hard time replacing one of the older professors who retired at the end of last term. And that this audiobook is creating a buzz. Luminaudio's advertising must be pretty widespread."

She pauses and tilts her head as if she's considering something. "Or maybe Hannah is talking it up on campus. I wouldn't put it past her."

"That's exciting." I turn around to stir some more cream into my coffee. I don't really need more, but I can't help the dread pooling in my chest, and I need something to do with my hands. I hope this isn't going where I think it's going, but I breathe in slowly and count to four in my head before letting it out in a futile effort to calm my thoughts.

"Anyway, he offered me those classes on a trial basis. I think I told you I had asked for them before the term ended? He said I needed more field experience before he'd consider it. I guess this counts."

When I face her again, she's watching me carefully. If I didn't know her so well, I'd miss the stiffness in her posture, the slight set of her jaw, the hopeful way her eyebrows curve upward. She wants this. She might be conflicted about what it looks like for us, but there's no mistaking that at least part of her is excited about the possibility of something she's worked so hard for finally playing out.

As much as I want to beg her to stay, tell her there are community colleges here that would jump at the chance to work with her, remind her that Noah has more audiobooks lined up, I can't make this decision for her. I don't even want to sway her choice. Every decision she's made in her adult life has been for someone else. She shouldn't make this one for me.

My heart hasn't gotten the memo that I need to do this for her, though, and it takes all my strength to very calmly say, "That's great. How are you feeling about it?"

Lark immediately slumps, the dam that was holding back her wariness breaking before my eyes. "I don't know. I was qualified before this, and it's annoying that they didn't see that. And a trial basis?" She rolls her eyes. "Come on."

I chuckle. "You know I think that's bullshit."

She points at me with her palm up. "Right? But, I don't know... This is something I've wanted for a long time."

The coffee scalds my tongue as I sip it too quickly. "You've worked so hard for it," I say carefully before putting the mug down to cool off more.

She studies me for a moment, then drops her gaze to her tea again before setting it on the counter and folding her hands in front of her. "What would it look like if I declined, if I stayed here? In LA?" she asks quietly.

I wish I could tell my stupid heart to slow the fuck down, but it registers my hope before my brain can catch up.

"Is that something you'd want to do? For real?" Of course we've skirted around the idea, but we haven't seriously talked about it yet. It felt too soon, too new, and I wanted to wait for her.

She shrugs. "Depends."

"On?"

"If you and your giant biceps can make room for me."

Using humor to deflect has always been her stalling tactic, but I play along. I grab her suddenly and wrap her up in a tight hug. "Oh, I don't know," I say into her hair. "These biceps seem like the perfect fit for you."

She wraps her arms around my torso and sighs into me, which only further proves my point. "They're pretty nice," she admits.

"They are," I agree. "And I'll not have you insulting their size again."

"My mistake. Sorry, Lennon's biceps."

We stand there, silently embracing each other in my kitchen while I breathe her in. It's not lost on me that this is another thing I could have been doing for the last ten years if I hadn't been too chickenshit to shoot my shot earlier. But she's here now, and even if I only get to have her for a little while, she's mine for as long as she'll let me.

"I don't want to make this decision," she says into my chest.

"I don't envy you," I say honestly. She bats at my arm with her hand, but I hold her tighter. "I can't help you with this, Songbird."

"Why not?" she whines.

I laugh quietly and kiss the top of her head. "You deserve to have everything you want in this new chapter of your life, but only you know what that looks like."

She's quiet for a moment before she whispers, "But do you want me here?"

I reach behind me and unclasp her hands so I can hold them between us and properly look at her. The desire to tell her I can't imagine living another moment without her here with me is so strong, it catches me off guard. But I've already committed to making sure she makes this decision on her own, so I simply incline my head slightly.

She presses her lips into a tight line, then nods once in return. "We'd better get going. I can't have Noah thinking I'm slacking now that he wants to work more with me."

As much as I want to continue this conversation with a list of pros and cons that are heavily weighted in my favor, she's not ready. I can see the uncertainty written clearly in the lines of her face and the curve of her spine. So I tuck it away for later, like she has seemed to do as she makes her way back toward her bedroom.

"Five till we leave," I call to her back.

"Thank you, five," she tosses over her shoulder with a beautiful, wicked smile.

I bend over and grip the edge of the counter until my knuckles turn white. "Dammit, woman." I shake my head. "Be careful with that."

She tips her head back and laughs her musical laugh. "Stop setting me up, then."

Shaking my head, I eye her from across the apartment. "Never."

Lark lingers there with her hand on the doorknob of her bedroom as her soft lips stretch into a warm smile.

I don't know what she'll decide, but I know that every time we're apart, the piece of my heart she keeps with her gets bigger and bigger. I worry that eventually, there won't be any of it left for me.

CHAPTER 23

LARK

"Please tell me you're calling because you're finally fucking Hot Lennon," Hannah says by way of greeting.

I scramble to turn the volume on my phone down as I glance past the screen to make sure his door is still closed. "Oh my god," I whisper. "Could you not? He's in the next room."

Her brown eyes go even darker through the screen as she pins me with a look. "Don't think I didn't notice that wasn't a flat-out denial."

Unsure of what to say, I stare at her for a minute. "Fucking Hot Lennon" is both exactly and not at all what I've been doing for the past week or so. He has been my entire world, and we've barely come up for air. I had hoped calling Hannah would anchor me, or at least remind me of what I would miss back home if I stayed here.

On one hand, it has only taken me a matter of days to completely fall for Lennon. On the other, it has taken twenty-five years. It has been a whirlwind summer romance where everything is happening too fast, but it has also been a lifelong slow burn where nothing is happening fast enough, and I want more of everything I've been missing.

As I study Hannah's face, hoping to see something in it that will bring me to my senses and remind me that shifting my life in such a significant way is madness, the very specific color of sage-green paint behind her registers. I squint at the wall. "Are you at my place?"

"Uh..." She tries to shift, but that only results in me being able to see my couch where there are clearly blankets strewn about and her legs which are clad in very comfortable-looking joggers. Piles of books I don't recognize litter the cushions.

"You are!" I exclaim, happy to have a distraction from the whirring of my mind. "You look pretty cozy. Are you staying there?"

Her mouth spreads into a smile that looks more like a grimace. "That depends. Would you be mad if I were?"

"No," I say slowly. "But why?"

"It's so much bigger than my place," she whines. "I only have the one tiny bedroom, and the office is so lonely without you, so one day I just...brought some stuff over here to check up on the place like you asked me to."

"And then you, what, didn't leave?"

She nods guiltily. "Please don't be mad!"

"I'm not!" I exclaim through my laughter. "Why didn't you tell me?"

The image on the screen bounces as she shrugs. "I kept meaning to go home." She ticks an eyebrow up, and I know before she even opens her mouth what's coming. "Are you going to bother coming back and kicking me out, or can I squat here indefinitely?"

"You sure are jumping to a lot of conclusions."

She starts to tick things off on her fingers. "I know the audiobook is going well, because you texted me last week. I know you turned Silas down for a date, though I still think you're absolutely bonkers for that."

I roll my eyes. "You could always come visit for a weekend before we're done recording. I could introduce you."

"I might actually take you up on that," she says before returning to her list. "I also know you get googly-eyed whenever you talk about Lennon—"

"I do not!" I interject.

"You do." She raises a hand to stop me from protesting further. "At the very least, you're a single, hot-blooded woman in her sexual prime who is living with her *very attractive* best friend for the summer."

"Women are in their sexual prime at forty?" I ask skeptically.

She slips into her professor voice. "Some studies suggest it. Each individual is different, of course, but it makes sense. By forty, most women have finally figured out what they like in bed and how it works for them, and you're going to want more of something you're finally enjoying." She props her chin on her fist. "So, tell me, Lark. Are you enjoying it?"

I'm an actress. Or at least, I have been. My entire life's work has been teaching students how to present the emotions of the roles they're playing while essentially masking their own. But even I can't help the slow smile that spreads across my face.

"Aha!" Hannah's image shakes again as she pumps her fist in triumph. "I fucking knew it. *Please* tell me it's amazing and Earth-shattering and has made you rethink everything you thought you knew about pleasure."

I cringe. "That's a little intense."

"Sex with your high school best friend is intense!" She pauses as she reels back a bit. "Do not tell me you're pretending this is some summer fling that'll end when you're done recording."

I shake my head. "No. This doesn't feel like that at all. It's just..." I trail off and sigh. Hannah waits patiently for me to continue, adjusting her dark glasses higher on her nose. My right foot starts wiggling as if the jittery movement could somehow alleviate the pressure of everything I want to tell her.

I check that Lennon's door is still closed. He's been editing all afternoon with no sign of taking a break, so I curl into the fluffy armrest of the couch. "Carl emailed. He said there's been a buzz about the audiobook. I don't suppose you had anything to do with that?"

She tilts her head back and forth. "I may have been talking very loudly about how excited I was to hear your narration and how cool it is to have someone on our faculty doing such a high-profile project. He might have been within earshot."

"I had a hunch. Anyway, it's apparently enough to justify giving me some of the higher-level classes on a trial basis."

Hannah scoffs. "Trial basis. What bullshit."

Lennon said the same thing, and they're both right. I've worked hard at Arbor Hills for fifteen years to prove myself. The implication that I would have to continue to justify my expertise is slightly insulting. "You don't think I should take it?"

"I'm not going to tell you what to do. I know how hard you've worked for this job. But I also know how amazing you are. Carl apparently hasn't caught on yet."

"Maybe he's catching on now."

"On a trial basis." She imitates him with a nasally voice and squinty eyes.

"You think it's too little too late," I guess.

"It doesn't matter what I think." She's all serious now. "What do *you* think?"

"I think I'm too old to make this massive change in my life. I think Lennon and I will probably try to make it work no matter what, but either of us can do the jobs we're doing here from anywhere. The only job that's not movable is mine at Arbor Hills, so it feels like a no-brainer to try to make it work there, even if LA is objectively better. Not to mention that I haven't told Devin yet. This is all so new still, but it feels strange keeping something so giant from the most important person in my life. What is she going to think?"

"I'm going to stop you right there," Hannah interrupts. "Devin is important, but she can't figure this out for you, either. It's okay for you to take some happiness for yourself, Lark. You can't always be doing everything for other people."

"Ugh, did you and Lennon talk, or something? He more or less told me the same thing," I grumble.

"He's a smart man."

I sigh deeply. "I'm stuck," I admit. I bite my lip, wondering if I should let her in on the next part or not. But she's my only friend back home, and I need advice, so I say quietly, "I watched Lennon's parents make decisions that didn't have him in mind all through high school, and I've seen how it still affects him, even now." I close my eyes against the image of Lennon standing in the open door, eyes bloodshot and shoulders slumped. "I don't want to do that to Devin."

Hannah isn't completely in the dark about this. I've told her before about Lennon's parents and their nomadic nature. I'd be lying if I said that wasn't a big deciding factor in my staying in Michigan through the divorce. I wanted Devin to have some consistency. I'm just a little unclear now about whether or not she'll still need it while she's away at school. And yet a nagging voice in the back of my head is telling me that leaving Lennon in LA now that we've started this won't end well for him, either.

I open my eyes. "I don't want to leave him. I'd never *leave* him. We'll always be friends," I clarify uselessly. "But...you know."

She nods and draws in a long breath through her nose, which is something I've seen her do with students who aren't quite getting the point. "You do notice none of the things you've said are about you or what you want, right?"

I blink rapidly because no, I hadn't noticed that. Lennon and Devin are so inextricably wound up with me that I almost wonder what would be left if I pulled the threads of them out of the fabric of my being.

As if Hannah can read that realization on my face, she hums. "You've got some soul-searching to do."

"Thanks for the help," I intone.

"Anytime!" she says brightly. "So, have you had an occasion to wear that bombshell bathing suit I picked out for you yet?" She waggles her eyebrows as Lennon's door swings open.

"Bombshell bathing suit?" he asks from the doorway, his own sandy eyebrows raised in curiosity.

Hannah's face lights up. "Oh my god. Is that Hot Lennon?"

"Hot Lennon?" He can barely hide the smirk creeping across his features.

I roll my eyes. "Careful, Hannah. His ego really can't take much more inflation before it bursts."

In several long strides, he crosses from his bedroom to the couch, where he plops unceremoniously next to me. He leans right into my space so he can see the phone screen. His cheek is practically pressing against mine, and he slings an arm over my shoulders to squeeze me in tight.

"Oh my god, Lark." Hannah fans herself. "He's even hotter than that picture on your desk."

Lennon turns so his lips are brushing against my ear. "You have a picture of me on your desk?"

I eye him sidelong. "Why wouldn't I?"

His goofy grin spreads even wider, and I have to roll my lips together to keep myself from kissing it right off his face.

"You and..." He trails off, glancing at the screen.

"Hannah," I say flatly.

"You and Hannah look at it and talk about how hot I am?"

"No. Hannah talks about how hot you are. But to be fair, she talks about how hot everyone is." I'm not above throwing her under the bus to end this insufferable conversation.

"I do not," she protests weakly. I simply raise my eyebrows at the screen and wait until she tips her eyes up and wiggles back and forth. "Maybe Lennon and the new guy in my department."

"And Silas," I remind her.

"Matthews?" Lennon asks.

She nods. "Oh yeah. He's unattainable, though, so I don't count him." She pauses to consider, then says, "And Lark's delivery guy is sexy as fuck."

"My delivery guy?"

She shrugs again. "I may have had a thing or twelve delivered here."

"How long have you been staying at my place?" I ask incredulously.

"Oh, did you hear that?" She looks around in the most overexaggerated way possible. "That hot delivery guy must be here with another package. Gotta go!" The screen shakes as she fumbles with the phone before she finally hits the button to hang up and it goes blank.

Lennon backs off slightly but remains close on the couch, and he's still sporting a self-satisfied smirk. "So, that was Hannah."

"Yes," I say simply.

"And you two have conversations about how hot I am."

I pin him with a look. "You heard her. You're not special in that regard." But even as I say it, I can't help but notice how his sandy hair falls in waves over his forehead. How it curls at his ears because it's a little too long. How one of his dimples peeks out from behind that smile, and how his eyes sparkle with boyish mischief and a touch of desire. How the strong column of his throat works against a swallow as my gaze rakes over him.

Not for the first time, my memories of high school Lennon merge with the image of him sitting in front of me. His dimples are the same, and so are his eyes. But all of the soft edges have hardened. He's fully a man now, and my cheeks heat at the more recent memories of exactly what that age and experience has given him.

"Lark," he warns darkly. "If you keep looking at me like that, you have about five minutes until I tear your clothes off."

"Hmm." I wet my lips with zero intention of changing the way I'm soaking in his body. "Thank you, five."

His eyes flash, and he stills. I can see the evidence of his desire starting to press against his shorts. My own begins to pool between my legs as I drag my lower lip between my teeth. When my gaze meets his again, those hazel eyes are practically on fire.

"What should we do with the next five minutes?" I tap my mouth with my pointer finger as I consider. "I think I'd like your shirt off first."

Lennon doesn't hesitate. He grabs his T-shirt by the neck and tears it over his head. Ink and muscles are on full display, and I want to trace my tongue over every inch. I swing a leg over his so I'm straddling him. His hands land on my hips, fingers inching toward the tops of my leggings. "I intended to use those five minutes to get you ready for me." His voice is an octave lower than usual. He sounds like a man on the edge.

I roll my hips against him, and he tilts his head back against the top of the couch with a moan as his fingers grip me tighter. Pure, unadulterated desire fills me from my toes to the top of my head. I'm high on the power I have—that I can bring this man to his knees with a touch.

"They're my five minutes," I taunt. "I can do what I want with them."

"Tell me what you want, Lark."

You. The word rings as clear as day through my head. He's what I want. He's all I've ever wanted. There is no life without Lennon near me. Not anymore.

I lift his wrist to my mouth and kiss it. His pulse makes quick, staccato pulses beneath my lips, pounding out the beat of his need for me. I run my thumb over it as I trace the tattoo of a compass over the back of his forearm. "What does this one mean?" I whisper.

"I thought it looked cool," he says sheepishly. "But after I put those larks above it, I liked that it pointed north to you."

Well, fuck. I'm surprised he can't hear my heart cracking open. "That's...nice," I manage to choke out.

"Nice," he repeats in a daze, his voice as full of emotion as mine is. He traces two fingers lightly over my lips. "I'm glad you think that's nice, because I'm thinking a lot of very not-nice thoughts about you right now."

"Me, too." I huff. As his fingers make another pass over my mouth, my tongue darts out to meet them. I draw them between my lips, swirling my tongue around them.

"Dammit, Lark." He lowers his head to my shoulder as I continue to taste his skin. He grunts as I suck his fingers even harder. "I want to fuck that mouth," he groans.

I release his fingers, and he trails a wet line down the V of my shirt, just over the swell of my breast. "That sounds like a good use of the time we have left," I pant. "Are you...clear?"

He barks a short laugh and nods. "I got tested last week after we..." He almost looks embarrassed as he trails off. "I don't want to presume, but I figured it was a good idea."

Removing myself from his lap and kneeling between his powerful thighs, I look up at him. "It was a very good idea." I hook my fingers around the elastic waistband of his gym shorts and pull them off along with his boxers. He lifts his hips to help me and kicks the rest of his clothes aside. My mouth waters at the sight of his cock as it springs free to stand at attention for me.

I don't know if I'll ever get over the sheer size of him. Longing for him to fill me collects in my core, but I temper it. Not yet. We still have some time, and I plan to use it.

Gripping the base of him, I lick up his shaft. Lennon sighs and sinks into the couch cushions. I taste the precum dripping from the tip and hum my approval before taking him into my mouth. I let my saliva drip down to wet my hand as I work with it in tandem with my mouth and in time with the Lennon's movements.

His hands make fists on either side of his legs. When I look up at him, he's already watching me with hooded eyes, and his parted lips curl into a dazed smile. "Such a pretty mouth wrapped around me," he rasps. "You want more?"

I nod, and he palms the back of my head to gently bring me further. His tip grazes my throat, and I relax it to take as much of him as I can. The smooth skin of his cock slides in and out of my lips in time with his thrusts. He tastes like salty ocean waves, and I want to drink him in.

"You're taking me so well, Songbird, but your time is up." He grips my hair and pulls me off of him with a pop.

"But I want more," I protest.

Lennon shakes his head, his hazel eyes dark with desire. "It's been five minutes. Clothes off. Now," he orders.

"Touch yourself while I get undressed," I demand. He's not the only one who can boss someone around, and this power I have over him is still heady, humming in my blood. "I like watching you get excited."

He complies, his hand working as his powerful forearm flexes with the motion. I swallow hard as I remove my shirt first, then my leggings. My bra goes next, my breasts bouncing as they're freed from its grasp.

Lennon lets out a validating moan as he watches me, his hand still working slowly over himself.

"Panties," he chokes out.

"You want them?" I drag a teasing finger over the top of them.

"Yes," he says on an exhale. "Give them to me."

I peel them off slowly, then dangle them in front of him. He snatches them out of my hand and brings them to his nose to inhale deeply. "God, Lark. You smell like heaven."

My whole body is on fire, begging to be touched. Luckily, I don't have to wait because he releases himself and leans forward to drag a finger through my center. When he circles my clit, I all but fall forward, my hands meeting his strong shoulders.

"I need you, Lennon," I whisper. "Please."

"You're already so wet for me. You must have liked the taste of my cock." He watches his finger disappear inside me. When he hooks it forward, I shudder. "Tell me how much you liked it," he demands.

"A lot," I whimper, squeezing my eyes shut. "I want you in my mouth again."

"There'll be time for that," he assures me. "We have the rest of our lives."

My eyes fly open and meet his questioning glance. Between my legs, his movements stop, almost as if he's hesitating.

"You mean it?" I ask.

"It's you or no one," he says softly, his expression sincere. Hopeful.

Slowly, I lower myself onto his lap again so I can cup his face with my hands. There's so much uncertainty, but at least we are on the same page about the most important thing.

Him and me. Forever.

I crash my lips into his in a bruising kiss, and he meets it with equal fervor. His hand continues working between us, building an exquisite pressure in my spine. But it's not enough. I pull his hand from me and raise myself up so I can adjust him underneath me.

"No condom?" he asks.

Shaking my head, I bite my lip. "You got tested. I have an IUD. And I want to feel you. Can I?"

"Yes," he says on a breath.

I don't waste any time as I lower myself onto him, his cock stretching me deliciously, almost to the edge of pain. "Oh," I groan as I raise and lower myself to take him further. When my ass finally meets his legs and he's all the way inside me, I pause, relishing in the fullness of him.

Rocking my hips back and forth slowly, I find the spot where my clit meets his body. He grips my ass hard with one hand, guiding me. Showing me what he likes. Moving me closer to him and building even more pressure at the base of my spine.

His gaze meets mine, and I can't look away. He lifts the two fingers that were inside of me to his mouth and sucks on them, never removing his eyes from mine. I lick my lips, my core warming even more as I watch him.

"You want a taste?" He offers his fingers to me, and I open my mouth for them again. My arousal meets his skin in an explosion on my tongue. I moan and lean my head forward more to take it farther into the back of my throat.

"Yes," he hisses. "You're such a good girl, taking my fingers and my cock. Look at you." There's an edge of awe in his voice, and when I open my eyes, he's staring unabashedly at me, watching with a slack jaw and a slow release of his breath.

And that's what sends me over the edge. My orgasm rocks me unexpectedly, and I clench the muscles of my core around him. He removes his fingers from my mouth and wraps his arms around me, pulling me tight as I cry his name into his shoulder. "That's it, Lark. I love feeling you come. Fuck, you feel good." He continues to voice his encouragement as waves of pleasure wash over me. In a few more thrusts, he's shuddering inside me, too, tightening his grip and moving as far into me as he can get. I shout out again at the exquisite feel of him stretching me even further.

Our breaths come in heavy gasps for a moment before he lifts me off of him and flips me sideways onto my back. It's so unexpected that I giggle. "What are you doing?" I say, but my laughter is cut short at the way he's looking between my legs.

"I've never...done that before." He sounds unsure, but there's no mistaking the heat in his gaze as he watches his cum drip out of me. "Are you okay?"

Reaching between us, I lace my fingers with his. "I'm great. Are you?"

"Yeah." He laughs lightly, his gaze dipping between my legs again. "I liked that probably more than I should have."

"No such thing," I assure him. Biting my lip, I look down my body.

The grin he flashes me is so relieved, so boyish, that my chest physically aches. I don't know how to tell him that I've never felt more safe or more willing to explore my own pleasure and someone else's than I have with him these past few weeks. Nothing feels shameful, only new. I know I can tell him I don't want to do something at any time, but he hasn't yet found anything I don't like. As I'm lying here, deeply satisfied and so well-loved, all of that is too big and unwieldy to broach. So, instead, I just say, "I'm right there with you."

He slides up the side of the couch so he can squeeze himself between my body and the back of it. Tucking a piece of hair behind my ear, he studies me, his hazel eyes bouncing back and forth between mine. "For the rest of our lives?" he repeats on a whisper, like he's checking to make sure that wasn't the heat of the moment talking.

"For as long as you'll have me."

He chuckles as he throws his arm over my torso and draws me closer. "Buckle up, Songbird. I'm not going anywhere."

We settle into each other, the late afternoon light casting beams of gold and orange across the apartment as Lennon traces the lines of my body and we whisper sweet nothings between kisses. And just for today, I let myself believe that it could be this easy to just stay here and never let him go.

CHAPTER 24

LENNON

Watching Lark from the audience and not the sound booth was a different experience, but when she asked me to fly back for a weekend to see her as the lead during her junior year of college, who was I to refuse? I'd certainly never say no to her if I could help it.

She had sent out a mass email and bought tickets for all of us, so I was sitting between Richard and her parents. Richard had insisted that he needed an aisle seat to stretch his legs. I had bitten my tongue against reminding him that I was two inches taller and this newly renovated theater was designed for people of average height, like himself. Comparing height for no reason felt like a juvenile thing to do, and we were adults now. So, instead, I sat happily next to Lark's mother and indulged her proud, whispered comments every time Lark sang or danced. When she came out in a poodle skirt and cardigan, her mom practically squealed about how cute she was. I had to agree. Richard, however, made no comments at all. It didn't even seem like he was all that interested.

Watching Lark was a joy, as always. Her blue eyes sparkled in the stage lights, and she looked almost weightless as she danced. Every joke landed, and the audience ate it up. It was no surprise to me. I had seen Lark own the stage a thousand times before, but it was no less special to see it now.

Richard, however, looked around at the audience every time they laughed at something funny, almost as if he was surprised. When she leaned in for a kiss with the male lead, he visibly bristled, and I had to fight against the urge to lean over and remind him that she was acting.

At intermission, Lark's parents left to use the restroom in a flutter of happiness. Richard stood to stretch, and I averted my eyes from the swath of hairy skin that appeared under the hem of his shirt when he raised his arms.

"I'm so ready for this show to be over," he said as he settled back into his seat.

"I hadn't realized you did a lot of work on it," I said drily.

"No." He scoffed. "I mean I'm sick of these late nights. Lark wants to be home with me, not killing herself for this." He waved at the stage.

I eyed him sidelong, then shifted my gaze to the red velvet curtain currently blocking the view of the stage. Shadows of feet moving set pieces hustled back and forth under the yellow fringe at the bottom. I remembered those days with a pang—all hands on deck to move a giant set. Assistant directors and stage managers whispering directions and brandishing clipboards. Actors shimmying in and out of costumes for the second half. I pictured someone back there calling, "Five till curtain!" And Lark and the others responding, "thank you, five." The energy was palpable, even from here. Even as an audience member.

I couldn't imagine anyone wishing for the end of a show's run. Certainly not Lark.

"She loves this," I muttered, unable to help myself.

"She loves me more." Richard shrugged. "A lot has changed since you've been gone, Johnny. She's just getting this out of her system so she can settle down and marry me. And then we can put all this behind us."

He only used that nickname for me because Lark wasn't here. It scraped against the raw edges of my emotions, which were already on high from seeing her onstage again. I had to be comfortable taking the moral high ground and not responding by calling him Dick, which he also hated.

But he knew exactly what he was doing, striking up this conversation with me. He was staking his claim on her by telling me things had changed. He wanted me to think I was the outsider here. And maybe I was, but I didn't want to spiral into heart palpitations and anxious thoughts on the one night I got to see Lark, so I gritted my teeth and took a couple of deep breaths until her parents came back and the lights dimmed again.

The second half was even better than the first, and when it was over, we waited for Lark in the lobby. I held a simple bouquet of pink lilies. Richard cradled a giant one of probably about two dozen red roses, and I had the dim thought that he was overdoing it to cover up his annoyance at the whole thing.

I heard Lark's effervescent laughter rise up over the din of the crowd before I saw her. But as soon as she came into view, her eyes landed on me. She had been so busy backstage and my flight had been delayed, so I hadn't seen her before the show, but now it was like the whole world stopped in the moment before she ran and launched herself into my arms. I dropped her bouquet to the ground so I could squeeze her to me.

"You came." She laughed into my neck. "I'm so glad."

"Of course I came," I said into her hair, which was still stiff and smelled strongly of hairspray.

"Honey," Richard's condescension grated on my last nerve. "You're getting makeup all over his shirt."

Lark pulled back, but her eyes didn't leave mine. "He doesn't care, do you, Lennon?"

I shook my head. Who the fuck cared about a little makeup when I was holding Lark again after almost a year of being apart?

"Well, you'll have to wash your face before I take you out to celebrate," he insisted.

At that, she removed herself from my grasp, and I immediately felt the lack of her. My fingers itched to touch her again, to remind myself that she was real and I was here.

She frowned in his direction. "What do you mean, before you take me out?"

"I have reservations for us at that Italian place you like," he said. "I thought I told you."

She shook her head. "I would have remembered that, because I would have reminded you that my parents and Lennon were going to be here and I want to go out with everyone."

Richard pouted, and the motion was so childish, I had to shove my fists into my pocket to avoid decking it right off his face. "But I haven't gotten any time with you lately."

Lark faltered. "I know, but..." Then her eyes grew fierce as she subtly planted her feet. "Richard, don't make me choose. You won't like the choice I make."

I awaken to sunlight streaming through a crack in my curtains and music coming from somewhere outside my bedroom. In that daze between dreaming and fully awake, I roll over and try to snuggle Lark closer to me, only she's not there. And then it registers that what I'm hearing isn't music playing. It's Lark singing. I lie still and listen for a while. It's mostly humming, but the melody is clear. It's a song about summer love from her lead role that year in college. No wonder I was dreaming about being there with her.

There's no questioning it anymore. After a week and a half of having her in my bed, I'm sure of it. I want to wake up to Lark's beautiful voice every day for the rest of my life.

I emerge from my bed and quietly open the door to lean against the doorframe and watch her. She's already dressed, and from this angle, I can just see the outline of her perfect ass where it meets the curve of her back as she wiggles to the beat of her song.

Something clatters on the counter, and she laughs quietly at herself before leaving the bathroom. That's when she notices me, and as soon as she does, her cheeks turn a gorgeous pink that matches the airy blouse she's tucked into her jeans.

"Sorry. I didn't mean to wake you," she says with a shy smile.

I shake my head, unable to take my eyes off her. "I haven't heard you sing in a long time."

She shrugs a shoulder and averts her gaze. "I haven't really felt like singing in a long time."

My heart breaks and soars in equal measure. I had thought that I hadn't heard her sing because why would she spontaneously break into song over the phone? But to hear that my Songbird hasn't been singing at all is devastating. And yet the knowledge that I've had a part in making her want to sing again blooms in my chest.

I push off the doorframe and close the distance between us. One hand lands on her hip, and I use the other to thread through her hair, still warm from her curling iron.

"I make you want to sing," I practically whisper as she tilts her head up and leans into me.

A breathy laugh escapes between her lips, and I know before she even says anything that she's going to give me shit. "That's a bit presumptuous. There could be a lot of reasons why I want to sing."

I shake my head and tighten my grip on her hair. "Mm-mmm. Admit it—it's me."

"*Such* an ego." She smirks. "I don't know how you carry that thing around with you."

"It's heavier than you are," I say before I quickly swoop in to pick her up and throw her over my shoulder.

She shrieks in surprise. "Lennon, oh my god. Put me down!"

I take a few steps toward my bedroom. "Not until you tell me how happy I make you."

"This is a ridiculous display of toxic masculinity," she protests, even though her voice is edged with laughter. "Your need for me to fawn over you speaks volumes." She squeals again as I toss her onto the bed. "I just did my hair!"

"And I'm going to mess it up if you don't do as I say." I wink.

She props herself up on her elbows to look up at me as I stand over her. I palm my hard-on over the fabric of my boxers as I watch her eyes go dark and her teeth nab her bottom lip.

"In that case, I'm definitely not going to stroke your ego." Her hooded gaze drops to where my hand is working against myself. "But I might be persuaded to stroke something else."

I can't help the laugh that falls out of me. "And you think I'm ridiculous? What kind of a line was that?"

She just shrugs and reaches up to grab my shirt and pull me on top of her so we're a tangle of limbs and teeth and tongues.

***

I gape at him, my mouth opening and closing like a fish out of water. And that's how I feel—completely out of my element. Floundering. I can't believe he had the audacity to suggest I'm nothing more than his intern. After a weekend away at his lakeside cabin where we did little more than fuck and drink wine, no less.

But if I'm being honest with myself, the person I'm angriest at is myself. For thinking this could ever be anything more than a fling. For daring to hope his feelings had grown in time with mine. For falling for Marcus despite the ground rules we set out for this tryst at the beginning.

I've known Lark for my entire life. Or at least, for all the years that have mattered. But she still continues to surprise me, and this audiobook is no different. I've read *Sizzling Secrets*. Jessica handed a copy to almost everyone she knew before she published it and begged us all for reviews. Acutely aware of how hard it is to be a struggling artist looking for some traction, I read through it and tossed a quick review on a couple of sites just to pay it forward. Turns out she didn't need any of us as the thing topped the charts within a week of its release, but it still felt like I had done a good deed.

The book was fine. Not my favorite genre, but I could see why people would like it. It would have probably been forgettable for me if not for being written by an acquaintance. But listening to Lark and Silas becoming these characters has brought this book to life. Sometimes I'll be so engrossed in their performances that I'll have to go back through and make sure I edited out all of the mistakes. When I'm making a list of pickups for each chapter, I have to listen through at least twice to be sure I caught everything because Lark's performance is so distracting.

She and Silas have undeniable chemistry. A few weeks ago, their clear star quality was making me antsy, like I was being torn apart with envy for the connection they had, and I maybe even wished I had been more interested in being onstage in my younger years to have had a shot at throwing my hat in the ring just to be the one in that booth with her. Shit, a few weeks ago, her sultry voice moaning about cocks and tattoos had me crawling out of my skin. But now that Lark and I are together, it's almost as if we are back in our little impenetrable bubble from high school. It's her and me. Silas's narration can be as sensual as he wants, but it doesn't matter. She's mine.

But they are sexy. Incredibly so. It's no wonder Noah and Jessica asked them both back for the next book. In fact, if this audiobook does as well as Noah has projected, it would be bad business if they hadn't. And I've started to dare to hope that it might mean she will stay here with me. It seems like all but a done deal. She's having fun. She loves the sunshine. She's always loved me. Why wouldn't she jump at the opportunity?

When I left Michigan after high school, I never intended to settle here. I wanted to travel, and I chose to work freelance gigs so I could do them from anywhere. But traveling alone didn't really appeal to me, and no woman I spent any time with stuck. Before I knew it, undergrad in LA turned into half my life here, and my quest to find someone turned into a parade of lovely women who all seemed to be missing something.

Turns out it was just that they weren't Lark.

As if I conjured her here, the citrus-and-sunshine scent that is characteristically *her* overtakes me. I close my eyes and breathe deeply. Lark's slim arms circle around my neck, and her hands snake down my pecs until her chin is resting on my shoulder. I rub a palm over her forearms.

"How does it sound?" Her breath tickles the hair at my ear.

I let my hand come to rest where her arms cross under my neck. "It's brilliant."

She scoffs. "You're biased."

"Maybe," I admit. "But I've never lied to you about a performance, either."

Her lips graze my cheek before she nuzzles into my neck. "Mmm." The sound vibrates against my skin. It ignites something deep inside me, and I grip her arm tighter.

"I've liked doing this," she says.

"Touching me?" I tease.

Her laugh is a buoyant thing. It lifts and bounces and settles deep in my chest. "No. Well, yes, but I meant recording the audiobook. It's really fun."

There's that little kernel of hope again. If she likes it enough, maybe she'll stay.

I clear my throat, trying not to let that kernel expand too far. I watched Richard clip her wings and keep her grounded for years, and I don't want to do that to her again. I don't want her to stay here just because I asked, so I refuse to sway her opinion.

"Touching me is fun, too." I twist in my chair so I can wink at her.

She pulls away and smacks my shoulder. "You have work to do, and I shouldn't be interrupting."

"Okay, but I fully plan on having some fun later," I call after her as she walks out of the room, swaying her hips.

She pauses to give me a look over her shoulder. "You're the worst."

"That's not a *no*." I raise my eyebrows suggestively.

Her voice takes on the same, sultry quality of her audiobook narration as she says, "It's definitely not a *no*." And then she continues her sauntering out of the room.

I don't know what I did to get so fortunate to have kept Lark in my life for so long, for us to have finally found each other in this way. But I do know I'm the luckiest man alive.

CHAPTER 25

LARK

"I wish I never left Michigan," Lennon mutters as his hand trails a path over the hill and valley of my waist and hip. It's that predawn moment that feels perfect for whispered secrets and quiet declarations—a little fortress of hazy light and warm blankets that will keep them safe from the harsh reality of the real world.

I frown and search his eyes. They're even more gold in the early morning light than they usually are. "Why?"

His hand stills on my hip, warmth seeping into my skin. "I'm angry that I missed so much time with you. We could have gotten here a lot sooner if I had been near you."

"That's sweet," I say, "but I think you're overestimating how much cuddle time a kid allows for."

He huffs, and his hand resumes its idle exploration of my body. "You know what I mean."

I do know what he means, because I feel it, too. Of course, we will never know if we would have taken this step before now if we were in closer proximity, but it's possible. We've always loved each other. There were a few emotionally charged moments in high school. I may have realized Richard and I weren't a good couple much earlier if Lennon had been around in college, though it pains me to think that might have meant never having Devin. But even with Devin, if Lennon and I had been together, my life would have looked so much different. I might have been able to perform more or had the freedom to be happier at the very least. It's not that Richard didn't want me to be happy; it's just that we weren't, and we didn't realize it until it had grown so big there was no ignoring it anymore.

Anger might not be the word I'd use to describe it, but I certainly resent the time I could have spent feeling loved and cherished like I do now.

This isn't something I particularly want to talk about. It's water under the bridge. When Lennon decided to go to USC, it seemed like a good choice for him. Much as I tried to help him grow roots in Ann Arbor, he was always a little resistant, like he was ready for the next move. I suppose with parents who moved as much as his did, he had to be. So when he told me he was going to go, it made sense. And then I wasn't surprised when he didn't want to give up that California sunshine. Being here myself, I can see exactly why he wouldn't have wanted to come back. Everything feels lighter and happier here. I'm not sure if that's because of Lennon or the additional vitamin D or both.

But we are still in that security of predawn, so I ask, "Why did you leave?"

Lennon's gaze immediately breaks away from mine. It dips down toward the mattress, as if he doesn't want to look at me while he talks about this. "I was a stupid kid." Each word is a deliberate choice. He shakes his head a little as if he can't even believe his past decisions. "USC was great—don't get me wrong. Obviously, I loved it here enough to stay. But I never really meant to settle here. I've never settled anywhere in my life." He pauses, then runs his tongue over his teeth and shrugs. "I took some jobs, got set up, found a roommate...one job led to another, and all of a sudden, I was forty."

I huff a laugh. "It happened fast."

"Really fast." His eyes meet mine again, earnest and clear. "I told you I almost packed it up and came back the last time I saw you."

The sound of the pillow scrapes in my ear as I nod against it. "Why didn't you?"

He shrugs again. "You deserve someone who doesn't get the itch to just pick up and start over when the opportunity arises."

"You wouldn't do that," I protest. "You've been the most constant thing in my life since we were teenagers. You've lived in this city for almost two decades."

"Ten years ago, I almost did, though. I almost left here on a whim to move back to you. And I wasn't sure what I wanted," he says quietly. There's a vulnerability in his voice that makes my heart ache. "Richard had just left you. Devin was still little. Everything felt tenuous for you. I didn't want to add to the pile of projects for you to work on."

I narrow my eyes, studying him. "You're not a project for me to work on."

"Not anymore, maybe. But I was when we were kids, and I would have been if I had moved back then, too."

"I really wish you'd stop talking about my best friend like that." I tick up an eyebrow. The sass earns me a small smile, but I can tell these wounds still run deep. Decades of jokes and reassurances haven't mended them; they aren't going to fix it now.

That tiny upward bent of his mouth turns melancholy. "I don't want to ask you to stay, Songbird."

My mouth pops open to argue, but I can't get any words out around the sudden lump in my throat. I've been so busy rolling that email from Carl and the offer from Noah and the feel of Lennon's body around in my head with pros and cons and more than a little trepidation about the possibility of giving up a life I worked so hard for to start over somewhere new. For a man, no less.

No, not just a man. Lennon. My Lennon.

Nonetheless, underneath it all runs the knowledge that he can do his sound editing from anywhere. I can record from anywhere, too. But that stable job I fought through sleepless nights and rushing around to mommy-and-me classes and the tearful clinging at daycare drop-off to keep—that stability Lennon just said he didn't want to mess up—that's back home, in Ann Arbor.

And yet his words have a vice grip on my chest. I had thought we'd figure it out together, not that he'd send me packing.

He must see the entire war play out on my face, because his eyes go wide and he inhales sharply. "I mean, I don't want to ask you to stay because I don't want to pressure you. Not because I don't want you here." He laughs at himself. "I don't think I could live here without you if you decided to go. It wouldn't be the same, now that you've been here. Now that I've had you." He kisses me then—long and deep. It curls my toes and settles my heart.

"You could come back with me," I whisper when we pull apart. My eyes are still closed. "I know we said we wouldn't talk about it until I finish recording, but you said you almost came back ten years ago. Why not now?" I open my eyes to find his. They anchor me.

"I could," he says slowly. "But is that really want you want?"

His words land in the space between us. I can't fully absorb them, because I don't know how to answer. I wait, silently, for some revelation, but it doesn't come.

"I'll be honest," he says, offering me a lifeline, "I'd go back with you if you wanted me. I've been thinking a lot about it. But that's not what I want." He takes my chin between his thumb and forefinger so I have to look at him. "I missed *you*, Lark. Not Michigan. And if I were with you back there, I'd have you but I'd miss LA."

I crinkle my face at him. "Feels like a bit of a double standard. You don't think I'd miss Ann Arbor if I moved here?"

"Would you?" he asks.

The question is sincere, and I should retort that yes, of course I would miss the place where I grew up, where my kid grew up, where I went to undergrad and grad school and landed the job I've held for fifteen years. Where I got married, and where I got divorced. Where Hannah and my parents are.

But I'm going to miss it here, too.

"It's a lot to think about," I admit.

"Then think about it." He kisses my nose. "There's no rush. We have twenty-five years behind us and hopefully at least that many more in front of us. We have time."

He's right. I know he is. But now that I've had a taste of him, I know it'll never be enough. My time here is running out, too. We're wrapping up the primary recording of the audiobook this week, and I'll need to respond to Carl's email soon.

Lennon uses the hand resting on my hip to pull my body so it's flush with his so he can kiss me again. The hard length of his desire presses against my torso. The knowledge that I'm the one causing this reaction in him is still so new and exciting. I want to explore it every chance I get.

"I love you," I say between kisses.

"You're my favorite person in the world," he says back.

I try to tell myself that's as good as an *I love you*. He doesn't have to say it. This is just what we say—what we've always said. Maybe it's too soon to step from *love* to *in love*, even though I know I've fallen deeply and hopelessly in love with my best friend. It's been twenty-five years in the making; there's no point in denying it anymore.

He'll get there. If what he's said to me these past weeks is any indication, he's as far in as I am.

I push these thoughts away to worry about later. Lennon's right. We have plenty of time.

***

"So, Lark." Jessica leans her elbows on the small table outside the studio building and props her chin on her clasped hands. "I don't know if Noah has told you, but I'd love for you to come on board to narrate my sequel."

I glance at the man in question. He's still poking around his bowl, but he looks up at me. Silas pauses mid-chug of his water bottle, and a little of it drips down his chin. There are two empty bottles lined up in front of him. In retrospect, it was a bad idea to let Jessica ploy us with spicy burrito bowls, and we'll likely have to call it for the day. Luckily, we had a great morning and only have a chapter each to go.

I push my half-finished lunch closer to the middle of the table. "He has," I say simply. My phone dings from where it sits face down on the table. I pick it up quickly, hoping to at least buy myself some time before I have to answer the question I know is coming next.

> Devin: Dad and Rachel are already driving me bananas. And don't get me started on RJ. Did I ask this many questions when I was five?

I chuckle as I shake my head and type out a quick reply. She made it two weeks, which is actually pretty good.

> Lark: Yes. You did. You'll be out of their house and in your dorm soon enough. I'm excited to come help set it up with you!

> Devin: Yeah, you can be a buffer when you get here.

> Lark: Happy to.

I put my phone down and give my attention back to Jessica. "Sorry—that was my daughter."

"Awww," she croons. "I bet you miss her. Her dad's not in the picture?"

"I do," I agree. "And her dad is still around. She's with him now, in New York. She'll start at NYU in a few weeks."

"That's a great school," Silas chimes in. "Is she going to study acting like her mom?"

"No. She's declared a journalism major."

"Will you head out there to help her get settled, then?" Noah asks.

I nod. "That's what she was texting me about, actually. She's ready to be out of her dad's house."

"I remember I couldn't wait to be free of my parents, too. That's how I ended up in LA, thinking I could be a screenwriter." Jessica sighs wistfully. "Such a fun age. All that reckless abandon and trying new things on your way to your true potential."

I laugh lightly. "Funny—I feel like you just described me this summer. Maybe she and I can do it together."

Jessica tilts so far forward, I'm afraid her chair is going to tip right out from under her. "Yes! That's why I love your narration on this book, I think. It's full of new energy and bold determination. It's like you really *feel* Gia's character, you know?"

I wouldn't peg Gia as a woman on a journey of self-discovery, but I smile and nod anyway. *Keep Jessica happy* has been the mantra of the entire project, so I'm not about to present her with an alternate interpretation. "It has been a challenging role, so I'm glad you're satisfied with what you've heard so far."

"I am." She reaches over to cover my hand with hers. "Which is why you simply *have* to come on board for the next book. Silas has already signed on—right, Si?"

Silas nods and winks at her. "I'm yours for as long as you need me."

Jessica shoots what I imagine is her best puppy-dog look at me, though she looks more constipated than pleading. I stifle a laugh with my hand that isn't currently trapped by hers.

"Please?" she pouts. "It would be so cool to keep my narrators consistent, and I just love you so much, Lark."

There's probably no harm in signing on to this project, even if I haven't decided where I'll be recording. "Well, how can I say no to that?" I say.

Jessica gasps and covers her red lips with both her hands. "Oh my god. Really?" she squeals. "Ah! I'm so excited!"

My phone dings again, and I pick it up while Jessica gushes some more.

> Devin: My dorm will be cool, but I already can't wait to be home for winter break. I miss you.

I read and reread that message before it fully sinks in. Home. Michigan. Our townhouse. Her safe space.

I've been so selfish. Lennon and I haven't figured everything out, but I have more than entertained the idea of staying. And yet not once have I really thought about what moving to LA would do to Devin. She's already left the nest, which has been scary and new for her; how is she going to feel if there's no nest to come back to? No comfortable place for her to call home?

There's no question about it. I would lay down my life for my daughter. I have gone without so she can have everything, and I'd do it again and again. But I can't escape the pang of regret that shoots through my entire body at the realization that I can't stay here. Even if Devin only comes home on breaks, she has to have a home to come back to. She deserves that place to be somewhere she feels comfortable.

That pang turns to a physical ache when I remember what Lennon said to me the other morning. He won't be happy in Michigan. He'd move there for me, but he doesn't want to. I rub at my chest as if that could make the pain go away.

"Lennon will be so happy," Jessica is saying suggestively when I force myself to tune back into the conversation. At my confused look, she explains, "That you're staying here, I mean."

"I...oh. Well, I hadn't thought—"

"You two are finally an item, right?" she presses. "Noah said he saw you two kissing outside the studio."

He had seen us. Probably multiple times. We haven't exactly been hiding our goodbye kisses when he drops me off or our coy smiles when he picks me up. No one has said anything, but I'd be a fool to think they haven't noticed.

"I guess, yeah. We just haven't really talked about logistics yet," I say, stumbling over the words.

Silas looks between the two of us, and he must pick up on my distress, because he comes to my aide. "This is really none of your business, Jess," he warns quietly.

"I think we can take the good news that Lark is on board as a win today and come back to finish recording tomorrow." Noah starts to stand, clearly trying to help me end this conversation.

"Sorry," Jessica sings, completely unaffected as she stands and starts to gather the garbage from her lunch. "I was just excited to hear it. That man is a hard one to nail down, if you know what I mean. It'd be a shame if someone *finally* got him to commit only to turn around and leave."

Maybe I'm reading into it, but she says it like he has something fundamentally wrong with him. Like he's a loose cannon or someone people need to tie down. And despite the turmoil of all the possible decisions floating in the ether, protectiveness surges up and cuts through them. "He hasn't always had it easy, you know."

Jessica tilts her head and looks down at me. "What do you mean?"

"It's not really my story to tell, but he keeps a lot of people at arm's length. Especially ones he's not sure he can trust." The implication hangs in the air between us. I've probably just thrown *keep Jessica happy* right out the window, but I don't care. Our relationship is not her business, no matter who she is. No one suggests my best friend is anything less than amazing.

Jessica slinks back into her chair and covers her hand with mine again. "I'm sorry, Lark. I didn't mean anything by that. Lennon is such a great man, but you're right. I don't know him, or you, very well." She laughs, but there's no humor in it. "I'm a romance writer. I exist in boy-meets-girl, boy-kisses-girl, boy-and-girl-live-happily-ever-after. Sometimes I forget it's more complicated than that."

Her eyes widen, and her perfectly groomed eyebrows pinch upward slightly as she squeezes my hand. She's being genuine, and I probably overreacted as a result of all of these choices weighing down on me at once.

I dig deep for a sense of lightheartedness, for a joke that might clear the air. "Don't forget boy-fucks-girl." I smile weakly. Everyone barks out surprised laughter, which snaps the tension between us.

"I bet it's good, too," she says under her breath so only I can hear.

"You have no idea."

The door to the back patio bursts open, and Lennon steps out into the sunlight. My insides go all gooey at the sight of him in his sleeveless muscle tee and backward baseball cap. A slight metallic scent comes off of him. He must have gone to the gym before stopping by.

"Well, speak of the devil," Jessica teases. She squeezes my hand once more before letting go to finish gathering her trash.

"I'm glad you're here," Noah starts, always business. "I have a few notes to go over with you." He holds the door open, and they go back inside. Silas follows, tossing his water bottles into the recycling bin on the way.

I stand to also dispose of my garbage. Jessica lingers, and I can feel her dark eyes on me the whole time I'm gathering my things.

"You're not mad at me, are you?" She sounds so much like a lost, scared little girl that my heart breaks for her. "I'm sorry. I have a hard time making friends. Probably because I keep putting my foot in my mouth." She shrugs. "But I've been thinking of us as friends. I thought it was just a friendly conversation."

I shake my head. "No, I'm not mad." I sigh, searching her features for any sign of disingenuousness or malice. I come up empty. Maybe she really does want to be friends, so I give her the benefit of the doubt. "I have a whole life back home, you know? I haven't decided what I'm going to do."

Jessica's expression goes slack, and I'm almost certain there are tears glistening at the corners of her eyes. "Yeah," she says shakily. "I missed home a lot when I first got here. Still do sometimes."

"Where is home for you?" I ask.

"A tiny town in northern Maine. Population two-thou-sand-eighty-one. We don't even have a stoplight." She leans forward conspiratorially. "My name isn't even Jessica. My mom begged me to use a pen name so I didn't embarrass anyone out there with my smut."

I can't hide the look of surprise as it crosses my face. "Whoa. I never would have guessed."

"I know, right? Everyone out here is good at playing a part, and I'm no exception." She chuckles at herself, then gets serious. "That's what I like about you, Lark. You're playing a part in there"—she waves at the studio doors—"but out here, you seem really *real*."

I soften at her compliment. Admittedly, I have had my reservations about her since we met, but her willingness to open up and show me a piece of herself I get the sense she doesn't show many people warms me.

"Thanks." I smile a little. "I try."

"It'd be cool if you stayed." She shrugs. "I'd love to get to know you better if we had the chance." Her bright crimson lips split into a grin for a moment, then she nods and lays her manicured hand on the doorknob.

"What's your real name?" I blurt out. "You know, if you want to tell me. Between friends."

She faces me fully, her eyes shining with mischief. "Tanya Jacobs," she whispers, as if there were anyone else out here to hear her secret. "But if you tell anyone, I'll personally make sure your tea is only lukewarm for the rest of your life."

I burst into loud, bright laughter just as Lennon comes back out onto the patio. He looks between us, his wide eyes betraying more than a little apprehension. Maybe it's intimidating to him—Jessica still wearing an impish smirk and me bent over cackling. He smiles cautiously. "Noah said you're done for the day. Ready to go?"

I wipe the corners of my eyes. "Sure. Let me just grab my purse."

As I pass by both of them and back into the studio, I hear Jessica say quietly, "Hang on to that one."

And Lennon responds, "I plan to."

CHAPTER 26

LENNON

WE'RE ALL IN THE studio on the last day of recording—Noah, Jessica, and me. Even the intern decided to stay to hear the end. Lark and Silas are in their booths, and they share a little smile through the glass before he starts. After a few lines, Lark looks out the window facing the rest of us. Her blue eyes catch mine, and she winks just before she comes in with her dialogue.

I haven't been in the studio since we started this whole thing. First, it was because I didn't want to have to hide my raging hard-on every time Lark's voice dipped into the sultry, raspy tone I heard in her audition. Now I know that's part of the act. While it's still sexy as hell, the tone she uses when we're alone is much closer to her normal voice. The little moans and gasps I'm able to pull out of her are unlike anything I've ever heard from her before, and I like that she doesn't try to mimic that for this recording.

After a while, though, I stayed away to avoid messing her up, and also because by then, I had plenty of work to do on the chapters they had finished. Since we were behind from the start and switched to a more time-intensive duet at the last minute, Noah wanted me to edit chapters as they were finished. It worked well, and it also means the final product will be released within the next couple of weeks.

Seeing the way they work together, it's easy to understand how they have such incredible chemistry. This is what happens when you have two professionals in a room together. They check in with glances and quick nods or shakes of their heads. Once, Silas clearly doesn't like the way he delivers a line and winces. Lark doesn't miss a beat. She pauses before her dialogue, waiting to see if he's going to redo it, which he does. Their easy rapport is something really special to watch.

When Silas finishes his last chapter, he lingers in silence with his hands over his headphones for a second. Everyone in the studio is holding their breath before he takes them off, a smile slowly working its way upward as he continues to look down at the script in front of him. He nods once, and we all burst into a round of applause.

Noah glances at Jessica, who gives him a thumbs-up. He presses a button on the board so Silas can talk to them. "Really nice, Si. How do you feel?"

Silas swallows a sip of water and wipes his lips with the back of his hand. "Good. It felt right in here."

"Sounded great out here. Lark, are you ready, or do you want to take a break?" Noah asks.

Lark faces us, her face lit up and her eyes glittering. She's alive, practically vibrating from head to toe like she used to when she was onstage. She's so fucking beautiful. I can't breathe.

"I'd like to keep going, if it's okay with Silas? I don't want to lose this energy." She looks at him for confirmation, and he nods before taking another sip of water.

"Okay, let's go," Noah says, then clicks off his intercom so they can get started.

When any performance comes to a close, it's an emotional experience, and this one is no different. Even though the book itself has a happy ending, as Lark weaves her way through the joy Gia feels at having Marcus with her forever, Jessica sniffles next to me.

"I wrote that," she says quietly, a tear snaking its way down her cheek. "Those are my words."

I sling an arm around her shoulders and give a quick squeeze. "It's cool hearing it come to life, huh?"

"Mm-hmm," she says, her eyes glued to Lark through the window. She falls silent again as if she's absorbing every word.

"'Do you promise, Marcus?'" Lark reads. "'Will it really be forever this time?'"

"'Forever and a day,'" Silas promises in character.

They lock eyes through the window as Lark delivers her last line: "'I looked into his eyes and knew, without a doubt, that this man here—the man who kept all my sizzling secrets—was the only one for me.'"

She lets it hang there for a second—we all do—as if waiting for the curtain to close. Then, she rips the headphones off her ears and is out of the booth in a split second. Silas is close behind her, and they meet in the middle in a tight hug.

"That was so cool." Her voice quivers as she grips him tight. "Thank you for taking a chance with a rookie."

"You were a dream," he says as they pull apart.

Lark giggles and wipes at her eyes before Jessica darts between them, using an arm around each of their necks to pull them into a group hug. Silas pats her on the back, and she lets go of him to hold Lark at arm's length.

"I can't tell you what this performance means to me," Jessica says softly. "Thank you for taking care of my characters."

"It has been my absolute honor." Lark squeezes her elbows, then pulls her in for an embrace.

Noah leans over to talk to me as the two women continue chatting. "She's a natural. Thanks for finding her."

"She needed this," I tell him. "Seeing her performing again, excited..." I trail off because I don't have words for how wonderful it is. The Lark in front of me is an entirely different woman than the one I fell in love with in high school, but in so many ways, watching her today has been exactly like watching her then. Her talent and joy are a privilege to behold. I might have invited her here in a desperate attempt to help her find it again, but that magic I saw in the booth today...that's all her.

Noah claps me on the back as if he understands exactly what multitudes my silence holds. It's a show of solidarity; he knows what emotions these things bring up, and he stands there while they run over me.

As soon as Jessica releases her, Lark turns to me and launches herself into my arms. Her feet aren't even on the ground as I hold her tight, inhaling her citrus-and-sunshine shampoo and kissing her cheek.

I lower her to the ground slowly, angling her body so I can feel it dragging against mine. I cup her jaw and kiss her deeply. It's what I've wanted to do after almost every performance of hers I've ever seen, and I finally can.

Noah chuckles somewhere in the distance. Jessica swoons. Silas hums as if he called it from the beginning. But I don't care about any of it because I have my Songbird in my arms, and she just created something beautiful.

"I know you'll be honest," she says into my lips. "How was it?"

"Perfect." I smirk. "I doubt I'll have much to do on it. You're going to put me out of business."

She rolls her eyes and smacks my shoulders. "I'm serious!" she cries, then squeals as I catch her and spin her into my arms again.

"So am I," I insist. "It was perfect. You're perfect." I lean in to whisper the last part into her ear. The gorgeous flush of her cheeks belies the skeptical look she flashes.

I grasp her hand and hold it between us as we face the rest of the group. She rests her head on my shoulder and her other hand on my biceps, and I'm on top of the world.

"Are we celebrating?" I ask the group before looking down at Lark on my arm. "I've been wanting to take her to a LACMA jazz night. Anyone want to join?"

All of them eye each other, exchanging a silent conversation. "That sounds fun…" Jessica trails off. Silas clears his throat.

"We, uh, wouldn't want to crash your date. Again." Noah pulls at his beard, but I can still see it twitching with amusement.

Lark pinches my arm, and I look down. Her blue eyes are dancing. "I brought sparkling wine."

Jessica claps her hands giddily. "You did? Oh, that's brilliant!"

Releasing me, Lark walks over to where her purse rests on a chair in the corner. She reaches into it and produces a bottle. "Would you like to do the honors?" she asks Jessica.

"You just…carry a bottle of sparkling wine in your purse?" I ask.

"No," she says as if I'm an idiot. "I brought it because I knew we'd finish today."

"That purse is giant," Jessica says, taking the bottle from Lark's out-stretched hand.

"Mom life." Lark shrugs. "Once I started carrying a huge diaper bag, I realized how awesome it was to have that much space for everything and never looked back."

"And pockets!" Jessica exclaims, peeking inside.

"The pockets are the best feature," she agrees solemnly.

Noah shuffles around in a drawer and produces some cups while Jessica twists the wire off the cap. When she pops the cork, it goes flying. Silas and I duck while Lark's bright, beautiful laughter rings through the space.

Once everyone has some, we tap our cups together, offering congratulations and praise. Eventually, the intern leaves—probably for something more fun—and we move to the small table out back to finish the bottle.

Lark's phone chimes from her purse as we're headed outside. I hang back with her as she checks her messages. She reads for a second, then frowns deeply.

"Everything okay?" I ask.

She sighs as she types. "Yeah. Devin has a stomachache. I think Richard is probably stressing her out. It happens every summer." She finishes her message, then pockets her phone before we head outside.

I've worked on a lot of audiobooks over the years. It's always special finishing one, but this feels unique somehow. I don't know if it's because Lark is here, at the center of it all, or because of the clear camaraderie the four of them have developed over the weeks, but sharing a bottle of sparkling wine outside of the recording studio in the late-summer Los Angeles sunshine feels good. Like I was meant to be here. Like Lark was meant to be with me.

As the sun is beginning its descent, I suggest quietly to Lark that if we're going to make it to LACMA, we should head out. There are more hugs, more pats on the back, and then we're in the Jeep, the wind whipping through our hair and our fingers interlaced over the center console.

A few hours later, we're sitting on a blanket in the shade, listening to the erratic, energetic sounds of jazz music. As the sun sets, rows upon rows of white wrought-iron streetlights illuminate the grounds behind the stage. The effect of it is almost like an M. C. Escher drawing, the lights in rows creating an optical illusion behind the band.

Lark and I drink wine and eat the spread I've brought with us between stolen kisses and gentle touches. When she stands and starts swaying to the music, I just watch her. I'm completely in awe of her, always.

I'm in love with Lark. I know I am. Sure, it hasn't been very long that she's been here or that we've been together. But then again, this has been decades in the making. And watching her move her glorious hips to the beat of the music, soaking up that smile she's always had just for me, seeing her eyes sparkle in the lights behind the stage, I've never been more sure of anything in my life.

A small part of my mind snags on the fact that we haven't quite decided what to do or how to fit our lives together, but I haven't had nearly enough time to simply enjoy this version of her—the one who dances freely, who sings in the bathroom in the morning, who whispers secrets to me under the cover of night. The one who is here, next to me, lowering herself so she can sit on a blanket in a pool of her floral skirt, leaning over to rest her head on my shoulder. Sighing up at me, big blue eyes happy and at home.

"I love you, Lennon," she says.

And I should say it back. I want to. But I don't know yet what it would mean to fundamentally change our relationship in this way. If we're even ready for it. It's easy for her to love me out loud. She always has. But me? That's never been in my vocabulary.

Knowing it's not worthy of what she is to me, but meaning it with every fiber of my being, I say what I've always said, even though it's never been enough.

"You're my favorite person in the world, Songbird."

Chapter 27

Lark

THE CALL COMES SOMETIME between two and three in the morning. Parenting a teenager has meant that I always leave my phone on, even though the ringer is turned down. Doesn't matter; I'm a light sleeper. I answer it quickly, without bothering to look at who is calling. Lennon doesn't even stir as I whisper "Hello?" and swing my legs out of the bed. I step into the hallway and shut the door quietly behind me.

"Lark? Sorry to wake you," a woman's voice comes across the line.

I try to blink myself awake as I pull the phone away from my ear to look at the name. "Rachel?" I ask, panic starting to rise in my chest.

"Hi. Richard told me not to call. He said everything is fine, but I'm a mom, too, you know?" She sounds panicky, which definitely is not helping me calm down.

A few quick steps bring me to my bedroom, where I sit on the edge of the bed and take a deep breath. "What's going on?"

"Well, Devin's stomach started hurting this afternoon. We thought it was gas," she starts.

"She texted me about it," I say.

"Right. Well, it got worse. She started vomiting and spiked a fever. Richard just left with her to go to the hospital."

I pull my suitcase out from the closet and toss it onto the bed with one hand. The other is holding the phone so tightly, I'm starting to lose feeling in my fingertips. "What do you think it is?"

"I don't know. Probably nothing serious? But we thought it was best to take her to the ER, and I figured you'd want to know."

"What hospital?" I start opening drawers and throwing clothes into my suitcase as quickly as I can.

"I don't know. They left really fast. Richard said he'd text me with information once they got there."

"Okay." I try to stay as calm and collected as possible. Panic won't help me get my stuff packed and get to the airport. "I'll get on a flight out as quickly as I can. Will you text me updates?"

"Yes." She sounds relieved, like she wants me to come. Like she thinks I should be there. That doesn't feel like a great sign. "Fly safe. See you soon."

As soon as we hang up, I check for flights. The soonest departure is at five-thirty, which gives me about two hours to get to the airport if I'm going to have enough time to make it through security. I book the flight, then glance in the direction of Lennon's room. This is going to kill him. I already know it. But I have to be with Devin if she's as sick as Rachel's shaky voice suggested. In a last-minute decision, I also book a ride to the airport.

That done, I start frantically packing everything of mine I can see. I hadn't moved anything into Lennon's room, so all of my clothes are here somewhere. When that's done, I move to the bathroom, shoving bottles and creams and makeup into my toiletry bag. I'm zipping up my bag when the door to Lennon's room bangs open and his heavy footsteps sound in the hallway.

His big frame fills the doorway where he freezes, staring bleary-eyed down at me next to my suitcase. "What are you doing?" He rubs his eye with a fist and yawns.

"Devin is sick." I almost trip as I hurriedly pull on a pair of leggings.

Lennon blinks as if his brain hasn't quite caught up to what he's seeing. "What?"

I tug half of my short hair into a ponytail, then put on my bra and a T-shirt. "She's sick. Richard took her to the hospital. Rachel called to tell me."

"In New York?"

"Yes." I take one last look around the room. Funny how it felt like I had found a home here, yet I was able to pack up all my belongings in a matter of minutes.

"Wait, you're leaving?"

My hands land on my hips, and I start shaking from adrenaline. I press my lips together and breathe through my nose. Now is not the time. I can't freak out yet.

"I have to." I spell it out calmly. "My daughter is in the hospital."

"What are you going to do? Take the first flight out?" he asks incredulously.

"Yes."

He shakes his head. "By the time you get there, she'll be discharged."

"Maybe, but it doesn't matter. She's sick, and I need to be there."

"Lark, stay here. Wait for news. If it's bad, we'll fly out together," he says, as if he's trying to talk some sense into me. I bristle at his tone. How can he not understand that this isn't even a choice? My daughter is sick, so I'm going to be with her. He must see my reaction, because his face falls.

"If it's bad, I need to be there," I tell him. "I already booked my flight and a ride to the airport."

He gapes at me, all of the sleepiness completely wiped from his expression. "You were going to leave and not tell me?"

"I was going to tell you, but I knew what you were going to say."

Silence stretches between us as he folds his arms over his chest. "And what was I going to say?" he asks, his voice flat.

"This." I wave, encompassing the conversation between us. "You were going to beg me to stay and tell me I don't need to be there. But I do. She's my daughter."

From the grumble that starts in his chest, I can tell he's trying to hold back. He runs a frustrated hand through his hair before saying it anyway. "She's grown. She's going to college. Richard is with her. What are you going to do, jump on a plane every time she gets sick?"

It lands like a knife straight to my heart. I exhale a quick puff of air as I press my hand against my chest. "She's my daughter," I repeat slowly. "If she's in the hospital, yes, I will."

His expression turns pleading, all upturned eyebrows and wide eyes. "Lark—"

"Don't make me choose, Lennon," I cut him off before he can try to persuade me further. "Support me. Tell me it's going to be okay." My voice cracks. "Don't make me feel bad for leaving to see my daughter who is in the hospital."

"That's what I *am* saying. It's going to be okay. You're flying out there in a panic for nothing."

"I'd rather fly out for nothing than stay and have it be something. Why can't you understand that I have to go?" My phone chimes. I pick it up to see the notification that I have five minutes until my ride arrives. My breath is shaky as I draw it in, then let it slowly out. I heave my wheel-less suitcase past him, and he moves aside to let me.

"Are you coming back?" he asks quietly, his feet planted in the doorway.

"I don't know," I answer honestly. The past few minutes have been like a bucket of ice water thrown on the heat of our time together. I've been so consumed with the newness of our relationship that I never stopped to wonder what might happen when something like this inevitably came up. I stupidly thought we'd figure it out, but I can see now that he hasn't taken my very real responsibilities into consideration. It makes me wonder if he ever would because he's never had any. Not like this. And it dawns on me now that he knows I'm a parent in an abstract sense, but he isn't really aware of everything that means. I fear that he won't ever be happy with anything less than me giving my whole self to him. Which I can't ever do.

Neither of us says anything. He looks as hurt as I feel.

My phone chimes again. "My ride is here," I say as I glance at it.

"Lark—"

"I'll call you when I land, okay?"

His mouth snaps shut. He nods once, and I leave quickly, before the quivering in his lips can turn to the tears that might make me change my mind.

Chapter 28

Lennon

Lark is gone.

She was here one minute and gone the next. But standing in the hallway, my feet fixed to the floor as I try to push down the anxiety fighting its way out of my chest, she's still everywhere. She's in the two mugs sitting clean and overturned on the drying rack next to the sink. She's in the light that's still on in the hallway bathroom. She's on my lips, the taste of her lingering even a half hour after she's left. She's in the fucking *air*, her citrus-and-sunshine scent still swirling around me.

I squeeze my eyes shut so hard I see stars on my eyelids and press my thumb and forefinger into them. It's futile to hope that she'll magically reappear when I reopen them, but I take in a breath to the count of four, hold it, let it out the same way, and open them anyway.

She's not there. Because she left.

I'm ashamed to admit I don't know what to do. When my parents would vanish, she was always the one to save me from my anxiety getting really bad. Even when they'd stop by and leave just as suddenly like they did a few weeks ago, I'd always end up calling her. But now, who am I supposed to turn to?

When I promised her we'd remain friends no matter what happened, it didn't even occur to me that we'd ever be apart again. We'd figure out where to live, and everything would be fine. I never, ever thought we'd be physically separated. Which, in retrospect, was likely the result of not thinking at all rather than having come to any kind of conclusion about it.

But it's going to work out. She'll see that once she realizes Devin is okay. We'll talk. She'll land in New York, she'll call me, we'll hash out some details, and everything will be fine.

Don't make me choose.

I run a frustrated hand through my hair, tugging at it as my breathing quickens. I hadn't meant to suggest it was Devin or me. I'm not delusional enough to think I'd ever come out on top in that scenario, nor would I want to. My parents were shitty. They *never* chose me. I don't wish that on another person.

But Lark is reasonable. Steadfast. Rational. If that's how she read what I was saying to her, I must have fucked something up in the delivery. Or her fear for Devin clouded her ability to take what I was saying for what it was—a reassurance that everything would be fine. That we'd wait it out and go together if we had to.

Either way, this is all my fault. My therapist would probably say that thinking about it that way is destructive and not at all correct, but I don't see any way to share blame for this. I selfishly wanted her with me. I tried to hold her here instead of letting her go when she felt she needed to. Which, ironically, is exactly what I had been avoiding doing these past few weeks.

I dimly realize I can't stand in the hallway forever. She's not coming back, and I need to go through some motions to keep the anxiety at bay at least until I can talk to her again. Her flight probably leaves at five-thirty or six if she's on one of the first ones out. She won't land until eleven or noon. That's six or so hours. In the meantime, I can make coffee, shower, get ready, go to the studio, and explain to Noah what's going on.

Having a plan of small things to do helps calm me a bit, but when I glance at the sink and see our two mugs there again, I decide I can't face it. Instead, I turn right around and climb back into bed, pulling the covers up over my head and breathing in the scent of her that's still on my pillow.

***

Bang, bang, bang.

When I blink open my eyes, I immediately close them again as what must be late-afternoon sunlight streams through my open window. Lark and I had opened it last night to let the cool breeze in, and the loud sound of traffic floats through. It's also *hot*. And bright.

Bang, bang, bang.

And why is there banging?

I scrub a hand over my face to try to rub some life back into it. It's unsuccessful. But I have a dim awareness that the banging is coming from my front door, and if I don't stop it soon, someone on this floor is going to be pissed.

Grumbling expletives to myself, I throw on a shirt as I shuffle to the door. When I pull it open, Noah is standing there with his fist raised, ready to pound on it again. From the set of his jaw when he sees me, it looks like he might follow through anyway and bang my face in to knock some sense into me. I kind of wish he would.

"Oh, good. You're alive." He doesn't sound at all happy to have found me among the living, but I step aside to let him into my apartment anyway.

"What are you doing here?"

The hoarseness of my voices must surprise Noah because he halts on his way into my kitchen and gapes at me. "What the fuck happened to you?" He wrinkles his nose and takes a step backward. "You sound like shit, and you stink."

I lift the collar of my shirt over my nose and take a whiff. He's not wrong. I shrug and pass by him toward my coffee machine, forcing myself to swallow the lump in my throat at the sight of the two mugs next to the sink. "The window's been open in my bedroom, and it got hot. I must have been sweating."

"Lark lets you walk around smelling up the place like that?"

Nothing to do but state the obvious, I guess. "Lark's not here."

Noah looks around as if he's just noticing her absence, which is funny considering the lack of her is so big to me that it's practically squeezing all the air out of the room. "Where is she?" Each word is careful, deliberate.

"Gone."

He narrows his eyes. "What do you mean 'gone'?"

I put my mug underneath the spout of the coffee machine and push the button. It gurgles to life. "She left at around two-thirty."

"This morning?" Noah asks incredulously.

"Couldn't very well have been this afternoon yet, could it?" I snark, but then I hazard a quick glance at the clock. Four-ten. "Fuck," I mutter and all but run to my phone in the bedroom. She said she was going to call when she landed, which would have been hours ago.

But when I snatch the phone off the nightstand and look at it, there are eight missed calls, all from Noah. He must have come over because he was worried when I didn't answer.

She didn't call. She landed in New York and didn't call me like she said she would. Which either means Devin is not well or she's pissed. Or both.

My knees give out, and my ass meets the edge of the mattress as I continue to stare at my phone. Noah comes into the room holding my coffee. He sets it on the nightstand and crosses over to the window to close it. "I think you'd better shower, have some coffee, and tell me what the fuck is going on," he says. "In that order."

He sounds a lot like my therapist used to, and I have a vague awareness that I should probably make an appointment with him again. This is getting out of hand.

I practically drag myself to the shower, and I have to admit that the warm water feels good as it runs over me. It doesn't go as far as to wash away the past fourteen hours, but it clears away some of the haze. By the time I leave the bathroom, my brain is a little less foggy, and about halfway through the steaming cup of coffee Noah left for me to drink as I get dressed, I'm starting to feel human again.

He's waiting for me with his own cup of coffee at the kitchen counter when I emerge, and the asshole has the audacity to sniff the air when I approach. "Better," he declares. "Sit."

"I'm not a dog," I grumble, but I do as he says.

"No, but you clearly need some direction."

I pout into my coffee. "Fuck off."

Noah refills my cup for me, then does the same for himself. "Get it out of your system if you need to. You're not mad at me, and I can take it. But I'm not leaving here until you tell me what's going on. Did you two have a fight?"

"Yes," I admit. "But that's not why she left."

"Why did she leave?"

"Her daughter, Devin. She had to go to the hospital." They're cave-man sentences. Short and choppy. But it's all I have the energy for.

Thankfully, Noah seems willing to prod me for more information. "Oh, shit. Is she okay?"

I shrug. "No clue. Lark said she'd call when she landed, but she didn't."

He grunts, then clears his throat. "What did you do to piss her off?"

"Why does it have to be something I did? Why can't it be a mutual disagreement? Normal growing pains that come along with falling for your best friend?" I sip my coffee to avoid the glare Noah is shooting me from his end of the counter.

"Is that what it was?"

"Probably not."

He lets out a long and exasperated sigh. "Listen, Lennon. You ignored my calls, and I got worried. My schedule is cleared now. I've got all day, and you're not in great shape. So you can either tell me what happened and get it off your chest, or we can sit here in silence until I'm satisfied you're not going to stink up the place again. Your choice."

Don't make me choose.

I dip my head forward so I can thread my fingers through my hair as my elbow rests on the countertop. "I'm such an idiot."

"You're not going to get any argument from me," he quips.

I don't even have the energy to give him a look. The only thing I can do is breathe. For now, that has to be enough.

After a minute or so, Noah softens. "Tell me why you're an idiot, Lennon. It's probably not as bad as you think."

Taking in a deep breath through my nose, I lift my head and say to the space in front of me, "I told her she couldn't get on a plane to see her kid every time she got sick. I tried to suggest she stay here until she knew more, or she might be flying out there for nothing."

Noah hisses a breath in through his teeth. "Oof. That wasn't a great move."

"I see that now."

"Her kid was being taken to the hospital. The one who just moved out of the house. And you told her to wait it out?"

"It's more than that, though." Finally, I turn to look at him. "She's not sure where she's headed after this. She hadn't decided if she was going to stay at all. And now I'm worried I pushed her away and she's never coming back."

"You wanted her to move here permanently?" he asks. "Don't get me wrong. That would be great for us, but I didn't realize things were that serious yet."

I shake my head like I also can't believe it. "I didn't see this coming, either. When I invited her out here, it was because we needed someone for the audiobook—and because I was watching her fade away over a phone screen. She needed this, too."

Noah rubs his beard. "Let me guess. She's unsure about giving up her life and a job back in the Midwest?"

I nod. "I offered to move back, but I was honest. I told her I would do it for her even though I didn't want to. She was an entirely different person here, Noah. You didn't know her before this, but it was like she found herself again. It was the brightest I've seen her shine in a while. She belongs here with me."

"And you moved around your whole life, so now that you've found some permanence here, I imagine that'd be hard for you to give up," he suggests.

I hadn't really thought of it that way, but he's probably on to something. While settling in LA had never been intentional, it happened. That and my tattoos and desperately hanging on to my friendship with Lark was all probably, at its core, an attempt to prove I could make something last. Which would explain why the thought of packing up my life and moving it across the country gave me a lot of anxiety.

"Yeah," I croak out, swallowing and gripping my mug so hard my fingertips turn white.

"You love her?" Noah asks.

It's a simple question, and there's a simple answer. Yes. Of course I love her. More than anything or anyone in my entire life. So much that it consumes every waking thought, that her body near mine causes tiny explosions in every one of my cells.

But a simple *yes* isn't big enough to encompass everything she is to me. And I'm suddenly too emotional about it to say anything, so I just nod.

"Did you tell her?" he prods.

And this is where I know I'm the dumbest man alive, because no. I've done a million things, big and small, over the years to show her how much she means to me, but I've never told her. Not really. And when she needed me to do the biggest thing and get on that plane with her, come what may, I let her down. Even though she didn't ask me to come with her, she shouldn't have had to. I should have offered. And when she inevitably said no, I should have done it anyway.

Noah doesn't need me to admit it. My silence is admission enough. He sighs and sips his coffee, setting his mug carefully on the counter.

"What do I do?" I ask, my voice like sandpaper.

"You get on a plane. You find out where her kid is, and you go there. You wait until you know her kid is okay, then lay it all out. You tell her you fucking love her, and you do what it takes to fix this."

I huff a sad laugh. "You make it sound so easy."

"Because it is." He takes his phone out of his pocket and taps a few times. "There's a red-eye that'll get you there around six in the morning local time. Get some shit in a bag. I'll drive you to the airport." He smirks at me. "See? Easy."

"It's the rest of it that scares me," I say quietly.

"Well, yeah. Love is scary as fuck." He shrugs. "Take it one step at a time. And for the love of god"—he shoots me a pointed look—"don't forget to pack deodorant."

CHAPTER 29

LARK

SOMEWHERE OVER COLORADO, SMASHED in the middle seat between a heavy breather and a kid who can't be older than fourteen who looks nervous as hell, I remember Davey McMan, who somehow landed the role of Puck in *Midsummer* his freshman year. He was also nervous all the time during that show, but he was short and sprightly. When we slathered him in green face paint and an artfully torn sack of a costume, he somehow looked exactly right.

A ghost of a smile dances on my lips at the memory of Davey as Puck with a voice newly hit by puberty proclaiming to whoever played a blue-horned Oberon, "Lord, what fools these mortals be!"

Mr. Jensen, the director, paused rehearsal once after Davey exclaimed the line a little too artificially. I was waiting in the wings for my entrance when he said, "Do you know what that line means, Davey?"

"No, sir," Davey had responded with an exuberant innocence only a freshman could have. The rest of us would have made something up to try to impress Mr. Jensen, but Davey didn't know enough to pretend.

"The lovers onstage, they're pretty serious about this whole thing, right?" Mr. Jensen asked. Davey nodded, and Mr. Jensen continued. "And Puck is the one who caused this mess in the first place. Yet he still blames the mortals for all of it. It's their foolishness that has prompted this whole plot, according to him. But it's Shakespeare's way of saying that love turns mortals into fools."

I wish I had known at the time that Mr. Jensen was not only giving us an acting lesson but a life lesson. Love does, indeed, turn mortals into fools. Maybe Lennon was right in a way. Maybe my love for Devin has made me foolish enough to book a flight without knowing more about what was going on. But I've never been so glad that I trusted my instincts as I was when Richard himself called me as I was waiting at the gate and told me Devin has appendicitis and they were taking her back for emergency surgery.

I suppose I was a fool for ever loving Richard, too. We were always so different, even from the start. But I won't pretend I didn't love him. I know Lennon would prefer I didn't—he's said as much over the years—but I did.

My jaw clenches against the inclination to admit that I was a fool to fall for Lennon. I shake my head to myself to fend off more of those thoughts. Loving Lennon is a given. As simple and necessary as breathing. Falling in love with Lennon was inevitable. Being in love with Lennon is a privilege.

I am in love with Lennon. I doubt I'll ever love anyone as deeply and broadly as I do him. If that makes me a fool, so be it. I'd rather be a fool who has had a great love even for a short time than someone who's kept their wits and never really loved at all.

The teenager next to me purses his lips and breathes out slowly. A quick glance tells me his knuckles are white and his foot is bouncing up and down erratically. I bend over to retrieve my bag from under my seat and pull out some gum. I take some for myself, then tip the pack to him.

"Need some?" I ask.

He smiles weakly up at me, takes a piece, then returns to staring out the window. I wish I could offer him something more, but gum and a reassuring smile are about all I can muster up. He'll be okay. Hopefully we all will.

***

When we land, it's about two-fifteen in New York, even though my stomach is suggesting it's closer to lunchtime. Devin was going into surgery when I boarded the plane, so she's probably out by now. As soon as I can, I power up my phone and check my messages. There are three from Richard, but nothing else. My heart falls, but I don't know what I expected. Only that it's weird not to have any reassurances from Lennon. He has always gone through the hard stuff with me.

I guess I'll just have to do this one alone.

Gritting my teeth, I tap on Richard's messages.

> Richard: She's going back for surgery now. The surgeon says it should be over in an hour. Will update.

> Richard: I'm in the recovery room with her. She's not awake yet, but everything went fine.

> Richard: She's pretty groggy, but she seems okay. They're moving us to room 405. See you soon.

He attached a picture of a sleepy Devin flashing a goofy smile and a thumbs-up to the last one. If I were alone, I'd burst into relieved tears, but I don't have time for that. Getting to the hospital as quickly as possible is my top priority.

I check the time stamp on the last message to see it was sent at almost noon. She's probably been moved into her room by now, so I quickly get my suitcase from baggage claim and jump into one of the cabs waiting outside the airport.

It doesn't take me very long to find Devin's room when I get to the hospital. When I get to the wing where she is, one of the nurses stops me and asks who I'm here to see and if I'm family. She checks my ID and waves me through.

The scene that greets me when I arrive is one of the sweetest I've seen in a while. Devin is lying in her hospital bed playing a card game with Richard and Rachel's five-year-old son, RJ. He's giggling and smacking cards, and she's rolling her eyes and pretending she didn't just let him win. Richard and Rachel are sitting on a small couch underneath the one window in the room, smiling at the two of them.

I have flown with Devin out here and come back to get her, but she and Richard and I have only ever had lunch before I've left them to have their time, usually flying back home to teach during the summer term. I know Rachel, of course, but in the more recent years since Devin has been in high school, I have come out here less and less, opting instead to stay home and tutor or teach and save up as much as I can to cover some of her college tuition. I haven't ever seen the four of them interact like this. It equally warms my heart and throws me off.

They look like a family. Devin's easy rapport with RJ is obvious. Richard's adoration of both of them is painted right there on his face. And Rachel leaning on his arm, correcting RJ's behavior when he gets a little too rowdy completes the picture.

I'm on the verge of feeling like a true outsider here when Devin glances up from the card game and breaks into a huge grin. "Mom!" she exclaims. "You came!"

"I told her as she was heading back into surgery." Richard stands and hugs me. "She must not have remembered."

"Oh yeah." Devin squints like she's recalling it. "You did say something about her." She shrugs at me. "It's been a long day."

"No kidding." I let out a short laugh. "How are you feeling?" I place my suitcase in the corner of the room as far out of the way as possible and sit on the edge of the bed opposite RJ. He climbs off and sits in his mom's lap.

"Better now. Appendicitis is no joke." Her eyes go wide, and she shakes her head. "That *hurt*."

I pat her hand where it lies on top of the hospital blanket. "I'm sorry I wasn't here with you," I whisper, the tears I've been holding back all morning threatening to break through.

Richard clears his throat from where he's standing next to the couch. "It's about time we got RJ home. How about we give you and your mom some time, and I'll be back later. Where are you staying, Lark?"

Eyeing my full suitcase in the corner, I shrug. "I hadn't gotten that far."

He nods as if he assumed that much. "They want to keep her here tonight, so how about you stay in her room at our place until she's discharged, and we can go from there?"

I shoot him a grateful look. "Thank you. That would be great."

Rachel collects RJ's things. He gives Devin a quick fist bump on their way out. As Richard passes me, he squeezes me on the shoulder. And then, the room is silent except for the humming and beeping of all the machines Devin is hooked up to.

"So," she hedges. "Are you missing the end of your audiobook for this?"

"No. We finished primary recording yesterday. I just have some corrections left, but that's easy. I can do that from anywhere." I move over to the couch to give her some more room.

She frowns down at me. "Wouldn't you go back to do it?"

"Oh, honey," I say on a sigh. "I don't think so. I'd have to turn right around and head back here to move you into your dorm and then to Ann Arbor anyway."

Being a parent is so weird sometimes. You can see your kid for who they are, but you're sort of always seeing a previous version of them overlaid in your mind. Like now, when her face is scrunched up and one eye is squeezed shut, she's both eighteen and ten, looking at me with a mixture of confusion and skepticism.

"So you are going to stay here for a few weeks?"

"I really don't know, kiddo." I smile weakly. "I got on the first flight out of LA to be here, and I didn't think much past that."

A nurse comes in then to ask her a few questions and check her vitals. She makes a joke about me being Devin's sister, which we get all the time, so we both politely smile and make some small talk before the nurse leaves again.

After a few moments of painful silence, Devin asks, "How's Lennon?"

"Good," I say a little too quickly. "Good. Good, good."

"Mom." She sounds annoyed. "You're being weird. What is going on?"

"Nothing!" I insist. "I'm tired. I've been up since Rachel called me at two-something this morning."

Devin's unimpressed face is a thing of legend. She's been perfecting it since she was a tween. Sometimes I'd tease her about it, trying to make light of her hormonal tendency to be completely irritated with pretty much everything I said or did. But when she pins me with it now, my heart skips a beat in trepidation. I almost feel like I'm in trouble.

"Can we skip the part where you try to hide whatever it is you're hiding from me and you just tell me like the adult I am?" Her eyebrow ticks up at the end of her sentence as her lips form a tight line that leaves zero space for objections.

I gape at her. "Stop doing that. It's creepy."

"Doing what? Reading you like a book? It's not that hard."

"It's like you can see into my soul, and I don't like it."

She flashes me a tight smile. "I learned from the best." She pauses, then says, "That's you, in case that wasn't clear."

"Yeah, I got it. Thank you." There's probably no sense in hiding any of this from her. I was going to tell her eventually anyway. But I still pick at a loose thread on the couch to avoid looking at her. "LA was great. Working on that audiobook was... It was magical. I want to keep doing it."

"You should." She wiggles excitedly in her bed. "Oh my gosh, I've been thinking a lot about this. I've never been to LA. Real estate out there is super expensive, but I could come stay with you for a while on breaks, and—"

"Whoa. Hold your horses there. I've been looking into renting studio space in Ann Arbor. Maybe even soundproofing a room in the town-house so I can work from home."

"Pardon my French, Mom, but why the fuck would you do that?"

My eyes just about bug out of my head. "Watch it, young lady."

She unsurprisingly doesn't back down. "Seriously! Look at you! I mean, you look like crap because you've been worried since before dawn, and you smell like an airplane, but underneath that. I've never seen you seem so...what word am I looking for? *Relaxed. Confident.* Dare I say *tan*?"

I open my mouth to respond, but all that comes out is an incredulous bark of a laugh.

"You're practically glowing," she adds. Her mouth twists into a cocky smirk. "So, let me ask you again. How's Lennon?"

Frantically, I search my brain for something—anything—to tell her to get her off this train of conversation but come up empty. I shouldn't be surprised. It's been her and me for ten years. I've tried to protect her from a lot, but we've shared almost all of each other's vulnerable moments for the past decade. This isn't all that different. And while I don't want to shake up her entire world by telling her I've fallen in love with my best friend, she's going to find out eventually. It might as well be now.

"Lennon and I have been... Well, we..." I sigh. Okay, this is going to be harder than I thought.

Devin tries to come to my rescue. "Did you go out there and finally fall in love with him?"

"What do you mean, 'finally'?" I blurt out.

She gives me her epic eye roll, and I realize just how much I had missed her, because I even missed that, of all things. "Mom. Please. I'm *your* kid, but I'm not *a* kid. So, what? He's not here, so I'm guessing you had some kind of fallout, and now you're trying to pretend you don't want to run back to him in LA now that you know I'm okay?"

"What the hell?" I mutter under my breath. "I've got to say, this is really throwing me off."

Her face softens. "I want you to be happy, Mom. You've done so much for me, but it's your turn now. Lennon makes you happy. He always has. Go be with him."

"What about your home in Ann Arbor? You said you already couldn't wait to be home for break." It's a feeble protest, but I have to know. That text from her really made me reconsider some things.

"You're my home," she says simply. As if that single sentence isn't meant to fill me with joy. As if it doesn't change my entire life.

I've done a pretty decent job of holding back the waterworks. Until now. Silent tears stream down my face as Devin sits in her hospital bed with a dopey smile on her face.

"Don't get all emotional," she deadpans. "I already told you I want to visit you in LA. This is mostly selfish on my part."

I stare at her in awe. "How did I get such a great kid?"

She shrugs. "You basically made me. Must be that thing about the apple and the tree. So"—she claps her hands together and rests them in her lap—"are you going to patch things up with Lennon and move out there and live happily ever after?"

I wish it were that easy. But I can't get past the look on his face when I said I had to go. The suggestion that I should ignore my instincts about my kid for his benefit. The fact that I was scared and he didn't offer to come with me. And that nagging knowledge that he has never really told me he loves me. What if he doesn't, really? What if this is too much too soon? What if we can't ever figure out how to fit our lives together? It's crystal clear to me that this is more convoluted than just picking a place to live.

But Devin doesn't need to know all that, so I tilt my head, sigh, and say, "It's complicated right now, kiddo. Let's get you healthy, and then I can worry about the rest of it."

CHAPTER 30

LENNON

FLYING ACROSS THE ENTIRE country is the fucking worst.

Flying on a red-eye across the entire country is fucking hell.

At least it's quiet, so I try to sleep, but there's not really any sleeping on an airplane. There's especially no sleeping on an airplane when your best friend is on the other end of the flight and you're on your way to tell her you love her.

In between fits of sleep, I stare at the pitch-black nothingness outside the window and think about Lark making this same trip not twenty-four hours ago. She must have been so scared the whole time. Scared and sad. I let her down at the first real test of our relationship. I'm a better man than that. Now I just have to prove it to her.

Noah hit the nail on the head when he said I've been searching for something permanent for the better part of my life. But the most dependable, steadfast thing has always been Lark. She's been so permanent, in fact, that I never thought I could ever lose her. And while I hope the promises we made to always be friends no matter how this works out between us weren't meaningless, I don't want that anymore. I want her in my arms. I want to kiss her every chance I get. I want to shout out loud how much I love her every day for the rest of my life.

When the plane finally lands as the sun is just peeking over the New York City horizon, I remember what Lark told me the second day she was in LA. That she's a sunrise person, and I'm a sunset person. At the time, I had written it off as one of the funny eccentricities of our friendship. She wanted to be onstage, and I wanted to be behind the scenes. She had roots, and I was a traveler. She got married young, and I never settled down. She woke up with the sun, and I watched it set on my way to the club.

But here I am, contemplating the sunrise on my way to her. And I think I could be a sunrise person, too, if she wanted me to.

She still hasn't called or texted by the time I've turned my phone back on at the airport. I only have a backpack with essentials, so I go straight to the bathroom and freshen myself up as best I can. I brush my teeth in the sink, put on some deodorant—which Noah made me promise to do about ten times on the way to LAX—and change into an extra-soft T-shirt. Just in case.

Then, I grab a cup of coffee from the nearest café so I can use it to swallow my pride as I text Richard to find out what hospital Devin is in. I'm beyond grateful that he not only texts me back with the information but he does it without any snark.

I'll take all the good omens I can get.

And with that, I hail the cab that will take me to the love of my life.

CHAPTER 31

LARK

WHEN I LEFT THE hospital last night, the doctors were pretty sure they could discharge Devin today, so Richard and I are up early to get there as soon as visitor hours start. Rachel opts to stay home with RJ, so Richard drives me there. I slept most of the way to his house from the hospital last night, so it's really the first time we've been alone for any significant amount of time since the divorce. It's awkward for a million reasons. I can't stop thinking about Lennon, for one, and Richard clearly doesn't know what to say to me. Which is super great, because the drive from his house to the hospital is thirty minutes on a good day, and we run into traffic about ten minutes in.

"So," he starts slowly, "Devin said you've been in Los Angeles this summer?"

"Yeah. I've been recording an audiobook with Lennon."

He nods, drumming his fingers on the steering wheel. "Nice." After a long pause, he adds, "You had fun?"

"We don't have to do this," I quickly reassure him as kindly as I can. "You don't have to pretend to be interested in the shit I've been doing. It's really okay."

Frowning, he glances at me before returning his attention to the road. "I'm not pretending. It sounded really cool."

I lean my head against the headrest, looking out at the scenery slowly passing by his car. "It was."

We're silent for a while longer. Richard's phone buzzes in the center console. At a stoplight, he takes it out to look at it, taps it a few times, then returns it. He smirks to himself briefly, but it's gone as soon as it came on. Just when I think we're going to settle back into silence, he takes a loud, quick breath in. "Kind of incredible you and Lennon have remained friends for so long."

My eyebrows pinch together in thought, but I don't take my eyes off the landscape. "What do you mean?"

"He was in love with you in high school," Richard says matter-of-factly. "I always kind of thought you'd get together after we split."

I eye him sidelong before shrugging and slumping farther down in my seat. I'm not in the mood to have a conversation with my ex-husband about my best friend and our complicated reality. They don't even like each other.

"Yeah, well..." I trail off. "You can't be right about everything, I guess."

"Hmm," he hums, unconvinced. "Okay."

The way he says it grinds my gears. He doesn't buy it, but he also doesn't want some kind of confrontation about it. Which is fine, because I'm lying, but I also don't need to sit in a car with him for the next twenty minutes while he's all smug about it. I'm already miserable enough.

"I know you don't believe it, Lark," he says after a while, "but I do want you to be happy."

"I am happy," I retort without thinking. Another lie.

"Really? You don't seem very happy."

"It's been a long couple of days," I counter. Not a total lie.

He nods thoughtfully. "I was jealous of Lennon back then. You two have always had something special. If he makes you happy, you should run with it."

Dammit. Am I always this easy to read? I slowly face him with my mouth agape as we finally pull into the hospital parking lot. "Thanks, Richard," I finally manage. "That's...really decent of you."

He smiles at me, and then he's out of the car while I'm still sitting there, dumbstruck and very confused about where that conversation came from and what to make of it.

By the time we're in Devin's room again, I've shaken off most of the weirdness. The three of us chat for a few minutes before Richard goes off in search of some coffee. The nurse comes in to check the machines Devin is still hooked up to and then leaves with assurances that the doctor will be by shortly and that she should be able to leave the hospital later today. It's great news, but it also means I need to figure out what I'm going to do quickly. Noah will be needing those pickups soon, and I have to find a place to stay that isn't my ex-husband's couch.

On the way out of the room, the nurse stops. "Good morning, sir. Can I help you?"

A muffled voice comes from a little farther down the hall, but I could swear he says he's looking for room 405. Love really does turn mortals into fools, because I want so desperately to believe that it's Lennon out there, asking to be let in. That, somehow, he found me. That he can forgive me for leaving in the middle of the night.

But Devin goes still at about the same time I do, and we both look at each other. She must have heard it, too. Her face lights up, and mine might look like a deer in headlights because she cackles.

"I'm sorry, sir, but only family is allowed in at this time. You'll have to come back later," the nurse is saying, and I'm on my feet in a heartbeat.

But then I hear Richard's voice, clear as day. "He's family." My heart soars, just as he says, "Come on in, Johnny. She's just inside."

I cringe. Devin woefully shakes her head.

I guess Rome wasn't built in a day.

None of that seems to matter when Richard swings the door open and announces, "Look who I found outside." He winks at me, and that's when I know exactly where that conversation in the car came from. Lennon must have texted him to ask where we were. He knew this whole time.

As soon as Lennon steps out around Richard and into my line of sight, I want nothing more than to launch myself at him, bury my face in his shirt, and cry. But I hold my ground.

His hazel eyes meet mine, the gold flecks shining in the morning light. "Hey," he says, clearly uncertain.

"Hi," I respond before glancing at Richard, then Devin. "Um…do you want to take a walk?"

"Actually, I'm here to talk to Devin." He gives me a shaky smile, his dimples appearing under sandy stubble that tells me he must have flown overnight to get here.

Richard claps him on the shoulder, and I can tell Lennon tries desperately not to make a face. "I'll give you three a minute," Richard says. "This coffee sucks anyway. Good luck, man."

Lennon mumbles something incoherent as Richard leaves. And then it's just the three of us. Lennon's open-sky scent makes its way to me, and it takes all my strength not to wrap my legs around his torso and kiss him as he crosses over to Devin's bed. He pulls up a chair and sits next to her. I lower myself to the couch in a daze.

"Hey, kiddo. How are you feeling?"

"Better now." Devin is trying unsuccessfully to hide a giant grin. "Pretty cool I got not one but two of my favorite people to fly all the way across the country just because I got a useless organ removed."

Lennon chuckles deeply, and the sound of it pools in my stomach like honey—sweet and thick. "Well, you're pretty important to your mom, and your mom is pretty important to me," he says.

"She's a special lady," Devin agrees.

"That she is." He leans forward and rests his forearms on his knees. "I want to ask you a question, if you're up for it?" Devin nods, and he pulls in a steadying breath before he continues. "Before your mom came to LA, you asked me to take care of her."

"You what?" I exclaim. They both ignore me.

"You weren't supposed to tell her that," Devin mutters.

Lennon shifts in his seat. "Sorry." He winces apologetically. "Anyway, at the time, I couldn't think of any reason I'd have to not fulfill that promise I made to take care of her. But when she found out you were sick, she didn't hesitate. She booked a flight and came right out here." He swallows hard. Devin glances at me, but before she can say anything, Lennon jumps back in. "I messed that up. I panicked and asked her to stay with me instead. I knew you'd be fine, and I didn't want her to go. That was dumb, because she'll always be your mom and you'll always be her kid, and if she feels like she needs to see you for any reason, I should go with her. Don't you think?"

"Sure," Devin says slowly. "But you two can't be showing up at college unannounced or anything. There has to be boundaries."

A harsh laugh escapes me, and I'm not at all surprised to find it's wet.

Lennon leans in conspiratorially. "I promise I won't let her do that," he whispers.

"Hey!" I shout, but they continue to ignore me.

"I think she thought that I was asking her to choose between me and you, which was never my intention," Lennon assures her. "That's not even a choice. It's you, every time. I'm going to need to apologize to her in a minute for how I came off, and I will. But I wanted to ask you first if it'd be okay with you if I love your mom for a while."

Devin regards him for a moment, all the playfulness gone as she considers what he's saying. And just for a moment, she's six again, carefully deciding between two pieces of candy in the checkout line. "You've always loved my mom," she finally says. "But it's okay if you want to be *in love* with her, too, if that's what you're asking."

"That is what I'm asking." Lennon smiles, and it happens to him, too. Just for a second, he's not a forty-year-old man sitting next to my daughter's hospital bed. He's sixteen in the sound booth—all limbs and teeth and dimples. The boy I've always loved and the man I'm in love with, all in one.

"I need you to do something for me, though," Devin interjects.

"Anything."

"You said it's never a choice between you and me." Her lip starts quivering, as if she might cry, too. But her voice is steady as she says, "That was nice and all, but can you get her to choose herself once in a while? She doesn't do enough of that."

I let loose a shaky exhale. Lennon locks eyes with me over the hospital bed. "I'll do my best." He faces her again. "I think I need to go talk to her now."

Devin wipes her eyes, nodding. Lennon hands her a tissue before he comes over to sit next to me on the couch. He doesn't offer me a tissue, but he cups my face with his hands and wipes at the wetness on my cheeks with his thumbs.

"I'm sorry," he whispers.

"Me, too," I whisper back. "I shouldn't have left knowing what it'd do to you."

He shakes his head. "My feelings aren't your responsibility. I was so hung up on whether or not you'd stay forever that I couldn't see past you leaving temporarily. That's not on you. I need to do better."

There's no point in arguing with him, even though I want to tell him that it's okay if we tackle these big things together. From what he's just said to Devin, I think he's figured it out. "So where does that leave us?" I ask.

His tongue darts out and nervously wets his lips. He searches my eyes, then smiles. "When we were fourteen, you told me you like *L* names. You said they sound musical. Do you remember that?" I nod, my skin brushing against the palms of his hands. "You were right," he continues. "*L* words are musical. *Lark. Lennon.*" He pauses for a moment. "*Love.* I love you, Songbird. I should have said it a long time ago, because I've always loved you. You're my favorite person in the world, and I love you."

"I love you, too." I laugh despite my tears. I don't think I've ever been happier to hear something in my entire life.

"I'll go where you go," he promises. "Always."

I glance at Devin, who flashes me a quick thumbs-up. She wants me to choose myself. And if money and time and a sense of obligation weren't factors, I know exactly what I'd choose.

"Seems like a sign," I say. "Let's go to LA. That sounds musical, too."

The words slowly sink in, and realization dawns on his face. "Really?" His voice is quiet, as if he's afraid to break whatever spell we're under.

"Really," I assure him. "I've never been happier than I was out there with you. And the same person who thinks I need to choose myself would also really like to visit on breaks." I cock an eyebrow at Devin, who rolls her eyes.

Lennon laughs. "I can't wait." He grows serious as he threads his fingers through my hair. "Twenty-five years," he says, reverent. "I've loved you for twenty-five years."

"And I'll love you for at least twenty-five more," I promise.

He kisses me deeply, then. I sink into it, grabbing his soft T-shirt to pull him closer, letting him fill my soul in the way only he has ever been able to.

I've waited twenty-five years to be loved like this.

And it was worth every minute.

EPILOGUE

LENNON

ONE YEAR LATER

"This is so exciting," Devin whispers as we shuffle into our seats at the Valley Community Theater. "I've never seen Mom perform."

"Me either," Lark's friend Hannah says over my lap as we sit down. She flew out for the show the night before. She winks at me. "I heard the costumes are particularly sexy."

I don't tell her about the more indecent fantasies we've played out with Lark wearing a similar black leotard, tights, and heels. That would be inappropriate, and I'm nothing if not a gentleman.

I did, however, thank Hannah profusely for that bombshell swimsuit she bought Lark a year ago when she first came out to LA. When Lark came back with me, I made sure she had occasions to wear it. And then I asked Hannah where she got it and promptly ordered three more in different colors. It's Los Angeles. My Songbird needed more swimsuits. See? I'm a gentleman.

Noah, Jessica, and Silas all scurry down the aisle and slide into their seats in front of us just as the lights flicker to warn everyone that the show will be starting soon.

"Thank god we made it," Jessica pants. "I thought we were going to be late."

"That wouldn't be because a certain someone had to change three times before we left, would it?" Silas asks drily.

She tosses her dark hair over her shoulder. "You never know when you might meet the love of your life!" she singsongs. Noah shakes his head incredulously.

"Holy shit," Hannah breathes next to me. She leans closer to whisper, "Is that Silas Matthews?"

I nod and flash her a mischievous grin as I tap him on the shoulder. "Hey, Si," I say. "This is Hannah. She's your biggest fan."

"Ohmygod." Hannah squeals it all as one word. "Hi."

He shakes her hand. "A pleasure."

Devin giggles, and Jessica bounces her eyebrows suggestively at him. I'm surprised Hannah doesn't fall out of her chair right then and there. There isn't time for that, though, as the house lights dim and a spotlight illuminates a man in a pageboy hat and suspenders at stage right. He says a few lines, the joke lands, and the pit starts up their jazzy overture. Dancers come and go on the stage, hitting a few moves in time with the music as they pass in and out of sight. Devin moves back and forth in her seat to the beat. I can see Jessica's wide eyes from here. Hannah watches, scrutinizing.

As the overture leads into the first song, everyone in our group is hooked. It doesn't take long for the magic of theater to cast its spell over everyone in the crowd. But when the music moves into a more somber tone, that's when I lean forward in my seat.

Lark enters and hits her mark. Most people won't notice her in the frenzy of the other dancers still onstage, but I do. I can't take my eyes off her. She's the most beautiful woman I've ever seen.

I've been in the audience each night for this show's six-night run, and she does it flawlessly every time. The other actors disperse, and she's left standing there, still as a statue, her hip cocked and her head down, holding onto a black bowler hat with a gloved thumb and forefinger. I watch, mesmerized, as she practically vibrates with energy. Devin is holding her breath. Hannah is sitting straighter in her seat. Silas is smiling and tapping his fingers against the armrest. Jessica twirls her hair in anticipation. Even Noah's eyes widen from where I can see his profile.

Two bars. That's all it takes for her to hold every single audience member in the palm of her hand. Two bars, and then her head pops up, she flashes a brilliant smile, and her blue eyes find me.

Her smile widens just a fraction, and then she's off, singing and dancing like she was made to do this. She's at home on the stage.

And later that night, after our friends have gone home and Hannah and Devin are settled in the guest rooms of the house we bought together, she's home with me, too. She hums quietly as she rests her head on my chest, and I stroke her hair, just listening.

She laughs quietly at herself. "I'm really happy," she says into the night, the notes of her voice lifting into the air. "I love you, Lennon."

My heart is a light, bubbly thing. It could float away on those words alone. I don't even have to think as I kiss her forehead and breathe her in, all citrus and sunshine.

"I love you, too, Songbird," I say into her hair. "And you're my favorite person in the world."

ACKNOWLEDGEMENTS

I'VE SAID OVER AND over again that this is the book of my heart, and it is such because there are so many nods to so many people in here. I couldn't have written this without them.

First and foremost, thank you to my husband for the boring stuff—taking the kids, offering me quiet, cooking dinner so I can write. But thank you for believing in me, for encouraging me to chase these dreams, and for never trying to hold me down. You're my favorite person in the world, and I love you.

Thank you to the best of friends and my alpha reader, Hannah. Every time you told me you loved the prose in this book, I glowed for hours because that's the biggest compliment you could give me. I've said it before, and I'll say it again, if I wrote something even half as beautiful as your books, I'd be happy.

A huge thank you to my early readers: Jillian, Cait, Lexi, Jess, Stefanie, Brooke, Elizabeth, Sandy, and (eventually) Kayla. Hot Lennon reigns supreme! Thank you for listening, helping, commenting, and generally loving me (and my characters). I couldn't do this without you.

And thank you to my street teams! There are now too many people to name here, I think, but you know who you are! I know I can count on you to hype me up when I need it most, and I hope you all understand how important that is. There are times I've wanted to throw in the towel, and you all are always there to remind me to keep going.

Lark @_thebookchamber! Thank you for going on Threads one day and randomly asking if an author would use your name in a book. I love Lark, and I hope you do, too.

I consulted so many people on this project, and I am so grateful for their willingness to share their knowledge with me. Thank you to Megan for walking me through how an audiobook is produced and bouncing initial ideas around with me. Your insight is invaluable.

Thanks to Joe for answering random theater questions and never questioning what the hell I was doing with that information. But, more than that, thank you for being such an incredible friend. If you hadn't asked me to join the team all those years ago, I don't know where I'd be. Thanks for always reminding me what it means to be a good coach, teacher, and human.

And Deven. How do I thank you for being such a constant in my life? From middle school until now, you've celebrated my wins, shared my losses, cheered me (and my kids) on from afar, and kept me from my introverted tendencies. I bet you never thought you'd be listening to musical soundtracks and creating imaginary set designs and choreography for a book, huh? (Thanks for that, too.) There aren't adequate words to thank you for a friendship that has lasted over twenty-five years.

A giant thank you to my agent, Katie Monson at SBR Media. This book might not have gotten a deal, but I think it taught us a lot...and led to some other pretty great things, too. Thanks for being in my corner and fighting for my stories.

To my editor, Mandi Andrejka of Inky Pen Editorial Services—you have been an absolute dream to work with. I will never shut up about the fact that you gave me not one, but *two* crying Zooey Deschanel GIFs in this manuscript. Thank you for loving these goofballs.

There is no way I can do justice to a thank you for Lorissa Padilla for being the best friend *and* designer. I mean...look at that cover! Just look at it! It's my favorite cover you've done. Ever. And I know it took a little while, but I'm so glad everyone gets to see it now. Perfection. Seriously.

Thank you to my family and friends. There are too many people to name, but your support does not go unappreciated. And to my mom, dad, brother, and sister-in-law who have been endlessly and unconditionally supportive. I am so fortunate you're all in my corner.

And last but not least, thanks to you, dear reader. May your love be loud and bold.

About the Author

Allie Samberts is a romance writer, book lover, and high school English teacher. She was voted funniest teacher of the year for 2023 and 2025 by her students, which is probably her highest honor to date. She is also a runner, and enjoys knitting and sewing. She lives in the Chicago suburbs with her husband, two kids, and dog. You can follow her on Instagram @alliesambertswrites, TikTok at @alliesamberts, sign up for her newsletter at alliesamberts.substack.com, and get other updates at www.alliesamberts.com.

ALSO BY ALLIE SAMBERTS

Leade Park Series:

The Write Place
The Write Time
The Write Choice

Standalones:

Common Grounds

Novellas:

Pumpkin to Talk About
Christmas by Design
Love in the Time of Conversation Hearts (with Hannah Bird)

Coming 2026 from Page & Vine

Not a Strong Enough Word
(Plus two untitled books in this series)

www.ingramcontent.com/pod-product-compliance
Lightning Source LLC
Chambersburg PA
CBHW050025120726
47903CB00006B/1914